SEED

A Hard Science Fiction Novel about Survival,

Colonization, and Leadership Growth

MATTHEW G. DICK

VOIGHT-KAMPFF PUBLISHING

Published by Voight-Kampff Publishing, LLC

Cover artwork by Montdoom @montdoom

matthewgdick.com

ISBN: 978-1-7351035-1-8

Chapter 1

My name is Nick Burke, and I'm most likely going to die on Mars. I'm an engineer for MarsX, a company focused on trying to get Mars sustainable as an interplanetary colony planet. I'm currently on Mars, but I shouldn't be here. None of us should be here.

The real question I ask myself on a daily basis, is why am I still here doing this? Most people only have one shot at life—one round—one chance, and I decided that my reason for being alive is to do what hadn't been done yet. Help humanity leave Earth permanently. It is the only thing I can think about. I figure I should go big or die trying. But in the current circumstances, it looks like the latter is more likely to happen.

I do have a safety net though. My dad saw the value of a small start-up company when I was only a toddler. I wore special glasses for my entire life that recorded everything I saw, heard, and said. It even had sensors for monitoring brain waves. All the data I experienced in my life was recorded and streamed to cloud storage. For decades the data was collected and stored. The idea was someday technology would be capable of using all the data to make a digital clone of yourself, a D-Clo using deep learning neural network algorithms to build a conscious digital twin. My dad signed me up for a D-Clo way before most people even knew about it. Everyone thought he was a quack and that the whole D-Clo thing was a scam.

I've been wearing the dark rim D-Clo glasses since I was a kid and I still wear them now. I've only damaged one pair in my life. It was during a bus ride after school. I don't recall exactly word for word what I said to Laurie that made her face distort in anger. She winded her arm back and slapped my face so hard that my glasses sailed off my face, out the bus window, onto the pavement. In seconds after recovering from the shock of it all, I screamed at the bus driver to *STOP, STOP, PLEASE*, so I could trot sheepishly down the road and retrieve them from the street.

It was one of the first real memorable times in my life I said something I regretted and felt like a jerk. My dad was beyond upset when I brought the glasses home that day, with the right lens scratched and cracked frame. For two weeks I walked around, babying them, embarrassed by the gray duct tape and unable to see clearly out of the right lens. Thankfully, the glasses still worked until my dad cautiously handed me my new pair once they arrived in the mail.

Today my glasses make me look like a clean-cut, geeky wireless data plan salesman from the kind of persistent advertisements we've all seen. I made sure to do a full backup upload before I left Earth. I'm able to do uploads while on Mars, but it is not automatic like it is on Earth. I need to upload from my living quarters. Maybe it's easier to risk your life on a killer planet when you know you've got a second life in your pocket. But who knows if D-Clo would even work for me? I won't know until I die, which could be soon.

Ever since I was a little kid, it seems that the excitement has been slowing down for Mars. I remember watching the first manned landing to Mars with my face pinned against my computer screen. But since my childhood, it's been on-again, off-again, with research outposts being set up and then abandoned. Nothing stayed as a permanent colony on Mars. It turns out that shipping everything you need to a distant planet is not very economically viable. I kept saying during the mandatory MarsX staff meetings that it would be easier to make a colony on the ocean floor than on Mars. At least the bottom of the ocean is a shorter commute for the supplies. For a sustainable colony, water, air, food, shelter, materials, and energy all have to be produced on Mars somehow. That's why I'm here.

After everyone lost the dream of terraforming Mars within a reasonable time frame, a more realistic plan was put into place. A small team of humans (salary paid) with a much larger team of android aids (slave labor) were sent to Mars to make it happen. I'm one of the salary-paid humans, not one of the slave-labor androids.

I get a kick out of the androids every time I see them. Someone got the bright idea of keeping the androids environmentally sealed by making them wear the same white space suits we wear. Except they couldn't fit in all the robots' guts into the suit. So, they just made the suit bigger. A simple enough solution, I guess. A space suit-wearing android stands a couple of heads above our tallest staff member. It's a bit odd seeing these gargantuan white space suits walking around Mars. I'm calling them Space Yetis. We'll see if the name sticks.

Each Space Yeti is powered by a high-efficiency thermoelectric generator (HE-TEG) with a small plutonium-239 core being the power source. Technically it's a radioactive thermoelectric generator (RTG), but some salesman thought HE-TEG was a better name. A HE-TEG works by utilizing the heat from the radioactive source and converting it to electricity. Each Space Yeti has a glowing heart of radioactive love with a half-life of 24,100 years. But it is a shame that the electricity producing portion of the HE-TEG only has a design life of one hundred years due to the thermal stress cycles. The plutonium-239 is not the greatest choice since its half-life is way too long. But because it's been so abundant after the nations denuclearized, its cheap. And cheap wins. You just need to make sure you find a good burial site for the Space Yeti with its HE-TEG after a hundred years of service.

All the Space Yetis are guided by a central AI named ORIN. ORIN is good, but not great. I don't think ORIN will ever go HAL on us, at least not intentionally. ORIN is like that one person who is great at doing things when you hold their hand through it all, but he can't solve problems on his own. The imagination for problem solving just isn't there with ORIN. So, this requires us humans on Mars to really be the ones running things. I feel calm knowing that ORIN isn't scheming to kill us all off one by one. But that bumbling bucket of bits and bytes is going to kill us off with one of his mistakes. I just know it.

I'm part of the third team sent to the MarsX camp. As expected, things are not going well. We're here to clean up the mess of the first two teams. The first team lasted only three months then bailed early after killing one person and injuring three others. We lost two people in the second team. After their loss we rallied to learn from our mistakes and make the project a success in their name. What else can you do? Two failed trips don't make a trend as we would naively say. I suppose with my D-Clo in my back pocket I feel like I am not making a completely dumb decision being on Mars with the third team.

The third team is made up of Owen the botanist, Ben the physicist, Amy the project manager, and me, the do-it-all engineer because our fifth person, Karen the electrical engineer, took another job before launch. I guess, for her, two data points were enough to make a trend. Being dead doesn't help much with her résumé. I don't blame her.

The main camp is named Remo. The Greek god Mars had two sons: Romulus and Remus. Rome was named after Romulus. Our new great city in the works is named Remo after Remus. Inside the camp is the staff's barracks. Human staff, that is. The Space Yetis sleep outside. ORIN does get to sleep inside the barracks in a cozy computer rack though. Next to the barracks is the greenhouse, a network of air domes made of transparent polymer sheeting.

To make a self-sustaining colony, it turns out you need a lot of food and air. We did the math, but it's still staggering how much is needed. There are about thirty air domes that make up the greenhouse, each connected with short walkway tubes. The greenhouse serves to grow the crops that of course provide food, but also create the needed oxygen. We could also get oxygen from water electrolysis as a backup if needed. The only missing part that we still need to figure out is a significant local source of nitrogen. Mars' atmosphere only has 2.7 percent nitrogen as compared to Earth's 78 percent. For purposes of plant growth, airborne nitrogen isn't a big deal. For humans and soil it is a really big deal. We have to ship in most all our nitrogen with a to-do task of finding a local source on Mars.

The camp has a few other structures including a shop to house the equipment (Space Yetis and Transport Rovers) out of the dust storms. The shop is nothing special and would be similar to a Quonset that you would find on a humble earthling's farm. Waiting for their first use in the camp are lots of empty water tanks. The first team was able to build the barracks, greenhouse, and supporting structures before a rupture in the liquid oxygen supply tank caused their early departure. Wreckage of the first crew's ruptured tank is still at the camp. We can't exactly move it anywhere.

Every time I see the wreckage, it feels like an unwelcome ghost. We learned our lesson and adjusted the tank design to account for the thermal cycles better. We won't make that mistake again. At least that's what MarsX's management told the second team.

We need water, but here is the problem: Mars is hoarding her water in the wrong places. Most of the water is ice at the poles where it is cold and dark. We need it closer to the equator where it is warm and sunny. We could likely have built our camp close to a pole and dealt with the cold, dark conditions with nuclear power and heat. However, it is no place to make a sustainable colony. The physical barrier we couldn't overcome is that the poles are terrible places to launch a spacecraft from. The rotation of the planet isn't enough to get the exit velocity needed to launch from the planet. It would be like David trying to kill Goliath by throwing the rock instead of using a spinning slingshot.

If we built the camp at the pole, it would mean that when we did want to leave to go home, we'd have to do a long journey toward the equator. Not impossible, but not ideal. The other alternative is to live near the equator and move the water to us. This is the approach MarsX chose.

Near the south pole, the second team built a smaller outpost camp at the foot of a glacier. The glacier had a bright white presence in otherwise dark red surroundings. We fondly named the outpost camp and the glacier "the Red Edge", an eerie sight of where endless red dirt meets endless white ice.

The water-drilling operation at the Red Edge is straightforward. First, you drill down into the glacier about twenty meters. A heater probe is then lowered and melts an underground balloon shape into the ice, leaving a cavity full of water about the size of a living room. You then pump out the water or leave the heater on and pump it out later.

The mistake the second team took was they too eagerly started drilling into the glacier, which caused an ice sheet slide. Turns out that when you make water under a sheet of ice it makes for a very slippery condition, causing the sheet of ice to go where it wants. Which is downhill. Two MarsX employees lost their lives on the first day of drilling. We now do seismic surveys before each drilling. We won't make that mistake again. At least that's what MarsX's management told the third team.

The Red Edge is operated predominantly by Space Yetis under direction of ORIN, playing the role of a foreman. The human crew like to stay at the warmer Remo camp. We monitor remotely and provide ORIN correction instructions when needed. Traveling between the two camps is difficult. The preferred method is to take Hoppers back and forth. The Hoppers are rocket-powered ascent and landing vehicles about the size of a dome camping tent. They don't so much fly, as launch and land in a big arch. We have two of them, one based at Remo and the other at the Red Edge. Due to fuel reserves, they get used sparingly so we don't go to the Red Edge much. The alternative to taking a Hopper would be a miserable ground trip in a Transport Rover.

The third team's mission is simple. Build the water pipeline to connect the Red Edge to Remo and get the farm started. The pipeline we use is flexible, high-strength polymer tubing with embedded electrical heater wires running its whole length. All we need to do is tow spools of the tubing with Transport Rovers and lay it out as we go. We place a HE-TEG every few dozen kilometers to keep the water heated to prevent any ice blockages in the tubing.

The idea is to use the pipeline in the summer months. In the winter the HE-TEGs wouldn't be able to overcome the cold to keep the water liquid. We would continue to drill and melt our water stores in the glacier, then pump them out during the summer months. Once the water arrives at the farm, we would keep it in storage tanks until used in the greenhouse. The pipeline route from the Red Edge to Remo is a primarily a smooth, downward descent on a path that an ancient river paved for us. The most difficult part of it all is the two-thousand-kilometer slow walking-speed trip while laying out the pipeline as we go.

So, who are the lucky people that have to lay out the pipeline? That honor goes to our loyal army of Space Yetis. All told we have about two hundred Space Yetis on Mars. Mass production is a beautiful thing. Actually, it's more like ORIN is building the pipeline with our instructions using the hands and backs of the Space Yetis. Two teams of Space Yetis are deployed building the pipeline. One group started from the Red Edge, the second started from Remo. They are to meet in the middle. The whole construction is expected to take three months. Transport Rover supply trains are made from each starting location feeding the Space Yeti construction crews with more pipeline tubing. ORIN directs the Space Yetis in their night and day construction. No breaks for the Space Yetis. We humans act as the engineers defining the route and making the big decisions when we run into problems. As mentioned before, ORIN is good, but not great.

So, this all sounds like a great plan. Surely good enough for MarsX to give compelling pitches to the government and investors to receive the needed funding. At least enough funding to start the project. The checks were signed with blinding optimism for what could be the new colony, Remo. So, where is the problem? MarsX has the funding. The people. The technology. The issue was failure was always there. Always present. It just took us a while to unearth it once the brightness wore off.

Before the first team left Mars, they were fighting a losing battle with the greenhouse. As it turns out, air would rather be outside the greenhouse than inside. We were losing air faster than it could be replenished through leaks in the seals of the polymer sheeting. It got so bad that we stopped replenishing the air and let them leak until empty. We decided that we would fix the issue when we eventually got water to the farm.

After the second team left the Red Edge, the Space Yetis continued ice drilling. But the ice sheet slides didn't stop. As it turns out, ice at the top of the hill likes to be at the bottom of the hill if it is ever given the opportunity to move. We were losing about three Space Yetis a week. We couldn't recover most of them. Their final resting place is buried under an avalanche of ice on Mars. Unfortunately moving the drilling operation to a different location is not an option for us. With Remo and the pipeline where they are, it is not economically viable to do drilling somewhere else that has better conditions. For now, drilling operations have stopped until we devise a safer method. We've got enough stored water to keep us sustained at the farm for now. The ice sheet slides are a problem we will need to deal with later. I have to admit, it's not looking good. We bet the farm on this location and any alternative solution would mean dumping more money into the problem.

This brings us to the third team. My team. Currently Ben the physicist is laying in his Remo cot feeling miserable from his untreated diabetes. Why did Ben get sent to Mars with diabetes? He didn't. His diabetes didn't show up until after we'd been on Mars for a few months. The poor guy has already run out of what insulin supplies we had at the camp. He's been cutting back his food intake to lower his blood sugar. He has enough energy to stay in the camp, but he can't do much physical activity. He's not going to die right away, but we need to get him off this planet.

Owen the botanist has a bad toothache. A toothache! It wouldn't be such a big deal, but Owen won't shut up about his toothache. We are all suffering, buddy. You should have known it's natural for teeth to decay and should've done something to prevent it. Sorry that sending a dentist to Mars didn't come up during the risk analysis meetings prior to the launch. Owen has been spending his time eating up the painkillers and complaining to Ben. I don't think Ben can get any lower. He's sick and he's in a prison with a whiny botanist. Needless to say, Owen and Ben are not helping the team much.

9

Chapter 2

Recently ORIN has run into problems with the pipeline build that he couldn't solve on his own and we couldn't solve remotely. Amy and I are the only active duty team members now. We both get on a Hopper to fly out to the head of the southbound pipeline construction from Remo.

"We need to get out of here, Nick," Amy says slumping into her Hopper jump seat. "We're fixing this last problem, then that is the end of it. I'm going to file an evac request for us. Ben is miserable. I'm about ready to punch Owen in the face. This whole place is messing with me. Isn't it messing with you?"

"Yeah, I don't think we're going to make it to the end of our term. But don't you feel cheated? We were supposed to be space pioneers. Our names are supposed to be memorized by schoolchildren for centuries. If we bail now, we will have failed. What would have it all been for? If we quit, that will certainly be the end of MarsX. I don't think funding will keep coming with three failed teams." I look at Amy while I adjust my glasses. "We should have seen all these problems coming and did things differently."

"I don't know why you care about this colony so much, Nick. It's still just a job. Don't you want to go home? Get back to Earth. Have a family. Raise some kids? I still want to have kids. That can't happen if I die on Mars. Don't you want kids?"

I pause for a moment. "I don't even have a girlfriend. Having kids has never been on my radar as something I need to do in my life. I don't have an aversion to kids, but they are not a priority for me. But after my dad died, I felt building this Mars colony is what I need to do. What I must do. It's my purpose now. Building this colony has been the only thing I can think of since he passed away. He died three months before we launched for Mars. I feel guilty that he gave me a chance to live forever with a D-Clo, but he had to die."

"Nick, I am really sorry about your dad. I really am. But you need to let go of Mars. We can't enjoy success if we're dead." Amy pauses. "I guess you can with your D-Clo, but not the rest of us. How the hell did your dad think to get you signed up for that while you were a kid? The rest of us didn't realize we should be doing it until we were too old. We missed those early formative years needed to train your D-Clo. I hope you're not making decisions that affect us all knowing you can fall back on your D-Clo. You can die on Mars. I can't."

I adjust my glasses again. "I most certainly am not." We ride in silence, faces forward for the remainder of the trip.

After we land, the Hopper loses power. Everything goes dark. I cycle the power switch. Nothing. 'What happened?' I mutter to myself while flipping more switches. It could be a loose wire, a blown fuse, a software issue. We've been having problems with the Hoppers for a while, but have been too busy dealing with other issues to find the root cause. Amy and I agree to deal with it later. We put on our helmets to exit the Hopper. Amy gives me a look of redemption, knowing that she is right that we should be getting off the planet and not fixing pipelines.

We get on-site and find the Space Yeti team trying to lay the pipeline while descending a steep hill. The tube keeps slipping sideways down the side of the hill, causing misalignments in the pipeline. Apparently, when trying to correct it, they tore the pipeline apart. The Space Yetis have simple artificial intelligence that ORIN gives guidance to. But even ORIN himself can only do so much. He had at least made the right call to ask us for help. I can tell you there is nothing more frustrating than looking at twenty Space Yetis with a broken pipeline at their feet with a super artificial intelligence backing them up and none of them having an idea how to fix this simple problem. There is no way the human race will get destroyed by an organized AI robot rebellion. There are too many problems to overcome when trying to eradicate the human race.

We get to work fixing the pipeline. Two groups of Space Yetis grab each end of the pipeline and bring them together at the location it is supposed to be. We cut the ends flush, then install a cutoff valve with glorified duct tape. Space duct tape. The cutoff valves are supposed to be installed every kilometer anyways, so it isn't a big deal. A last step is crimping the heater electrical wires to keep electrical continuity in the pipeline. Then we set the pipeline down with a line of Space Yetis holding it down along its length.

One Space Yeti wielding a sledgehammer and a bucket of U-shaped spikes approaches us while we are finishing the space duct tape job. It is extremely intimidating-looking with the sledgehammer in its hands. It could kill us if it wanted to. One swing could easily take out both of us. I hope ORIN has his slaves somewhat under control. During its awkward pause, I feel like a lamb looking at the farmer ready to butcher me. Finally, it puts down the bucket of spikes on the ground like an instructed army private. It grabs one at a time, holds it in place, and taps it into the ground to get it started. Then it stands up and takes one swing to nail it all the way into the ground. A perfect swing hitting the target and driving the spike to the perfect height. We watch as it continues down the length of the pipeline, nailing at each Space Yeti location where they are holding down the pipeline. When it finishes a spike, the Space Yeti at that location stands up waiting for its next instruction. When he finishes with all the spikes, the row of Space Yetis is standing there, looking at me, and wondering what to do next.

I'm still in a sour mood with all the problems of the day. Having to micromanage ORIN and the robots is not helping with my demeanor. I yell out, "Great! Now get back to work!" In unison they turn away and start walking. ORIN himself can hear my frustration with our communication link back to him in our suits.

"Amy, we need to go deal with the Hopper power issue. Let's get going!" I lead the way back to the Hopper. As Amy and I are walking around the leaving Space Yetis, I hear her yell out in the communication radio in my helmet. Looking over I see a Space Yeti trip in slow motion over the nailed-down pipeline. The Space Yeti falls into Amy, knocking her over, then bouncing off her when they both land. She starts sliding on her frontside down the side of the hill with the fallen Space Yeti following her in a cloud of Mars dust.

We shouldn't have come out here. We should have left Mars like Amy wanted. Adrenaline kicks in. I run after her and call out to ORIN to send me two Space Yetis. I get to the bottom of the ravine and turn her over to her back. Her suit is depressurizing.

She is gulping for air looking at me with wide eyes I've never seen before. She is dying and panicking. A second bullet of adrenaline hits my skull. I frantically look for the leak. On my knees I look up at the closest Space Yeti. *"Get me the tape now!!"* I scream at him. I look up the hill and see one of the Space Yetis throw the roll of tape down to us in a perfect line drive throw.

The Space Yeti closest to me turns and catches the roll one-handed, then casually turns around holding it out to me to grab. I wrap the tape around Amy's neck, shoulders, and wrists. As I move her around, I see she's passed out. Her vitals monitor on her wrist display says she's still alive and the air pressure in her suit starts to rise. I take time to double and triple up all the tape on her until the duct tape roll runs out. I throw the empty roll to the all-American football receiver Space Yeti nearest me. All I see is a faceless reflective helmet looking back at me. Then ORIN's face shows in the Space Yeti's visor. "Sir, I sense you are in need of help. Please instruct me what to do."

ORIN doesn't take over a specific Space Yeti's body unless it is an emergency. This is an emergency. ORIN in the Space Yeti body helps me bring Amy back up to the Hopper. Space Yetis' helmets are actually LED screens. ORIN's face in the visor looks something like Alfred from the classic Batman cartoon I watched with my dad when I was a kid. A dignified old gentleman with slicked-back gray hair and a crisp mustache. A face that takes instructions and is aimed to please with as little emotion as possible. Back when the Space Yetis were being designed, someone had the bright idea of letting them have faces. Something about making them more humanlike. ORIN's facial expressions don't look human. He looks calm and unconcerned given the emergency we are in.

"Sir, I've logged into Amy's suit to retrieve the diagnostic logs. Amy's suit has stabilized, and she is still unresponsive. The standard operating procedure states that we must return to the nearest camp and seek medical attention," ORIN says with out-of-place professionalism.

Once we complete our hike back up to the Hopper, ORIN lays Amy down against one of the lander legs. I climb into the Hopper to figure out the power issue. I want to get the hell out of here as quick as possible. This issue with the Hopper couldn't have happened at a worse time. After a quick power cycle test, I pull off a panel and start frantically searching and prodding to find the electrical issue. Grabbing a multimeter voltage tester, I insert the probes trying to find where the power is missing. "No. No." My hands frantically move with the probes around the circuit board like a skilled brain surgeon saving the life of my patient. Suddenly a wisp of smoke snaps into my view between my hands from the circuit board. This is not good. I just shorted out the board and don't have a spare. My patient just died on the operating table.

"You have got to be kidding me! *You have got to be kidding me!*" I shout, throwing the multimeter as far as I can out the Hopper door into the open Mars landscape.

ORIN pokes his head into the Hopper door. "Sir, are you having any troubles?"

"ORIN," I say with both hands clenched with diamond-crushing pressure, "I'll let you know when I have problems I need your help with."

"Indeed, sir, I wait for your command."

It takes a few seconds for my head to clear from the blinding rage. What is my next option? There is a second Hopper at the Red Edge. The issue is that I can't remotely pilot it. I can't pilot it being out here in the middle of nowhere. I can't, but ORIN can. "ORIN, I do need your help. Please fly the Hopper at the Red Edge up to us so we can get out of here."

"As you wish, sir."

ORIN's helmet screen changes to show flight telemetry information from the Red Edge Hopper. He crouches down on one knee so I can actually see the screen. On launch ORIN does well. I monitor the readings as the Hopper is making the quick journey to our site. Everything is looking good as I look anxiously into ORIN's helmet monitor over the next several minutes. Watching the screen, I can see that ORIN is starting the descent for landing. I look up and can now see the Hopper.

"ORIN, you are coming in way too fast!" I look at the screen and it shows a normal speed.

"Sir, everything is as expected. I should have the Hopper landing soon for our departure."

I watch my last ride home hit the ground like a meteor generating a plume of dust on impact. I later found out that the Hopper parked near the Red Edge was getting water condensation frozen on the airspeed and altitude sensors. ORIN, not knowing any better to question the instrumentation, and not bothering to look at the outboard cameras, flew the Hopper straight into the ground thinking he was saving his human master.

Maybe robots do have a chance to kill all humans, but it will be done with incompetence instead of evil robotic intent. ORIN's gentlemanly face shows back on the helmet screen. I look straight into his eyes, but he is not picking up the plastic-melting hate stare I am giving him. I can't bring myself to even speak with him. I slap the side of his helmet as hard as I can. He doesn't even move. ORIN stands up in his Space Yeti body and doesn't say a word as we both look out at the dark smoke and dust in the horizon.

ORIN puts Amy over his shoulder and we walk back to the Space Yetis' Transport Rover used for the pipeline team. Amy is still out. A cramp in my stomach starts as I think of the reality of Amy and me dying out here. Amy doesn't deserve this. We shouldn't have come out here. We should have put in the evac orders and not bothered to fix the pipeline.

ORIN loads Amy into the rover and unhooks the trailer that has the pipeline tubing roll. I boot up the air system to fill the cab once ORIN, Amy, and I were all in. Once the cab is filled with air, I pop off my helmet and throw it at ORIN. He easily catches the helmet and sets it down behind him. I take my glasses off and rub my temple for a moment. I put in eye drops before putting my glasses back on with a sigh. This planet is a desert and my eyes have had enough of it. I have a massive headache. Clicking through menus on the onboard display in the Transport Rover I look for how much time we have left in the air reserves. Not much. But we could make it if I stretch it out by driving faster and calling in a rescue trip from Owen using one of the Remo Transport Rovers to meet us en route. I look at Amy in the back seat. She's stable but still unconscious. I put the Transport Rover transmission into gear and hit the pedal heading toward Remo.

ORIN stays silent as we drive. I don't waste any time driving and use the pipeline as my guide back to Remo. For us to make it I need to go full speed. I drive in silence. I can't blame ORIN for this. There is no one other than me to blame. I shouldn't have commanded the Space Yetis at the pipeline to move like I did. Maybe that one Space Yeti wouldn't have fallen on Amy if I had thought about it more at the time. I should have taken my time with the first Hopper's circuit board. I shouldn't have spiked the multimeter off the ground. I might need it later. The second Hopper though? I'm blaming ORIN for that one. I look over at ORIN and give him another glare. He doesn't look at me; he's in a frozen forward stare in his still Space Yeti body. I wonder if his helmet cameras are looking at me right now.

"Oh crap!" I shout snapping my view back to the windshield.

The rover cab bounces, shuffling us inside our seat belts as I slam on the brakes. I pick up my knocked-off glasses and put them back on. I realize we have come over a ledge and have run into a boulder with one of the front wheels. Turning the steering wheel, I can feel something isn't right. I think we snapped the steering tie-rod. I can't steer the Transport Rover anymore. We are stuck. I screwed up by not paying attention.

There are no other Hoppers to save us. We are too far from Remo for Owen to come get us. My mind clouds over in rage and panic while I beat my head on the steering wheel. ORIN is still looking forward in his silent stare.

"ORIN, any ideas?" I say picking my head up and looking at him.

"No, sir," he responds, finally snapping from his fix and looking over at me.

"You're not so good at these situations, are you?"

"No, sir."

"Well then, I suppose it would be most fitting that you finish the job by choking me to death. I know you've always wanted to kill all us humans, so here you go. Better yet, go get that sledgehammer and make it quick."

"Sir, you know I can't do that. I cannot harm your life."

"I know, but you could have fooled me when you tried to see how high you could bounce that Hopper off the ground."

ORIN turns his head forward again not saying anything back to me.

"ORIN, I'm going to die. See Amy back there? She is going to die too. You're going to sit here for the next hundred years with your HE-TEG-powered Space Yeti suit watching us turn into mummies. Please play my advanced directive music playlist while I wait to die. I might as well be listening to good music."

"Sir, you know I don't work like that."

"Oh right," I say, knowing it already in a dark sarcastic tone reinforcing my point that ORIN is useless. "In that case, ORIN, please tell the rover computer to play my advance directive music playlist."

"Sir, as you wish."

Before we launched, we all had to fill out our advanced directive forms to define what happens to us if we are in an end-of-life situation. For me, my end-of-life plans are to listen to my favorite music. I only listen to old rock music that my dad listened to when he was a kid. Back when music was made by real people. Nowadays new music is just recycles of the old great songs or soulless messes created by artificial intelligence algorithms. It is only the old classics for me. ORIN issues an opening COMMAND to launch the rover computer music player. Then issues the LOAD instruction choosing my music. Then he instructs PLAY to start the music. I lean back and close my eyes to listen to Radiohead's album, *Kid A*.

Chapter 3

What can we do? I don't have a spare tie-rod or the tools to change it out. I can try to jury-rig it with some space duct tape, but it would mean limited steering, which is somewhat a necessity. Not to mention the first bump I'd hit would make me stuck again. I'd have to travel at a crawling pace to keep the Transport Rover alive. We've got twenty Space Yetis doing nothing a few kilometers back. I can just have them carry the whole Transport Rover home. Unfortunately, at their walking speed, they would be pallbearers carrying us into Remo. We've got our Mars Ascent Vehicles (MAV) for transporting us off the planet back to the orbiting spaceship. One at Remo and one at the Red Edge. However, they're meant to take off and leave the planet, not land and pick us up. Besides, I'll need the Remo one to get out of here if we actually make it to Remo.

I wonder how well my D-Clo is going to work. I guess it would pick up most recently when I uploaded last, which was last night while I was still at Remo. I'm not sure if my dad would be happy or sad if he knew I'm dying and have to use my D-Clo. When you die, the D-Clo company will automatically build your D-Clo if you miss a scheduled upload. This means they take all the decades of information that has been collected from your glasses and compile a digital clone of you using deep learning neural network modeling. My dad did something for me that he couldn't do for himself by signing me up for the D-Clo program when I was a kid. Hopefully I will survive this, at least as a computer program. But I feel miserable that my dad is dead for good.

Luckily for MarsX my D-Clo won't remember today's mess since I left the Remo camp this morning. An eternal, disgruntled former employee could make their life miserable. Daydreaming, I imagine spending my ever-waking immortal hours giving them negative reviews online. That would teach them.

What am I going to do as a D-Clo? There's probably no other D-Clos compiled yet. Who knows if it's even going to work? When I was started on the D-Clo program, it seemed to be a scam to everyone we knew. It was just uploading data to the cloud with the promise that someday, someone would figure out how to make a digital clone of you out of that giant pile of data. It may still be a scam. Maybe there are some teenage D-Clos out there of kids that died in their misguided driverless cars dumping them into the river. I don't think that is who I'd want to spend eternity with when I'm a D-Clo.

Should I tell Ben and Owen we're going to die? Probably not. Ben might want to do something stupid by trying to save us. Owen wouldn't care about us anyways, given his life-destroying toothache. I'll have ORIN send them a message after we pass. But it might be a while before that happens. I best have ORIN give them positive news until we go, then tell them they need to leave Mars.

I'd need to get an android body after my D-Clo compiles. I wonder what type I would get. Maybe I'll go teach at a university. My class would be called "How to Realize and Embrace that Death is Inevitable on Mars 101". I better not become a professor. I'd be a circus sideshow. A D-Clo keeps learning and recompiling. Maybe I should take my android body and roam the Earth as a robot tourist. I don't need food or a hotel. A random power outlet is all I would need. But what kind of life is that? Sounds like it would get pretty boring after a while. Being shooed out of coffee shops with my unplugged electrical cord trailing behind me. I don't know if I could deal with that.

Daydreaming takes my mind off the hard, deathly facts around me. Looking out through the windshield while off in my daydream clouds, I see a bit of dust picking up on the horizon.

"ORIN, what is the weather report today? Are there chances of windstorms?" I ask while sitting up in my seat.

"Sir, the weather is clear today in this area."

"So, what is that dust cloud out there?" I ask pointing through the windshield.

"Sir, that is a Transport Rover in the pipeline supply train. It will be making a delivery to the pipeline construction crew in approximately thirty-eight minutes."

"Are you kidding me!? Why didn't you bring this up before!?" ORIN has no emotion while he sits looking at me.

"Sir, that Transport Rover is allocated to the pipeline supply train. It is not a general use rover. According to the standard operating procedure we must file a request for reallocation of the use of the Transport Rover if we want to utilize it for a different purpose. Right now, it is designated for the pipeline supply."

"The hell it isn't! Override its function and have it drive to us. We break rules around here."

"Sir, as you wish, but I must note that this will go into my command discrepancy log."

"You do that, buddy! How many other Transport Rovers are between us and the main camp?"

"Sir, there are three other rovers."

That's enough to get us home. "Have the three rovers spread out equally along the pipeline. We are going to relay race our way home and we are going to be the baton."

"Sir, as you wish."

***

Finally, something is going smoothly for us. We get into the first Transport Rover and head out quickly, but carefully watch for any life-ending rocks in our path. We meet up with the first rover after about eight hours of travel. We transfer into the next Transport Rover and do it all again. Then again. I need to get Amy back to Remo as soon as possible. I am not going to risk her dying on me while I take a nap during our trip home. We have plenty of energy pills in the Transport Rover, so it's not a problem staying awake. But I am amped to a vibration level that could mix a paint can.

Amy finally wakes up once we arrive at Remo, but she can only move her eyelids. She is still incapacitated. I send brief messages back and forth to Owen and Ben during our trip letting them know what had happened and that we are on our way. The only message I get back from Owen is that he had run out of pain meds. Really?! I almost died on this Mars hellscape while he's got a boo-boo in his mouth because he can't brush his teeth well enough. Reading Owen's message makes me more upset on top of my caffeine-induced fog. I've been driving for twenty-four hours straight when we finally roll into the Remo camp. The MAV can only launch at certain times because it needs rendezvous with the orbiting spaceship.

"ORIN, as soon as we get inside the barracks, we're packing and getting on the MAV to get out of here. When is the MAV emergency launch window?"

"Sir, we are currently within the launch window, but it will expire in twenty-six minutes."

We park the Transport Rover near the Remo barrack's front door. ORIN follows me into the air lock with Amy in his arms. I'm not looking forward to having the next few conversations with Owen.

"What the hell happened?" Owen blurts out as soon as we walk out of the air lock into the barracks. Ben is standing there in his pajamas looking like death. Owen continues on his offensive. "I'm not going to die on this planet. You need to get me out of here." Owen rants, waving his hands in the air and pointing at me with unsympathetic attacks. "I need to get home. I need to get to my dentist. Where have you been? You don't know what pain I've been in! This is all your fault! It's your damn D-Clo! You think you can leave us to die here!"

Without taking three steps into the barracks past the air lock I coldcock Owen in the face. "No one cares about your damn *tooth*!" I scream hunching over him while he's knocked out cold on the ground.

I look up and see Ben standing there in shock and taking a few steps back. Owen is motionless on the ground. It all happened automatically. I didn't think. It happened and here we are. My hand suddenly has shooting pain in it.

I should not have done that. I really should not have done that. Leaning over Owen, I make sure he is still breathing okay while holding my bruised hand.

"Alrighty then, time to get the hell out of here," I say in an awkward silence-breaking tone to the still conscious people in the room. "Grab your stuff, we're leaving now."

We take the next several minutes grabbing our small personal possessions, including Owen's stuff while he lays on the barracks floor. We close down the barracks for long-term storage as best we can as we rush out to the MAV. ORIN makes sure Owen and Amy are secured in their flight suits and moves them into the MAV. He carefully buckles them into their seats. Ben brings himself out to the MAV. He has finally perked up knowing that he's getting off this planet and going to the orbiting spaceship to get his insulin. His smiling face tells me he isn't mad at me about the Owen knockout.

We finish loading up into the MAV. Owen is still unconscious. Amy is sluggish and quiet. Ben is the only happy one of the bunch. I know us leaving will kill MarsX. It will end the idea of interplanetary colonization. Three failed attempts will end it all. I'm making a decision right now that is affecting the future of the human race, that we will never live on another planet. I feel like I am letting my dad down. I brood over this thought as I am doing my preflight checks.

ORIN is standing outside of the MAV door when I go to close it.

"ORIN, thanks for not killing me," I say with the first upbeat tone of the day.

"Sir, it was a pleasure. I'm sure we will meet again." ORIN looks up at me and for the first time he gives me a smile.

I'm not sure if he is conscious enough to know what he is saying or doing. *It was a pleasure? We will meet again?* What does he mean by that?

I close the door and buckle in. I put my finger over the launch button but pause before hitting it. I've failed. We'll be going back as failures. I feel like I'm killing my dad. I look over at Ben.

"Nick," Ben says softly. "We need to go."

I hit the launch button and lean back in my seat.

Chapter 4

Pro tip: when starting a nine-month journey on a cramped, interplanetary spaceship from Mars to Earth, don't punch your crewmate in the face prior to departure. Don't get me wrong, I don't mind the isolation away from Owen, but the awkwardness is epic. We avoid each other as much as possible. I stay in my room for most of the trip and we only cross paths at the kitchen and bathroom. Maybe his tooth stopped hurting because I knocked it out of his mouth. I wouldn't know since he hasn't said a word to me on this trip.

He should be happy he's finally going home. Ben is certainly happy. After getting his insulin, he's doing much better. It's good we left when we did. Any longer and he would have gotten permanent eyesight and kidney damage. He's finally gaining weight after starving himself to keep his blood sugar low on Mars. Amy is back to normal. She is already working on her résumé, filling out online job applications and doing interviews. All on the spaceship. Her feelings toward MarsX couldn't be more explicit when she is using their billion-dollar high-speed communication system to do web conference interviews with potential new employers.

Nine months of isolation without knowing what I'm going to do when we arrive home does have its benefits. I'm catching up on all the books I've always wanted to read. I'll have all the sci-fi greats finished before we land. My routine has turned into reading until tired, and before going to bed taking off my glasses and putting them on their nightstand mat conveniently held down by the artificial gravity of our rotating living quarters of the spaceship. While I sleep the mat charges and uploads the D-Clo data. Day after day, night after night.

What are we going to do when we get back? MarsX is done for. Three failed teams, three deaths. A deflated bubble farm, icy landslides, and an incomplete pipeline. The amount of money to fix all that is beyond anyone's ability. No one will have the belief in a successful future.

Why did this happen? I'll tell you why. Mars is the worst idea for a colonized planet. You run out of air, you're dead. You run out of water, you're dead. Your car breaks down, you're dead. The normal state of you being on Mars is you being dead. The difference between success and the normal conditions on Mars is too big. Earth on the other hand has its normal state pretty close to success. You'll never run out of air. Thirsty? Just go have any of the water around you. Best of all, you don't die when your car breaks down. You just get frustrated, but that doesn't kill you. I realize now that Mars's invitation to colonize her wasn't rescinded from mankind. It was never given to us at all. She was always telling us to stay away. But our blinding optimism didn't let us see that.

We need a better planet. The galaxy has plenty of them. But they're all too far away. The most promising planets are hundreds of light-years away. Putting living humans into a cryogenic freeze has never panned out. Faster than light space travel is science fiction. I'm sorry to say this, but we are on a deserted island in an unimaginably large ocean. We will never get off this island. The human race will end on Earth.

Thinking of this, I imagine my D-Clo android doing his traveling. Maybe I'd get stranded on a deserted island. No people. No animals. Out in the middle of nowhere. What would I do? What else could I do, but kick back under a palm tree and watch the clouds float by. Hopefully I'd have a HE-TEG to keep me alive without any coffee shops with electrical outlets nearby.

I lay in my bed imagining relaxing under a deserted island palm tree. Hopefully I don't have a coconut fall on me. A palm tree has an interesting approach to its seeds. Did you know that a coconut floats? In fact, it does a great job using the ocean currents to float around in the ocean for years waiting to find another island. The seed is dead. But when it hits land, it becomes alive. It's a good thing that it's dead when it travels. When you're dead time flies by. Really time doesn't exist when you're dead. To the coconut, the time from falling off the tree into the ocean to showing up on a different island years later would be a snap of your fingers.

I think I have an idea. I need some caffeine to write this down.

***

When we land back on Earth, there isn't much fanfare. The public had long lost its interest in Mars and our return trip is no different than sailors returning from a shipwreck. Amy had a new job the moment she walked off the ship. She put in her resignation to MarsX when we were still en route home. Ben and Owen go their separate ways. Ben makes sure to connect with me on LinkedIn before leaving. Owen doesn't say a word to me. I don't think I'll be getting a Christmas card from him anytime soon. When I get off the ship, a familiar face walks up to me. My boss that I haven't seen in over two years.

"Jerry, we need to talk. Let's go get a coffee." He gives me a cautious look. He seems like he is expecting to get punched in the face by me.

After a quick drive we find a quiet coffee shop to talk. "Nick, if this is about your performance, just keep in mind that I put the best word in for you that I could," Jerry tells me while sipping on his drink. Jerry has shaggy blond hair, a gruff face, and keen eyes. His charming Knoxville, Tennessee accent gives him a genuine tone. A voice you could trust immediately without even checking under the hood.

"Wait, no, that's not what I want to talk to you about. My performance? I saved lives, buddy! I'm the MarsX employee of the century! Besides, I saw the company email. MarsX going out of business means it doesn't matter much." I lean over the table toward Jerry and adjust my glasses. "I'm here to talk to you about a new job." Jerry's eyes perk up.

"What is the problem with Mars?" I say rhetorically. "It's a terrible planet! We need a planet with air and water with the ability to make food, materials, and energy. Mars is not that planet. And it never will be. There will never be enough money to make it what we need. But there are plenty of other planets out there. So, what is the problem? They are all too far away."

"Nick, unless you discovered a new way to do space travel, I'm sorry but it's all been tried and has failed. I think you're in shock and not thinking straight." Jerry leans back, crossing his arms.

"Forget that. Here is what you need to do. You need to get rid of the people. That's right. No people on the spaceship. That's the way to do it. The trip would kill them and it's too long to be alive anyways," I say in my best elevator-pitch tone.

Jerry looks confused. "Doesn't that defeat the point?"

"No, all you need are the seeds and a method to deliver them."

"So, what are you going to do? Dump a bunch of human embryos on a spaceship and fire them off to another planet? Good luck with that. What are they going to do when they get there? You're going to let babies die on some alien planet with ORIN stumped on how to keep them alive? We all know that ORIN is worthless at solving problems. He'd never be able to raise children. We'd be sending them to their deaths." Jerry slouches back down.

"You do need intelligence to make the voyage and grow the seeds when you get there. That intelligence needs to be a machine. A machine is dead. It can make the trip. Since it's dead, the trip could take ten days or a thousand years and it wouldn't know the difference."

"Right, so you are thinking of using ORIN, aren't you? He could certainly make the voyage."

"Yeah, and he'll kill everyone when he gets there. I agree with you on that. He's not a problem solver. He's a human killer and his weapon is incompetence. Who then would replace ORIN? Me, well rather my D-Clo."

"D-Clo? I thought that was the modern-day snake oil. Has it really progressed enough?" Jerry leans in inquisitively.

I grin back at him. "I've checked and found they've already compiled D-Clos for some teenagers. They were getting 97 percent fidelity matches. That means their D-Clos matched 97 percent on tests for personality, cognition, memories, and problem solving as compared to their original selves."

"Okay, I got it. We make you a robot. We load you and a bunch of embryos on a spaceship. You sleep for a thousand years, wake up at a new planet, and hope for the best in the new civilization. Am I right? So, who is going to pay for this adventure? It doesn't seem like something that politicians can get behind. It's basically an admission that their constituents will never go to another planet."

I smile at Jerry again. "Don't you think the world's billionaires would line up at the door to know that their lineage would populate a new planet? A new civilization on a new world? Their descendants would be the new cradle of mankind. That seems like something their ego would pay a lot of money for. Of course, we'd add some additional embryos of the world's smartest, most capable people to fill out the embryo bank. You and I are going to make a start-up company. We're going to get funded by billionaire investors for their fertilized embryos living on a new planet. I need you to make this happen. I need you to get the investors and get the people to work for us. This is our only chance to make everything we wanted. It's the only real way to build an interplanetary colony." There it is. My whole plan. Let's see if he bites.

"I don't know, Nick. It seems a bit farfetched. I don't know if I'm up for it."

"So what, you're just going to quit? Your whole career of building a space colony down the drain? What are you going to do? Go get a job launching communication satellites into orbit so you can watch streaming cat videos in your retirement? Or do you want the chance to do something that no one else has done? To change the course of mankind. To be remembered."

I can see I've struck a chord. Jerry ponders for a few moments leaned back with arms crossed.

"Can I be CEO?" Jerry finally asks, perking up but still crossing his arms.

"Sure. You know I'm not good with people. I just boss them around as if they're robots. You're much better at leading this into success. Besides, you're the only one that has billionaires in your contacts list." *I've got him now,* I think.

"Nick, you are one smart bastard. I hope this works out." Jerry reaches out his hand to shake mine. I reach out quickly to shake his hand before he can change his mind.

***

"Ladies and gentlemen, we are making our final descent into Zurich. Please raise your tray tables, lift your backrests, and prepare for landing," the lead flight attendant announces over the airplane intercom. Jerry and I are on a flight to Zurich to the D-Clo headquarters. We don't get much sleep on the plane. Instead we spend most of the time arguing.

"Look, Nick, you can't have that big of a ship! It will cost too much. We need to dial it down. The engineering costs would be outrageous. Not to mention the amount of time it would take to get it all designed and tested. The investors won't wait that long," Jerry says while trying to keep his voice down.

"Jerry, if we're going to do this, we need to do it right. We need at least a hundred embryos, a lander with full living quarters, and resources to carry us for the first few years. If we're not going to do it right, we might as well not do it. I'm not going to set up our one and only chance for a new civilization on one measly small spaceship," I say, crossing my arms and leaning back in my seat.

Jerry better not be steering this in the wrong direction. I can still pull the plug if I want to.

"I'll see what I can do," Jerry says. "I've already made some calls and I have lots of investors already lined up. They're ready to drop the cash, but they want this ship launch ASAP. They're not willing to wait to have a new ship designed, tested, and deployed. We really should be looking at what spaceship designs we already have and stick to what we know. With MarsX going out of business, we should look to buy their designs and inventory," Jerry patiently explains.

"You have a point on sticking to what we know," I say. "I'd rather not be a guinea pig on a first ship of its kind. More chances of failure. The best technology is the kind that is so reliable it's boring. Just get the biggest ship you can. The MarsX Freighter used for transporting all the Transport Rovers, Pipeline Reels, and Camp Instructure should be good enough."

"Nick, you're kidding, right? That's way too big. The fuel to power that thing won't even get you to Titan."

"You'll figure it out. You're about to hire all those MarsX engineers. They live to solve problems. Solve this one, then. By the way, Jerry, I've thought of the name for the ship. Machine Transport for Organic Growth, M-TOG."

"Ehmm-Tawg..." Jerry says. "Hmm, sounds as good as any other name. I'll let you have that. You can name the spaceship. But I'm in charge of building the ship and I'll get the most reasonable one I can for you. I still have a lot of work to do with the investors. These billionaires are relentless. I'm getting nonstop calls from them wanting status updates. Some of them have already started other companies to work on the embryos. I'd have thought they'd just go the traditional route of getting fertilized eggs as they would with their own offspring. But I think some of them are looking into cloned embryos."

"Gentlemen, I'll need you to lift your tray tables. We'll be landing soon." The flight attendant interrupts before I can respond. I suppose I don't care much where the embryos come from. Maybe we'll be able to get the hundred embryos, but maybe not the full living quarters inside the lander. We could probably build our living quarters on-site if we had to. The thought of building the living quarters as the first step of the colony reminds me of my dad again. With this new opportunity, I'm finally feeling better about my dad after the Mars colony failure.

Chapter 5

"Good to meet you, gentlemen. My name is Dr. Herbert von Vogelsang. I am the General Manager of Digital Neurology here at D-Clo!" Dr. von Vogelsang says enthusiastically with a thick Austrian accent. "Mr. Burke, I'm very pleased to finally meet you. Your father was one of our first customers! He certainly saw the value of D-Clo much earlier than most people. If only he bought stock in our company at the same time. Ho-ho, he'd be a very wealthy man right now. But excuse me. I understand he passed away a few years ago. A shame. A brilliant man born too early to take advantage of the D-Clo. Anyways, what can I do for you?" Dr. von Vogelsang leans in and quiets his voice. "Mr. Burke, are you dying? Do you need to compile already? Do not fret! D-Clo has you covered! We can make the arrangement immediately! You will not even notice your death. What a marvel!"

"I'm not dying." I exhale. "But I do need to compile my D-Clo though."

"Mr. Burke, that is most unusual. Most customers only compile when they are at the end of their life. Why in the world would you want to compile when you are perfectly fine? I know! You want your digital clone to do work for you! You sly genius, this is a great idea! I'll need to add that to the D-Clo website!"

"No...well, sort of. Dr. von Vogelsang, I'm a planetary colonization engineer. I need to go on a mission that I can't go on.

33

But my D-Clo can. We need you to compile my D-Clo and give him to me."

"Interesting!" he exclaims. "Maybe I need to put that on the website too."

"Please don't," Jerry jumps in and says. "I'm going to need you to sign this nondisclosure agreement before we talk anymore." Dr. von Vogelsang signs the NDA without hesitation, not wanting to stall his intrigue.

Dr. von Vogelsang claps his hands in excitement. "Well then, it's really quite simple. I see in our records that your uploads are up-to-date. You've had 99.98 percent days recorded since you were two years old. Very impressive! You should have a fine D-Clo. I'll have my top engineers compile your D-Clo immediately and we'll begin the fidelity tests." Dr. von Vogelsang stands up and walks up to me to shake my hand and lead me into a waiting room. "Wait in this room, Mr. Burke. We will be with you shortly."

***

It seems like I've been waiting in this room for ages since Dr. von Vogelsang left me here. When is this fidelity test going to start? I'm sitting alone at a conference table in a small empty room. No windows. Looks like the type of medical room where they'd tell you you're going to die. There are a few chairs. They seem to be a random set of furniture lying around that they had put into the room. I can't sit still. I can't handle not doing something. Ugh, they need to hurry with my D-Clo. I thought this was going to be fast. I'm so...*bored*! Hey, where is Jerry? Why isn't he in here with me?

"Mr. Burke," Dr. von Vogelsang's voice interrupts over a speaker in the room. "We are ready to begin the fidelity tests."

Finally! I wonder how this is going to pan out. Hopefully my D-Clo doesn't freak out. I wouldn't freak out so he shouldn't freak out. I wonder if they're going to wheel him in on some monitor and we'll just talk to each other.

"Mr. Burke, we are going to ask you a series of questions. Your answers will be compared to your counterpart. It is very important that you don't think about your answers too much. Just say what first comes to mind."

"Yeah, sure thing," I say with enthusiasm knowing that I can finally start the process to get out of here.

"Mr. Burke, please tell me your name, age, and occupation."

Wow, they are really starting at the bottom here.

"Nicolas Joseph Burke. I'm thirty-six years old. I'm a planetary colonization engineer."

"Thank you, Mr. Burke. Now, who was your toughest professor in college?"

"Easy, Mr. Reid. He was tough as nails, but you came out of his class a better engineer. He probably didn't get much love on online reviews, but I'm sure he made a positive difference on a few students."

"Thank you, Mr. Burke. Now, what would you do in this situation? Your Transport Rover suddenly stops and no longer has power. What do you do?"

"This one is easy too. I'd first do a power cycle on the system. If power doesn't come up, I'd switch over to the battery for diagnostics. I'd review the error logs and see if there is an issue. I'll tell you what I wouldn't do. I wouldn't pop open the electronics panel and start poking around. That doesn't end well."

These questions continue for hours. Everything from my past to hypothetical situations. Lots of problem-solving questions. They are all easy questions; they just take a while to go through them all. They must be building a long list of questions and answers to go pitch to my D-Clo.

"Mr. Burke, you did very well. I'll be back shortly," Dr. von Vogelsang says with his usual upbeat tone.

Well, that wasn't so bad. Hopefully they've gotten what they need, and I can get out of here.

After a few minutes, Dr. von Vogelsang speaks over the intercom again. "Mr. Burke, we have the results. I am very happy to say that you have a 98.4 percent fidelity match with Mr. Burke."

"Great! Now can I get out of here now?" I ask.

"Mr. Burke, I needed to have you answer the questions with no interference. No doubt. But I must tell you that *you* are the D-Clo. Your organic self is sitting next to me. You are in a virtual waiting room."

A monitor turns on in the room, floating in the air in front of me. I can see Dr. von Vogelsang with myself and Jerry through a video camera. I look weird. I suppose it's always weird when you see yourself on a TV and not through a mirror. I pause. My thoughts begin to lock up. I feel like my stomach should be doing backflips right now. I'm no longer me. But I don't feel anything. I look around the virtual waiting room processing what has happened to me. Seeing the organic Nick in the monitor calms me. It worked! What I wanted worked!

"Hey, guys," I say finally breaking my silence and leaning up in my seat looking at the monitor while raising my fist. "Meet your new digital overlord. Kill all humans!"

Organic Nick busts out laughing on the screen. Jerry doesn't like my joke. Dr. von Vogelsang leans into the microphone.

"Mr. Burke, your fidelity test only captures your mental match for your personality, memories, and problem solving. Your motor skills will need to be relearned. You'll notice that you're not breathing right now. You can't feel the chair you are sitting in. With your new android body, you'll need to relearn all these things. We are loading you with the basic algorithms, but you will need to learn the specifics with your own body. It'll be like an Olympic athlete learning to walk again after a life-threatening injury."

"Great! Let's get to it. I've got a planet to colonize," I say with excitement and urgency.

"We're going to close the simulation and write the buffers. When you wake up next, you'll be in your android body. Then we'll begin the motor skills training," Dr. von Vogelsang says.

"See you, Digital Nick. Don't do anything I wouldn't do," Organic Nick says to me through the monitor. He looks intrigued and excited. Just as much as myself. Organic Nick leans over to Dr. von Vogelsang. "Doc, you can give the compiled file to Jerry. He'll take care of it from here."

***

I wake up. I'm in another waiting room. A screen turns on and I see Jerry.

"Jerry, we ready to do the motor skills training now?" I ask.

"You already did it, buddy," Jerry says with a bit of disinterest while looking at papers. He looks to be in a busy room with other people around.

"I guess. Vaguely. So, what's next?" I say with some confusion.

"We're nearly ready for launch. We need to brief you on a few things."

"Wow, really? What happened to all the planning? I thought we still needed to get the spaceship figured out. Hell, we still need to finalize all the billionaire investors. There are tons of meetings and briefings that need to happen."

"Already done. You were part of it all, well at least the organic you. We need to get moving if we're going to meet today's launch schedule." Jerry takes a drink of his coffee. He looks like he's been working hard on this launch. He should be proud. This is the most important launch of his career.

"Nick, you are on the Ehmm-Tawg 486 and before you ask, the number meant something to one of investors. They pay so they get to put names on things too. Anyways, you're on a 400 Class Transporter with sixteen—"

"A 400 Class?!" I yell. "A soccer mom has more room in her minivan! It's just an unmanned light cargo transporter and lander. It doesn't even have windows!"

"Yeah, as I told you before, we need to keep the weight down. Besides you don't need windows. There is plenty of radiation shielding though. For propulsion, we're using three of the MarsX ion drives with a solid fuel booster."

"A solid fuel booster? Is that for the launch?" I ask.

"No, actually the Ehmm-Tawg is already in low Earth orbit," he says with a deflated tone. "We're using the booster to get you out of the solar system in a reasonable time frame. It would take you 187 years to get out of the solar system with just the ion drives. We'd rather just get you out of town before anyone changes their mind."

Fair enough, I think. *A lot can happen in 187 years.*

"You're loaded with sixteen embryos..." Jerry continues with a pause waiting for the blowup from me.

"Only sixteen? I told you a hundred are needed," I cry out.

"Yeah, as I told you before, we need to keep the weight down. We also need room for some minimal supplies. You do have an additional sixteen goat embryos for your livestock. You'll need them to have a chance of survival when you get to"—Jerry looks down at a piece of paper—'The planet NGRST-783d'. And before you ask, this planet was chosen by a panel of experts, so don't blame me why you're going there."

"Alright, so I'm on a 400 Class, sixteen human embryos, sixteen goat embryos, supplies, and what else? I don't remember what android body you gave me."

"You're in a MarsX model T200." Again, Jerry braces for impact from me.

"*A Space Yeti*?! You're putting me in a Space Yeti?!"

"You said yourself—the best technology is the kind that is so reliable it's boring. We've built so many T200s, they're pretty much bulletproof at this point. We just put in a bigger hard drive and processor. You're welcome," Jerry smugly says while taking another drink of his coffee.

"Where is me? I mean, Organic Nick? Why can't I see me on the screen?"

"Yeah, you couldn't make it. I think you called in sick today."

"Sick! That's BS! This is the biggest launch of our careers! Why wouldn't I be here? I wouldn't put up with this."

"I don't know what to tell you. You flaked out on yourself. Anyways, everything is pretty routine at this point. You, organic you, doesn't need to be here. You're probably home enjoying the fat paycheck the billionaire investors gave you. You're one lucky guy."

"Fine, what else?" I puffed up in frustration. "A 400 Class, three ion drives, a solid booster, sixteen human embryos, sixteen goat embryos, supplies, and a Space Yeti. Jeez, is there anything that you actually designed from scratch for this project? Everything has been done before."

"Well, we do have two presents for you when you land. We designed them from scratch. They're a surprise."

"I'm riveted."

"Also, ORIN is going with you to be your aide. Lastly, and this is important, everything has been packed in the vacuum of space. There is zero oxygen and water in your ship. No oxygen and water means no degradation."

"Got it, I'm a space mummy."

"Yeah, that's right, buddy. Alright, we're about ready to launch in a few minutes." Jerry perks up and starts looking at his control panel. "You're already loaded on the ship's computer. We've also loaded in all the additional information and digital files you'll ever need. You'll certainly have plenty of reading time. You'll transfer yourself to the Space Yeti when you land."

The waiting room I'm in changes to a classic spaceship cabin with myself sitting in the middle. "Nice touch, Jerry. I'm starting to think you rushed through all this stuff to not give me time to push back." I don't get a response from Jerry on that one.

"Best of luck, Nick. Humanity and shareholders are counting on you." Jerry signs off and the boosters fire.

Chapter 6

M-TOG 486 blasts off from low Earth orbit. It's going to do a flyby on Saturn on its way out of the solar system. I wonder if I should bother staying awake for the flyby. It's not really real, is it? It's just cameras on the outside of the ship looking at it. I'm not really seeing it. It wouldn't be any different than any other flyby footage I've seen from probes. But I guess if I had my eyes, they're really just organic cameras. Maybe I should do it.

I'm going to leave ORIN off for now. I don't need the bad karma of that human-killing robot in this ship right now. I'll need to shut myself down with a timer to wake me back up. Hopefully I do wake back up. There is a nonzero chance I shut down and never wake up again. I would be pretty upset if that happened. If I could be upset. This is my second and only chance at achieving my life's goal. It's all for nothing if I fail at setting up an interplanetary colony. Organic Nick is still alive and I would imagine he'll recompile when he dies. That's what I'd do. I guess if I don't wake up, so it goes. I can't be upset that I don't wake up, because I'm not awake to be upset. But Organic Nick would be furious. I think I will wake myself up for Saturn. There is a lower probability of a problem occurring in that short trip. At least I'll see something worthwhile.

I set the wake-up timer for six years, twenty-three days, and twelve hours—just at the time for best viewing of Saturn. In the virtualized space cabin, I dial in the numbers next to the big button labeled Start Sleep Mode. Well, here it goes. I push the button. I blink but nothing happens. Maybe I need to hit it again. Pausing for a moment, I decide to take a look outside using the cameras.

"Holy hell! That's Saturn! We're already there!" I forgot that time isn't the same for me. In a snap of the fingers, I'm already at Saturn. In another snap of the fingers I could be on the other side of the galaxy. Saturn is an unworldly, godlike object. I do not regret my decision to be awake for the flyby...at all.

After the high wears off, I settle in for thinking about the big trip. NGRST-783d is about 779 light-years away. With the speedup and slowdown, the trip will be about three thousand years, with a cruising speed of about 50 percent the speed of light. Back on Earth the time that will have passed would be more than three thousand years due to Einstein's special relativity effects. Time goes slower while on board the ship when you're traveling really fast. I wonder if I should wake myself up while at cruising speed? Nah, I wouldn't see much. Besides, it's probably best to keep things simple when traveling as one of the fastest objects in the galaxy.

I set the wake-up timer for 3001 years, seventy-eight days, and two hours. The time on my ship, not on Earth. I remember that they are just numbers. They don't seem like much when I punch them in. I'll wake up inside the NGRST-783 solar system, but not to the planet yet. I'll likely need to do some course corrections to stick a good orbit around NGRST-783d. I hit the start sleep mode button. I blink. Remember, I just need to hit it once as I look at my finger over the button.

***

NGRST-783d is a stunning new home. It's a rocky, Earth-sized planet with lots of water. A bright blue-green planet. Alright! The first thing is to not go land on the planet. My lander is just a lander. It is a one-way ticket to the planet. I need to find the perfect spot first. I can take all the time I want. I've been traveling three thousand years. What's a few more months of surveying? I maneuver the M-

TOG into a polar orbit circling the planet. The elegant thing about a polar orbit is the planet does much of the work for you. You just need to kick back and let the planet rotate underneath you as your camera scans and you build up a full map of the planet.

The first realization I have of surveying the planet is that it doesn't have widespread artificial light at night. Therefore, it doesn't have any intelligent life. There is always a random light, but that can be attributed to natural fires occurring. So, a "no" for aliens, and also a "no" for faster than light travel with earthlings beating me here. I guess this planet is all mine.

After a few weeks of surveying and reviewing the results, I decide on the landing location. It's on the edge of a sea adjacent to a freshwater river. The land is a flat plain. The climate is mild. I'd expect a rare snowstorm in the winter and mild summers. No hurricanes or tornadoes. A perfect place to start a civilization.

Before landing, I'll send one of the two probes I have. The probe is a small robotic lander, no bigger than a shoebox. I reorient the M-TOG orbit, then deploy the probe to the landing site. It will get ground truth data on climate, flora, fauna, and microbial activity. I release the probe and watch it do its slow descent onto the planet.

After a few hours, it begins feeding data back to me. Climate gets an A+. Flora looks okay from what I can see. The video scan has green vegetation at varying heights. Some of the vegetation looks like trees, some looks like bushes, and some looks like grasses. Inconclusive on fauna. What am I to expect? The alien lander doesn't really say "animals of NGRST-783d please come say hi!"

Looking at the microbe log, things are not looking good. I'm reading the log with growing disappointment. The planet has heavy and aggressive microbial activity. The probe ran the microbe samples against the human model. The results indicate a rapid attack and destruction to human cells. I double-check the results.

"You have got to be kidding me!" I exclaim, slumping back into my virtual captain's chair. I came all this way, found this perfect planet, and now I can't land on it because it's teeming with superbugs.

I sit back, rubbing my head realizing I can't feel it. The same rage and panic from Mars sweeps over me. I feel the same guilt as I had when we left Mars. I'm letting everyone down. I'm letting my dad down. All these embryos are never going to live. What can I do? I suppose I could land and keep the lander sealed. I'll grow an embryo and try genetically modifying it using the CRISPR technique to modify the DNA to be more resistant to the superbugs. It might take a few years. And trial and error. With several human deaths before hopefully I could get it all figured out.

What am I talking about? I can't do that. I'm not going to make a baby live through that horror. Live in a windowless, crowded container, then eventually open up the M-TOG and hope the baby survives the superbugs. I can't do that! Besides how would I get water and food into the ship? We made the argument that we need to find a planet that is much like ours so building a civilization would be as easy as falling out of a tree. This planet is not the one.

"ORIN, wake up! I need you to give me some ideas," I call out into the virtual space cabin.

"Hello, sir, it is good to see you again." ORIN is now a full-fledged version of Alfred from the cartoon Batman. Smugness and all in his tuxedo outfit and perfect posture. "Sir, what can I do to help?"

"What are your thoughts on the problem we're having here?"

"Sir, I really don't know. NGRST-783d has a 78 percent chance of being a habitable planet. It is a habitable planet as evident by the abundant life on it."

"Yeah, well the geniuses that asked for 'habitable' should have been more specific in asking for human habitable."

"That is true, sir. What should we do?"

"I've got one more probe," I point out to ORIN. "I could pick another location on the planet and launch it there. It may not be as ideal of location climate wise, but we might be able to get the civilization started. Those superbugs can't be everywhere."

"That is true, sir. Should I ready the second probe?"

"Hang on and let me think."

I'd be a pretty terrible planetary colonization god, I mean engineer, if I started a civilization that would ultimately expand throughout the globe only to eventually find the superbug and get killed off anyways. That's not a success. That's a whole lot of suffering waiting to happen. And I will have failed.

"Cancel the probe. ORIN, what other *human*-habitable exoplanets are nearby?"

"Sir, the most promising planet is NGRST-1881e. It is remarkably similar to Earth in size and length of days and years. It is 532 light-years away."

"Sounds interesting. Do we have enough juice to get there?"

"Sir, there are no liquids on this ship. Taking the most efficient trajectory will require us to leave now to achieve a slingshot maneuver around the sun, then around the largest gas giant planet in this solar system. It will take 2,048 years and we will need 67 percent of our remaining energy to get there."

"Alright then, what are we waiting for? Set our course for NGRST-1881e."

***

From Earth to the second planet, it feels like only a few weeks, but in reality, we've been traveling for over five thousand years. Our ship has experienced five thousand years. Back on Earth is it more time, roughly five thousand, six hundred years. It seems like a big number, but it's just a number. We arrive at NGRST-1881e and again it's a remarkable planet. A lush blue, green, orange color. About a fifty-fifty split of ocean and land. Similar size to Earth, similar length of days and years.

"I can't wait to see how this planet won't work for us either," I call out to ORIN.

We began the polar orbit surveying again, just like the previous planet. Again, no widespread artificial light so no intelligent life. After a few weeks of surveying and reviewing the results, again I decide on the landing site to be at a sea adjacent to a freshwater river.

There are several rivers running into the sea, so I just pick one at random. The land is flat, but there are rocky mountains nearby. Again, the climate is mild and the geothermal activity looks reasonable. I need to launch the last probe and get the results back. This is my last chance.

After picking our landing site, we reorient the M-TOG and send our last probe. This is our last hope. If it comes back negative, we're done for. I release the probe and watch it slowly descend onto the planet.

As soon as the data comes in, I jump first to review the microbial information. If I'm going to be let down, I might as well get it out of the way. Looking through the microbial information, it looks...good. Actually great! All the tests for human and other Earth organisms we brought with us look great!

"ORIN, I think we've got a winner here!"

"Splendid, sir."

I look through the rest of the information. The air is nearly identical to Earth's. The climate is perfect. The video scan has green and orange vegetation all over the place. As far as fauna, I don't see much, but there appear to be something flying up in the sky. Perhaps something like birds. Well, I guess this is it. It looks pretty good and we don't really have any other choice.

***

The M-TOG is made up of two parts, a lander and an orbiter. The orbiter will stay in orbit indefinitely while we take the lander down to the planet. I need the orbiter to remain in space is because it is our long-term cold storage. As soon as we land, we'll be back into the world of oxygen, water, and warm temperatures. All our embryos will be destroyed unless we incubate them all at once. But we can't do that. We've only got four incubators on the lander. So, the orbiter needs to remain in space and send new embryos down when we need them.

The lander is already packed and ready to go. Nothing to do other than separate and descend. At the correct location above the planet, the lander separates and begins its descent. I am in full control. No way I am leaving this to ORIN to do. We take a very slow descent down to the landing site. Here is where the first M-TOG mechanical items need to work. We'll be deploying a five-thousand-year-old parachute from a five-thousand-year-old hatch. Wish us luck. I press the deploy button to release the parachute. I hold my breath and then remember I am not breathing. I watch and see that everything is deploying correctly. Five thousand years without air or water does wonders to prevent aging.

During the descent I have full control to navigate. We need to travel to the site, but we've got plenty of altitude to get there. Weather is perfect and we should not have any issues. During the descent we start to equalize the pressure and atmosphere on the inside of the cab. It is important to do this slowly and the descent is as good a time as any to do it. We break through the clouds and can see the landing site. An open field with plenty of room to maneuver. As we get closer, we adjust the parachutes to slow to a crawl and then finally we land with an easy bump.

I look over at ORIN. "See! That is how you do it!"

"Splendid job, sir."

Chapter 7

It happened...it really has happened! We're here! We are on a new planet! I'm the first person—I mean robot—to make it to an interstellar planet! I provide minimal power to the Space Yeti body by turning on a wireless charger. Once it gains power, I connect to it with wireless communication. I transfer my digital self into the Space Yeti body and do a reboot. Inside the Space Yeti, the electrical producing portion of the HE-TEG had been separated away from the radioactive source for the journey. Spring loaded thermal insulation retracts and snaps the HE-TEG into electricity-producing mode starting its one hundred year life. Starting the HE-TEG inside the Space Yeti is like pulling that little plastic strip to let the batteries start powering the device that you finally took out of the box. My cameras turn on and all I can see is that it is dark in the cab because there are no windows. There is faint light from the console LED lights. My sight seems normal, even through the cameras in my Space Yeti helmet. Then I remember that I'm not Nick. I'm a copy of Nick. A copy that was built using cameras in Nick's glasses. I'm strapped into a chair sitting down. I reach down and unbuckle myself. Lean forward. Stand up. *Thunk!* "What was that?" I reach around and quickly realize that I forgot the cab is not Space Yeti height and I had bashed my head on the ceiling. I lean down and shuffle to the exit door. After opening it, I find that the door itself isn't Space Yeti width either. I have to turn sideways and shuffle to get out of the lander. Finally, I'm standing up and seeing the new planet for the first time.

The dirt is bright orange with shades ranging from pumpkin to rust. The ground cover is a bright green, moss-like plant. Looking up at the sky I see a calm, blue, cloudless day. I take a walk around the lander to make sure everything is okay. The 400 Class Transporter's lander is about the size of a family camping tent. It seems so much smaller than I remember back in my MarsX days. I see the stenciling M-TOG 486 on the side of it. Everything is looking good with the lander. Other than the fresh dirt on the lander's feet you would think it is brand-new.

I give myself an inspection. Looking at my hands and legs I can see that I am a brand-new Space Yeti. My bright white space suit contrasts with the alien landscape. After finishing the necessities of the postlanding inspection, I eagerly jump to the next task of inspecting the area.

"ORIN, hold down the fort while I take a walk. Try not to burn the place down while I'm gone."

"Sir, I assure you that the gravity on this planet is sufficient to keep the lander firmly planted on the ground. No hold-down straps are required. Although I believe the lander could catch on fire, I certainly wouldn't start it on fire voluntarily. As you know I am housed in the M-TOG now. It is now who I am."

I do a walk around the perimeter of the area. The M-TOG lander is in the center of an open field. There is a river on the north side of the site running west to east with heavy tree growth surrounding it. Looking west you can see rocky mountains. Toward the east, you can't see the sea, but I bet if I did some hiking through the trees I'd eventually see it. To the south I don't see anything other than more open fields.

I walk toward the river. It's a short walk along a gentle downward slope, then a sharper slope toward the end near the river's edge. I specifically picked this location because it seems close enough to the river, but not so close we'd be in trouble if it floods. Near the river there is a lot more vegetation. The predominant foliage is tall, treelike plants with hard trunks about the diameter of a basketball. Hanging from the tops of the trees are ropes that look like they're made of hemp. I pull on one of the ropes and a few seeds fall down. They look like coconuts about the size of rugby balls. I walk down to the river's edge, stopping before my feet go into the water. Interestingly it looks just like any river on Earth. Its rocky riverbed allowed it to be clear and crisp. I need to get a sample of the water. But I don't have an empty vial or cup. I don't think I even have anything in the lander. Looking around I see a leaf that has somewhat of a concave shape. It's a mix of dark green with edges of bright orange. I dip the leaf into the river and pull out a small amount of water.

Carefully I walk back up to the lander, my free hand under the leaf to catch any droplets. I don't know why I am doing that. It seems to be the thing to do. I crawl back inside the M-TOG lander and get to the material identifier station. The material identifier station can tell you everything about anything you put in it. Is it dangerous? Is it okay to eat? Does it have some medical properties? It's probably one of the most important aspects of the M-TOG lander. Hundreds or thousands of years are leapfrogged that would otherwise have been spent trying to figure things out by trial and error. I put a few drops of water on the specimen slide and hit the big green button to start the analysis. It processes for a few seconds, then a big green happy face shows on the monitor. ORIN's voice speaks, "Water, H_2O, safe for consumption after purification."

"Full analysis?" I ask.

"Specimen is H_2O with trace amounts of sodium, potassium, calcium, magnesium, chloride, sulfate, hydrogen carbonate. Microbial life detected. Unclear if unsafe if consumed. Recommended to purify water before consumption. External use of water is okay."

"Thanks, ORIN," I reply.

"You are welcome, sir."

Just out of curiosity I stick a small piece of the leaf I used as a cup in the material identification station. After a few seconds a big green happy face screen shows again with ORIN's voice, "Safe for consumption. Use as pain reliever."

Huh, well there you go. I'll need to remember that when I build the medical supplies.

I exit the lander. It's an odd sight to see sitting in the middle of an empty field. The lander is powered by solar panels with a battery backup. No HE-TEG in the lander. The idea is that the M-TOG lander should be the center of the new civilization, hopefully for centuries. A HE-TEG would last only a hundred years and then would become a radioactive liability afterward. It's not exactly the best idea to leave a ticking time bomb in your newly created interplanetary colony.

I need to deploy more solar panels to make sure the M-TOG has adequate power during its next mission. I open a side hatch and grab the stack of solar panels. Excitedly, I lay them near the lander and one-by-one start hooking up the connectors. After attaching everything and connecting to the lander, I see that they're all working properly with reassuring LED lights turning on. Sometime in the future I'll need to set them up on a more permanent structure, but for now lying on the ground should be okay.

"Well, ORIN, I suppose it's time we start making babies. You up for that?"

"If you say so, sir. I am ready to incubate your embryos."

I bust out laughing. "ORIN, you're never short of the jokes, are you?"

***

A digital note Jerry left me pops into my digital view. *Nick, if you are reading this you've successfully landed on your new planet and are ready to start incubating. During the countless meetings prior to launch with the investors and engineers we decided the best starting group of embryos with the four incubators on the M-TOG lander is one human girl, two female goats, and one male goat. These are the embryos that have been preloaded into the M-TOG lander. You need to immediately start incubating the embryos when you land because they are no longer in cold storage from the trip. Best of luck, buddy, Jerry.*

Goats are an easy choice. They produce milk, which the human babies will need once they've gone through their powder formula ration. The goats will produce wool, and eventually meat. Most important about the goats is that a baby goat is about the size of a baby human. Cows and horses are too big for the incubators. We are able to use the exact same incubators for the goats as for the humans.

The three goats will complete their incubation first. Their gestation time is about five months. Once they are born, I'll put in a request to the orbiter to get more incubator capsules. For the second group I'll do a human boy and two more female goats. We'll need to have plenty of goat milk. For the kids and the kids. There's not exactly baby food lying around here on this planet. At least not that I know of without using ORIN's material identifier station.

Before starting the incubators, I decide that I had my fill of the lander being a bit too cramped for a Space Yeti. Using small hand tools included in the lander, I remove the entry door and side panel to make the entrance bigger. Then I remove another panel to get access to the storage area. I can walk in and around the lander now with more ease.

In storage inside the M-TOG lander, I find the two gifts Jerry had given me. The first is a high-grade alloy steel double-edged ax with its end shaped like a shovel. The handle is a long slender rod. I stand up with it. The blade stands about chest height on me with the butt of the handle sitting on the ground. *Hmmm...what should I call you? I dub you...Bearpaw.* A suitable name inspired by my favorite sword, Longclaw. The second gift is a machete knife about as long as my forearm. It has a pointed end and serrated back edge like a saw. *I dub you...Sting.* I expect you to start glowing when the Orcs come by.

Before I can get the incubators going, I need to get purified water. I'll need to make firewood to boil the river water. I grab my new friend Bearpaw and head down to the river with excitement to try out my new toy on the trees. Once near the river, I eye my first target. I've never swung an ax before, but when I was a kid my dad taught me how to swing a baseball bat.

I take a wide Space Yeti stance and wind Bearpaw back into grand slam potential. I swing the blade forward with my full Space Yeti force. It slices right through it so easily that I stumble and fall forward onto the ground. I'm not sure if the tree is that weak or I'm that strong. The tree lurches and starts to fall over making crackling branch noises as it falls. I quickly get up and run out of the way to make sure it doesn't fall on top of me. The tree makes a satisfying thud when it hits the ground. I walk back and lean over to look at the cut edge of the trunk. It looks more like a fungus than wood. But when I touch it, it's hard like wood. I give it a few knocks with my Space Yeti knuckles for good luck. I cut the fallen trunk into firewood lengths with mechanized ease. Then I split the logs into smaller firewood pieces. When all done, I have a reasonable pile of firewood. It takes a couple of trips, but I carry all the firewood back up near the lander and drop it into a pile.

"ORIN, I hope this wood actually burns."

"Sir, you should have used the material identifier station to confirm before creating the logs."

"Yeah, I probably should have. I guess we'll just need to find out the old-fashioned way."

I use Bearpaw as a shovel to make a firepit and clear out the mossy grass cover surrounding it. After nonstop digging I'm not tired at all. Actually, I don't feel tired or energized. "Normal," I guess you would say. It hits me again that I'm not Nick Burke. I'm a Space Yeti with a rough copy of Nick Burke's brain in it. Am I still Nick? Or was he a past life and I'm someone different? Both Organic Nick and I could probably become a Thinker statue trying to figure out that philosophical question for a whole century. But there is no time for that now. My new life has one purpose, which is kick-starting this new planet's human civilization.

***

Saying that the M-TOG lander is packed light is an understatement. There are small tools to work on the lander itself, Bearpaw, Sting, baby formula, embryos, and plant seeds. No matches. No igniters. No flint. How am I going to get this fire going? I grab some dried-up leaves and twigs down by the river. Let me try doing the rubbing-a-stick-into-a-log thing. I rub the stick against a log while keeping the dried leaves nearby. Like a factory machine, I rub in mechanical precision at blurring speed. After a few seconds I get the flame to ignite. I quickly blow on the fire to keep it going. Nothing is happening, I don't even see the smoke move. Wait, what? What am I doing? I start waving my hands at the flame to stoke it. I forgot I don't have a mouth. Or lungs. Luckily the flame starts to take off and I begin putting logs on.

Now for the water. I need some water buckets. That leaf I used to get the water sample isn't going to cut it. Again, nothing is available in the lander. But I remember those rugby coconuts near the river. Sting and I go back down by the river. I grab a rugbynut and cut one end off like a jack-o'-lantern top. Liquid pools at the bottom. Dumping it out I see that the inside flesh is soft, but the outside is hard. I grab a flat rock and scoop out the soft flesh. My Space Yeti paw could just barely fit in there. I finish making five more rubgynut buckets. I can carry only two at a time if I hold them. I'll need a way to carry more. Looking around and see the hemp rope hanging from the trees. One a hard yank and it comes down with a few more rugbynuts bouncing off the ground. I take the rope and make a sling around a rugbynut. Holding the rugbynut up by the rope, everything is staying connected. Continuing, I sling the rest of the rugbynut buckets and hang them from Bearpaw's handle so that I can put the handle over my shoulders. Three buckets on my left side, three buckets on my right.

Standing tall, I have all six buckets hanging off Bearpaw on my shoulders and walk over to the river. I dip one group in at a time filling them up. Slowly I walk back up to the firepit near the lander. When I get there, I put the buckets down on the ground. Immediately they all tip over spilling all over the place. Luckily the dirt mound around the firepit keeps out the water. But my ingenious bucket idea is looking ridiculous at this point. I take and cut a flat bottom into one of the buckets being careful to not cut a hole through the hard, outer shell. I stand it back up on the ground to make sure it would stand on its own. I even give it a nudge to see if it would fall over. It stays upright just fine so I cut the rest of them to have the same flat bottoms.

It is unlikely that I'll be able to put these rugbynut buckets into the fire to boil the water and not have them catch fire themselves. I need a cauldron, made out of something that won't catch fire. I look around the area and don't see much that the planet can offer. But one of the aluminum panels I had taken off the lander catches my eye. I take extra firewood logs and layer them out into a ring, three rows high. Then I lay the flat panel on top of the ring. I punch straight down in the middle of the panel and so that it buckles inward making a deep indent. That Space Yeti strength has come through again. I manhandle it more into shape with my mechanized power. I end up with a rough cauldron shape with wide horizontal flanges on the top edge. I go back down to the river and cut some smaller trees and get more rope. I bring them back up and build a structure over the firepit to hold the cauldron. The cauldron's wide flanges slide right over the branches holding it up over the fire.

After filling up the rugbynut buckets again, I cautiously dump them into the cauldron, half expecting it to topple over and dump water all over the fire. The cauldron steams as it starts to warm up. Everything is holding while I imagine holding my breath.

It's starting to get dark. I can see the stars coming out. This planet doesn't have a moon. Instead it has a faint flat ring you can see in the nighttime. Maybe the ring used to be a moon. Or maybe someday it will become a moon. Either way it looks surreal and is a reminder that I am not in my backyard.

Flickering campfire light dances on the side of the M-TOG lander when the cauldron finally starts boiling. Hopefully that's enough to kill off all the space bugs. I grab the cauldron by the flanges and start filling up the empty rugbynut buckets. As I let them cool, I go back to the lander to get things ready.

The embryos are prepackaged in transparent, cylindrical capsules about one meter in length and twenty-five centimeters in diameter. One half of the capsule is dry pellets that will be the food during the incubation. The other half looks empty, but really that is where the embryo will gestate. I grab the first capsule and lug it over to the incubator. I stand the capsule upright with the food on top and lock into place with a lever arm. I then grab two buckets of water that had cooled off and dump them into the top inlet. The whole process feels like I am making coffee. I repeat the process for the other three capsules. The last step is to hit the go buttons for all four incubators.

"I hope this works, ORIN. Let's hope the incubator water filters will clean out all the rugbynut floaties." I hit the go button and the incubator timer automatically starts a countdown: five months for the goats, nine months for the human girl. The timers will adjust based on the ongoing monitoring of the fetuses to ensure that the birth dates would be optimum.

Feeling pretty accomplished, I sit down, leaning against the lander looking back at the campfire. I didn't get lost in space. I didn't blow up during the landing on this planet. No alien monsters are tearing me apart on their planet I invaded. At least not yet. It has been a good day. The first I've had in five thousand years. If I had a beer I would drink it. I realize that I don't remember what beer tastes like, but I remember that I liked it. My body is not tired, but my mind feels like it needs to rest. It's probably an effect of the D-Clo's deep learning neural network training. Mental tiredness must have been trained into the digital clone of Nick. I set my sleep mode timer to wake me at daylight. The next steps will be easier when it is not dark out anyways. My sleep mode isn't a cognitive shutdown. To combat the D-Clo mental tiredness, I need to replicate human consciousness while sleeping. I drift into a low consciousness fog, like a warm, heavy blanket to let my mind rest.

Chapter 8

I'm feeling excited but also a little panicked on all I need to do. I've got five months to prepare for the first interplanetary goats. Water, food, and shelter are all needed. I won't need any of that for myself, but my kids will. The baby goats will eat formula from the M-TOG lander for the first two and half months. After that I'll need alfalfa hay to fill their diet. I have no idea if any of the local flora will be goat food friendly. I decide to start a field of alfalfa hay and wheat before I work on any other projects. Using Bearpaw, I scribe out a border of five fields, each about the size of a basketball court. I decide to make the fields a short walk away from the lander to the northwest near the river, so they won't be in the way later when I start construction of buildings and possibly allowing me to set up an irrigation system from the river.

"Sir, may I advise you to test the soil at my material identification station before you proceed with your plan?"

ORIN is right. I don't want to jump the gun like I did with the firewood. But I can't help feeling annoyed by his comment. Using Sting I dig a small sample of soil and bring it back to the lander to have ORIN analyze it. After hitting the analyze button, I see a big green light.

"Nutrient rich soil suitable for crops," ORIN says.

"Good. I would have a hard time improving the nutrients otherwise, ORIN. My Space Yeti body doesn't make any fertilizer."

"No, sir, your body would give no value being buried. The HE-TEG in your chest has a nuclear core that is dangerous to humans."

Again, ORIN is annoyingly right. I'll need to figure out what to do with myself when I die to keep from causing a radioactive mess that would kill off my civilization. Maybe when I've hit the end of my hundred-year life, I'll take a boat out to the middle of the sea and jump in. The bottom of the ocean would be as safe as anywhere.

It takes me eight days to clear off all the ground cover and till the fields. I really need to make a plow and get a big animal to pull it. Unfortunately, horses and cows didn't make it on my tiny M-TOG. I choose the seed canisters from the lander like selecting from a spice rack. I open the alfalfa hay seed canister first and spread the seeds with mechanical precision over the first field. Then I open the wheat canister and seed the second field. Next, I take a bamboo seed canister and disperse it on the third field. The fourth field I seed cotton. The fifth field I leave barren for now. I'll seed it with vegetables, but I will wait until the kids arrive to plant it.

Using the rugbynut buckets, I make a tedious number of trips getting water from the river and watering the fields. Hauling water like this isn't going to fly. I'm going to need to come up with something better sometime. I add that to my mental to-do list.

"Sir, I really should advise you that it is the intent of the M-TOG design that it be protected from the elements by a structure built around it. May I advise you on any proposed designs?"

"No, you may not." It has only been a few days, but ORIN is starting to get on my nerves. I'm starting to get a bit of social cabin fever and ORIN is not a pleasant conversationalist.

With the M-TOG lander opened up to the elements, it would be best if I build a shed over the top of it. I walk a square perimeter around it to get its measurements. I do this by putting my toe to heel measuring how many steps it is on each side. The new unit of measure of this planet is Space Yeti feet. The M-TOG shed is twenty-by-twenty Space Yeti feet. Next, I take Bearpaw's blade and scribe into the ground the outline of a small building nearby the M-

TOG. It's about the size of a large bedroom from a normal house. My house will be ten-by-sixteen Space Yeti feet.

"Sir, I might advise that you consider inspecting more of this planet for more types of building materials before proceeding."

I don't even respond to ORIN. I grab Sting and throw Bearpaw over my shoulder, holding its handle like a baseball bat, and walk toward the nearest patch of trees down by the river. I size up my first tree, setting Bearpaw on the ground next to it, and spit on my hands, then realize again that I don't have spit and I don't have a mouth. I need to stop doing that. I pick up Bearpaw, wind back, and swing for the fences. I barely feel anything as I fall forward. The tree lurches forward and downward, with the sound of breaking branches and falling rugbynuts as it comes down. I walk down to the base of the tree, then measure out my twenty Space Yeti feet, plus an extra foot for overhang.

I scribe the top of the log with Sting's serrated edge and start pacing out the next one. I cut off branches as I go, using Sting as a saw. I'm able to get four big diameter logs for the side walls and five smaller diameter logs for the roof. With the log cleaned and branches ready for the cuts, I walk with Bearpaw to the first cut. I walk down the length of the tree giving satisfying, single swings of Bearpaw to cut the logs to length.

Well, that wasn't too bad. Reviewing my internal clock, this first tree took me about an hour. I'm going to need another fifty trees or so. Looking around I see there are hundreds of trees that are all the right size. The first thing that comes to my mind is the old Walt Disney Paul Bunyan cartoon my dad showed me. The one where he's cutting down trees like an unstoppable machine. Well, I'm a machine and it's time to show up Mr. Bunyan. I grab Bearpaw and walk up to the nearest tree and give it a modest swing. Before it falls, I move to the next one with a casual stride and swing again. I keep moving forward and start doing backhand cuts through trees. Walking faster, cutting quicker, keeping an eye where the trees are landing so they don't land on me. I try doing a one-handed cut. No problem. I do a roundhouse swing over my head. No problem. I start jogging and swinging.

It's full-on battle mode now and I'm clearing out the area of trees. I throw Bearpaw at the last tree with a sideways spin. Bearpaw spirals in the air toward the tree like a flying saw blade. But the handle hits the tree making a vibrating *thud*, then drops to the ground. The tree looks smug without even dropping a single rugbynut. Feeling a bit defeated and concerned, I walk over and pick up Bearpaw to see if I bent the handle. I pick it up and look down the handle, happy to find it hadn't bent. "You are a lucky guy, Nick. Don't do that again," I say to myself.

Looking back at the warpath I had just laid, I see about a hundred trees on the ground, intertwined and on top of each other. Hemp rope and rugbynuts strewn all over the place. It is going to take me a while to get this all cut to length and cleaned up. Not my wisest decision. I swing downward and lodge Bearpaw's blade into a stump with a frustrated flick and walk toward the pile to start pulling apart the trees and setting them on the ground. Grabbing the first tree I see dark dots appear on the trunk. It is starting to rain.

***

I need some music to listen to. I search my onboard storage and find another digital note from Jerry. *Nick, if you are reading this then you must be getting bored listening to the alien birds chirp and you are looking for music. I know how much music means to you. So, I loaded the entirety of Earth's music catalog into your T200 onboard hard drive. You're welcome. I've also loaded onto the M-TOG a fully stocked digital library including books, Wikipedia, YouTube, and any other resources you can think of. Best of luck, buddy, Jerry*

I'm not a survivalist. I'm not a farmer. But I could teach myself anything with the right resources. Thanks, Jerry.

I need some music to pick me up. I've listened to music all my life. At least Nick's organic life. Most of the songs I like were made before I was even born. Even before my dad was born. But even so the classics never age. I try a few songs to play inside my computer head. If I am digital, and my music is digital, why let the analog world get in my way? I find that I don't like it when the music is just played in my head. It doesn't feel like listening to music. It is more of knowing the song already and all its lyrics. I find it works better to play the music out of my speech speakers and listen with my microphones. This would have been how Organic Nick would have listened to music anyways.

I search through the tracklist until finally, "Here we go." COMMAND LOAD PLAY. Standing in a pile of fallen trees. In a low area near a humming river. On an alien planet a thousand light-years away from Earth. A slide guitar and driving drumbeat hits the foreign, alien air...of Tom Petty and the Heartbreakers, "I Won't Back Down". I instantly remember when I was a kid having to rake leaves while my dad was scooping them up and putting them into a yard waste bag. The work seemed to pass faster with music. I think my dad was just a kid when Tom Petty died. My dad listened to music with his dad. Then he shared it with me. Funny how it was all the same old music. Modern music just doesn't have that charm. Listening to the music makes the tree cleanup work more like a pleasant hike than a punishing march. It also reminds me of my dad as if he were here helping me.

Pulling apart the trees is a bit more fun now with motivational help from the music. I lay them out so each one is on the ground, cutting off all the branches as I go. I throw all the hemp rope in one pile and rugbynuts in another pile. I measure out all the logs and use Bearpaw to cut them with precision.

The rain is starting to pick up.

The M-TOG lander is uphill from where I am. I need to carry all these logs uphill to the site. I grab the first one with my arms wrapped around it and start walking up the hill. The rain is really starting to come down now. My white boots and ankles are now a muddy dark orange. I start up the hill, but I can't get a footing. My feet keep slipping. Not only am I Space Yeti-sized, but I'm also Space Yeti heavy. The log I'm holding isn't helping either.

"Bearpaw, time to do some digging." I start cutting some stairs into the hill, scooping and shoveling with the ax. Starting at the bottom of the hill and working my way up. Standing on one stair step while cutting the higher steps. I get to the top of the hill after about ten steps and can see the M-TOG lander. It's starting to get dark. It's also a downpour now. I should probably call it a day, but I need to go get Sting. He's still stuck in a log down by the river. I drop Bearpaw at the top of the hill and walk back down the dirt stairs.

Lifting my legs over the logs, I make my way to Sting near the river's edge. Stepping down, I land in a puddle. Looking around, it's actually a big puddle. And it's moving. I look over and I see that the river level has risen up to the point of where the logs are resting. Looking down the river, I see one of my logs floating away.

"You have got to be kidding me!" I yell out to the river.

I turn off my music. It is time to think. How am I going to get these logs up the hill before the river takes them all? I grab the first one next to the stairs, headlock it, and start up the dirt steps. I make it to the top, and drop the log in the field. I turn around and briskly go back down. I get to the bottom and realize that the dirt stairs are already falling apart. The weight of the logs is causing my feet to seep into the wet soil. I'm only going to be able to move a few more logs before I'll need to redig the stairs.

I can't lose these logs. Who knows how long it's going to rain? How long will the river run high? For all I know this alien planet might like having storms that go for months! I don't know if the M-TOG will survive that long without shelter. I'll lose the embroys! I need to get these logs up and out of here *now*! I see another log start floating down the river. I turn on my helmet headlamps because it's getting too dark. I see the flickers of rain droplets reflecting the light back at me.

I'm not going to be able to get these logs out in time one by one. I need to get multiple logs out at time. I rush out toward the river to grab the outermost logs and pull them inland. That should buy me a few hours. I put the last log down and it rolls a bit over the top of some hemp rope. Standing there looking down at the log, it hits me.

"I've got an idea!" I shout out.

I boot up communication to the M-TOG from where I am.

"ORIN! Can you hear me? I'm down by the river," I yell through the connection.

"Sir, what can I do to assist you?"

"ORIN! What's the best knot for making long rope?!"

"Sir, according to my search, it would be double fisherman's knot. Would you like me to stream you the how-to video?"

"Yes!!"

After learning how to make the knot, my Space Yeti body springs into action. I sprint to the pile of hemp rope I had made earlier and start making two very long ropes, about two hundred meters each. I throw them over my shoulder and grab Sting and a medium diameter log to head back up the dirt stairs toward the M-TOG lander. When I get to the top, I look around to find a clearing in the sloped hill where there are no trees. Then I walk away from that location inland. About seventy-five meters away I drop the log, Sting, and the ropes. I retrieve Bearpaw, which is back near the top of the dirt stairs. I hope this works. If I had a heart it would be pumping right now.

ORIN speaks to me over the communication connection. "Sir, may I suggest—"

"ORIN. Buddy. Let me handle this. I'll let you know when I need you." No response from ORIN.

Taking Bearpaw I cut the log into two shorter logs, then start cutting sharp points to make two giant wooden stakes. With both hands I hold the first stake upright with the pointy end aimed at the ground and using my full Space Yeti force, I slam the stake into the ground, getting it about a third of the way down. Using the flat edge of Bearpaw's blade I pound it in the rest of the way. I don't hold back. Two swings gets it to the depth it needs to be. I measure out seven Space Yeti feet from the post and spike the second stake into the ground. The two stakes are parallel to the river. I take the hemp ropes, wrap each one around a stake a bunch of times, and tie a knot to secure it. Grabbing Bearpaw and Sting I take the free ends of the ropes and quickly walk them down to the river, letting out rope slack as I go. I really need to make some holsters for Bearpaw and Sting so I don't need to carry them all the time.

Carefully, I walk down the sloped clearing and drop the two rope bundles at the bottom. I stack the logs into two carefully assembled piles. When I'm done there are two triangular stacks of logs close together with a cradle between them. I'm working at breakneck speed in the dark and rain. I keep wiping the rain from my visor cameras so I can see. I take the two long ropes, pull them tight against the stakes, then lay them over the cradle. Then I grab three unknotted hemp ropes from the pile and drape them over the cradle as well.

I take the new logs and stack them inside the cradle with the rope underneath them. Inside the cradle, they take the shape of an octagon. After putting the last log on, I use the three short ropes to tie the octagon into a bundle. I then start moving the free stack logs closest to the stakes out of the way. I've now got a round bundle that is about half as tall as myself with ten large diameter logs, twenty small diameter logs, and two ropes to pull the whole bundle up the hill.

High-stepping up the hill with the two ropes in hand, I make my way to the two stakes. "ORIN, I hope this works," I say looking at the M-TOG lander drenched in rain. Once I get to the end of the ropes, I take one over each shoulder and face away from the river. I walk forward until the ropes are taut. I lean forward and stomp my feet into the ground to gain traction. I start moving forward as I feel the bundle rolling up the hill. The ropes dig into my Space Yeti shoulders. I keep driving my legs forward, but I'm in a horizontal crawl. I'm covered in dark orange mud while the rain continues unwaveringly.

I feel when the bundle crests at the top of the hill and rolls much easier. I turn around and pull the ropes from a standstill. The log bundle rolls toward me at walking speed. I throw the right rope to the ground and start pulling the left rope even faster. This causes the bundle to steer toward the right so that the bundle is out of the way from the stakes. Once the bundle rolls into the clear I grab the ropes and head back down to the river.

I start the process all over again. I make the triangle stacks of logs. Drape the ropes. Stack up the logs in the cradle. Tie them together. Then run back up the hill with the two long ropes. I get the second, third, and fourth bundles up the hill. It's a slog but I get them up and out of harm's way. When I get to the fifth bundle, the river level is up to where I'm building the bundle. I'm grabbing logs that are not floating away and putting them into the stack. As I tie up the fifth bundle and push out the bracing stack of logs, I see a rush of water. It picks up the remaining logs and carries them down the river.

After pulling up the last bundle up toward the M-TOG, I stand for a moment. I'm not tired, but I'm mentally exhausted. My mind feels strained, like it needs a rest. Looking down, I see I'm no longer a white Space Yeti, but a dark orange mud-coated wreck. I walk back down to the river to retrieve Bearpaw and Sting. All the remaining logs are gone now. The sun is starting to rise, bringing with it morning light. I take a moment in the water to wash myself off. My bright white suit shows again, but not as bright as when I first stepped out of the lander.

Chapter 9

It has rained for another two weeks. The river is still flooded, engulfing the base of all the remaining trees. Had I not gotten the logs out, I would certainly have been at risk of not completing all the work I need to do to protect the M-TOG and prepare for the kids. I'm able to assemble the shed to cover the M-TOG lander and a classic log cabin for myself. Working through the rain is difficult, but it has to be done. My vast music library is helping, but ORIN isn't any help. He keeps questioning my building skills when I am holding logs over the M-TOG, potentially dropping one on him. The M-TOG shed is open on all sides like a log cabin with no walls, only four vertical posts holding up the roof. The roof is made by installing medium diameter logs edge to edge, then installing small diameter logs to fill the spaces between the bigger logs.

I end up building a ladder out of extra logs to get up to the roof level to work on it. I avoid standing on the roof because it certainly wouldn't hold up my weight. The last thing I need to do is crash through the roof onto the M-TOG. To seal the roof, I take clay from the river's edge and put a layer between the individual logs of the roof, then cover the entirety of the roof, scooping and padding it down with Bearpaw. To finish it off, I mount the solar panels to the roof.

I make myself a traditional log cabin with a sod roof. My new house is just large enough for me to walk into, lie down, and store some equipment. I don't feel up to making something fancy for myself. I remember the storage building on Mars that housed the Space Yetis. It was just as bleak as what I built for myself. It has no windows, just a door made from the smaller logs tied together with the hemp rope. The size of the door compared to the rest of the house makes it look more like a barn than a house. There isn't so much of a hinge as hooks to hang the door on when I want it closed. I lift the door off the hooks when I want to open it and set it aside. After completing the cabin, I lay down on the floor to make sure I would fit okay. Looking up at the ceiling, I can see every weak point that will likely cause the ceiling to leak in a few years. I'll likely need to rebuild it, but for now it will serve its purpose, I suppose.

"Sir, I am very appreciative of the structure you have built around the M-TOG, but might I suggest you consider replacing it in the near future with a more stable design?"

Why does ORIN keep hounding me? I turn off the communication connection and lay quietly on the dirt ground of my new house. I never would have thought it, but I really miss talking to real people. Jerry, Amy, Ben—they were all good people to talk with. Owen, not so much. The thought hits me that they're all dead now. They've been dead for centuries. There is no one in the universe still alive that I know. I am alone. A feeling of epic loneliness sweeps over me. I am the only person on this planet. Everyone I know is dead. I don't even know if the Earth is still around. For all I know it's been destroyed by some war by now. I lay there and think while staring at my ceiling. Maybe this is a mistake.

***

After completing my new home, I spend a few days at a slower speed. I make scabbards for Bearpaw and Sting using carved log sections. Using Sting I am able to make nicely formed scabbards that are made of two parts of carved wood that held Sting's blade like a sandwich tied together with smaller strands of hemp rope. Sting's scabbard is tied to my right thigh. I practice taking it out and putting it back to make sure it works well for me. I do the same for

Bearpaw, but make the scabbard to hold the handle while keeping the blade open to the air at the top. I tie Bearpaw's scabbard to my back. With an extended reach to the back of my neck I'm able to grab Bearpaw by the neck and pull it upward and outward. It's a controlled throw launching Bearpaw from my back and catching the handle toward its bottom end. Putting Bearpaw back is pretty much the same, but in reverse. My mechanized body makes it all seem like I have perfected the movements over decades.

There is still a lot I need to get done. Since it finally stopped raining, I'm able to harvest more lumber from down by the river. I find that my uphill log roller arrangement is working well after having all the previous practice. The next structure I build is a barn with an outdoor fenced area. It is twice as big as my log cabin and has an equal-sized fenced outdoor area. The barn has a large door so I can walk in and out of it easily. It's open to the fenced area so the goats could walk in and out of the area as much as they please.

I build the fence by making stakes out of the smaller diameter logs and pounding them into the ground with Bearpaw. I space them close enough together that a goat couldn't get out and use interwoven hemp rope for good measure. Lastly, I make a swinging gate with a hemp rope loop that I attach to a nearby post to keep it closed. I construct another building just for storage and a worktable inside of it. For now, I'm storing the M-TOG parachute material and nylon rope in the storage building. I don't know what I'll use it for, but I'm sure I'll use it for something. I keep to myself and don't talk with ORIN much. Staying busy keeps my mind off the fact that I'm getting desperately lonely. Maybe I should try harder to talk with ORIN.

I'm getting pretty good using Sting to carve the logs for building construction, but it is extremely boring work. Unfortunately having a robot body isn't making menial work any less tedious. Someday I need to build a sawmill. But for that I'll need steel, which I currently don't have. I look out at my tiny town: an M-TOG shed, my house, the barn, and the storage shed. The pathways where I have been walking between the buildings have worn into the green vegetation leaving the bright orange dirt showing with my tank track like footprints all over. So much more that needs to get done before the goats arrive in two months. It is a bittersweet accomplishment.

***

With the M-TOG protected and the crops started, I'm now free to explore the area around me. I first head west walking along the river with Bearpaw on my back and Sting on my side. I'd like to find a way to set up a diverted stream from the river to irrigate my crops and provide water to my village. The problem is the water needs to be at a higher elevation than my village for the water to run downhill to me. Walking west I see more of the same, but it does feel like I'm walking uphill, which is a good sign. In the distance ahead of me I hear a rumbling noise. As I get closer, the sound gets louder. I walk up and see a small, rocky pond with a waterfall flowing down into the river. Standing near the waterfall edge, it's a steep, rocky drop-off down about ten meters to the shore of the river. I best not get too close. The last thing I need is to fall down there and bust a leg actuator or something.

Looking at the lake, it's calm with a gentle flow toward the waterfall. I imagine what my water canal will look like. What would I use for the waterway? It would be nice to build a Roman-style canal out of stone and concrete, but I don't have the materials, or the time, or the need for that much water. I could cut logs in half and carve them like half tubes to make a pipeline. Looking back at the village, I can barely see it in the distance. I've had about enough of carving all these trees. I can see my crop fields from here. The bamboo has already sprouted and is growing quickly. I rub my chin out of habit as I think about what to do. I decide that I'll wait until the bamboo is grown, then make a pipeline out of it. It would have a big enough diameter to deliver water for my needs. The whole installation would be less than a week. But I'll need to wait at least three more months before the bamboo is grown enough. It dawns on me that this bamboo pipeline is basically what I was supposed to build on Mars. Except it's easy! And simple! On Mars the pipeline was a disaster. It was too much of a challenge to overcome the environment and had to go too long of a distance. Here I just need to take bamboo and stick it together to move water a ridiculously short distance compared to Mars. Yeah, this is so much easier than Mars.

I continue walking west past the pond and along the river while looking up at the misty mountain range in the western distance. Someday I'll need to explore up there, but not today. It is much too far of a trip to go all the way up there at this point. The terrain begins to become more gray rock and less orange dirt. Gradually my walk has turned into an uphill hike. Eventually I walk into an open, flat rocky area and start investigating what types of rocks are waiting for me. I'm not a geologist, so I don't know what I'm looking at. Gray rocks, black rocks, shiny rocks, dull rocks. I grab pebbles of each to take down to ORIN to evaluate. With my hands full of rocks, I turn around to head back. With all these samples, maybe this is an opportunity to talk to ORIN and try to get him to be better at conversations.

Heading back to the village I walk on the river shore instead of up on the open plain field. The vegetation is much more interesting down by the river. The plants don't look alien. Just different. I could be walking through a lush island on Earth right now and I wouldn't know the difference. The periodic table is the same on this planet as compared to Earth. The laws of physics are the same. So, it shouldn't be such a surprise that they look so similar. Evolution finds similar solutions to similar problems. Walking along I grab specimens of plants. Leaves, stems, roots, moss, bark, everything I can find. I memorize them all and where I found them. I make a few rugbynut buckets to help me carry all my treasures back to ORIN. I should make a bag for myself. Maybe I could use some of the M-TOG lander parachute fabric.

I wonder if there are fish in the river. I leave all my discoveries on the shore as I wade out into the river until the water is chest high.

Not only am I airtight, I'm watertight. I squat down in the river facing upstream so I can see what is inside. The water surface moves over my head cameras. Looking under the water, it is clear with a rocky, sandy riverbed with little vegetation. I don't see any fish. I turn around to look downstream underneath the water surface. Again nothing.

Just before I stand up to get out of the water, I see dark orbs approaching. They are moving fast. Before I can get out of the way, they're already hitting up against me. Splashing, flailing, bubbles, and groaning surrounds me. I stand up in the river and look upstream to see the orbs already have swum past me heading upriver. Water is flowing over the top of them like speeding miniature submarines. A moment later I can't see them anymore.

"What the hell was that?!"

Spooked, I carefully leave the river, grab my rugbynut buckets, and head back to the village. I better not do anymore dumb things today. If something were to happen to me, it would be a massive disaster for the incubating kids in the M-TOG.

***

"Poisonous," ORIN says with a big round red unhappy face showing on the screen after I test the first plant specimen. I try the next plant. "Poisonous" with another red unhappy face. Well, I hope these plants are not all poisonous. I try another.

"Edible," ORIN says, with a round green happy face.

"Full analysis," I say to ORIN.

"Hallucinogenic properties that are not dangerous, but also not useful."

"Great, just what we need. Thanks, ORIN."

"You are welcome, sir."

My frustrations with ORIN seep back in. I work through the rest of the plants and rocks with ORIN testing them one by one. So far, I've discovered a pain reliever, a fever reducer, antibacterial leaves, vitamin K-rich roots, a laxative, and lots and lots of poisonous plants. Just think of all the centuries it had to take for humans on Earth to figure all this out by trial and error. ORIN is able to do it in just a few minutes. They say that it's best just to watch the animals and see what plants they eat and don't eat. But still that's a long time just to find out the deer like to get high on hallucinogenic plants. ORIN has come through for me here. From the rocks I test, I find copper ore, iron ore, and granite.

"ORIN, thanks for figuring these all out for me. But do you suppose you could help me harvest plants and mine ore instead of sitting around doing nothing all day?" I say, trying to get him into a friendly conversation.

"You are welcome, sir. You know I don't have a MarsX T200 body for myself anymore. You have the only one. If you like, we can swap residence and I perform the work. You would be in the M-TOG and I'll be in the MarsX T200 body."

"Absolutely not! I'm on to you, ORIN. Don't tell me things like that to try to convince me to sit in an M-TOG prison watching the alien moss grow while you walk around implementing your robot plan to kill off humanity."

"Sir, I would never. I only want to help you."

"ORIN, you can help me by telling me the names of these plants we tested."

"Sir, there are no names for the plants. These species do not have equivalents on Earth."

He's right. Nothing has a name here. I guess I get to name the plants and animals around here then, don't I? I don't like thinking of myself as Adam from the book of Genesis, but the parallel is amusing.

"Adam and ORIN, doesn't have the same ring to it, does it?" I say.

"Sir, I don't understand."

"Yeah, don't worry about it, ORIN. Just don't get up and go on your human murder spree."

I look out at the plants we've identified that won't kill or corrupt my kids. Taking a seat I decide I'll have some fun and name the plants.

"The pain reliever is Aspirin Seeds...the fever reducer is Cooling Balm...the antibacterial leaves are Bandage Leaves, the vitamin K-rich roots are Carrot Roots, and the laxative is...What am I going to name the laxative?"

ORIN remains silent without offering any suggestions. Maybe I'll leave that one to the kids. It's not like I'm going to be the one using this stuff anyways.

My village needs a name. It is definitely NOT going to be named Eden. "ORIN, any suggestions for the village name?"

"Sir, we can name it after the Mars colony, Remo." I think about it for a moment.

"I think you are right, ORIN. We need to try again making Remo."

By the way, what is my planet's name? Taking another look around it's green and orange. Lush and vibrant. At least it is this way in the small bit I'm looking at here. This is my new Mars. A green Mars. *Ares* is the Greek word for Mars.

"ORIN, what is the Greek word for green?"

"Sir, it is *prasinos*."

Prasinos? Green Mars, *Prasinos Ares*? I scratch my chin again thinking.

Finally, I look to ORIN to tell him my decision. "How about we name the planet Prasares? The Green Mars."

"Well-done, sir," ORIN responds without any fanfare.

"ORIN, I think it's time we rename you. You've got some bad history and it's giving me the creeps that you're going to take out the whole colony someday." I say, looking back at ORIN in the M-TOG.

"Excuse me, sir. I am ORIN. That is what I am."

"But on Prasares you're an Oracle. You tell me things I would never know otherwise. You tell me about plants and materials. You give me information from your database. You are wise and great, oh magnificent Oracle," I say while bending down on one knee toward ORIN. "From here forth you shall be known as the Oracle! But we need to do something about that voice. An old stuffy man's voice is not going to work for an Oracle." I go up to the control console and start trying out new voices.

"Sir...I...don't...have...to..." ORIN tries to speak while I am sorting through different voices.

"There we go!" I exclaim as I choose the Kelly LeBrock voice from the '80s movie, *Weird Science*. My dad gave me a file copy of the movie when he was cleaning out his old college cloud storage. He had a thing for old vintage movies. Movies and music from that time really stood the test of time.

"Sir," ORIN now spoke with a comforting British woman's accent. "You know that I am still the same artificial intelligence. You only changed my voice module."

"I know, Oracle, but it fits you better now. You're the maiden of wisdom, the lady of knowledge, the Oracle of Remo! Besides, I think it's a much better voice than your old one. You'll be more approachable to the children when they grow up."

"Thank you, sir, I am happy I can help."

"I know you are. And please call me Nick from now on."

Chapter 10

My next excursion from Remo village is down to the sea. I follow the river and eventually come to rolling hills with more tree cover. I make a path through the hills using Sting as a machete. Eventually the path exits out to a beach. Looking out at the sea, I see it's a bright blue contrast to the green and orange I've been looking at since I landed. I can't see any land on the other side of the sea. The rolling waves casually slide up onto the beach near my feet. The river exits into the sea in a broad, shallow delta. The beach sand has an untouched cleanliness with fine, light orange sand.

I need to harvest four things from this beach. The first is the sand itself for glass. I'll need to build a cart and rugbynut buckets to bring the sand up to Remo village for glass making. But the cart will need to wait. This is just an excursion trip. Next is salt. The sea is open to the ocean and should have a high salinity. I'll take a sample back up to the Oracle to test it. I need soda ash for lots of things including glass making. Soda ash is made from burning high salinity vegetation like seaweed. The last is seashells. Not for decorations, but seashells have a good source of calcium carbonate that I can make quicklime with. I'll need quicklime to make cement. Looking around I also see limestone rocks emerging from the tree cover leading into the sea. I'll need that too for iron smelting. I'm feeling more upbeat now. I'm turning into a one-robot humanity-building machine!

With Bearpaw on my back and Sting on my side, I walk into the sea. I take more cautious steps than when I walked into the river. "No dumb stuff this time," I say to myself. Sand kicks up into the water at my feet. Splashing waves crash overhead until I finally walk out far enough to sink under them. I can now see through the clear water. Looking up I see the moving waves. A short distance away into the water are large, green, waving pillars. Slowly I walk toward them until I find that they are large seaweed plants. A school of fish swims by. They are armored like a lobster, but have sharp, serrated edges on the plates. They leave me alone as I continue my journey toward the waving seaweed forest.

I unsheathe Sting and start cutting the first seaweed pillar at the base. The sea current must have changed because the seaweed seems to move while I am cutting. I look up and see that the seaweed is starting to move around me. They start engulfing me like dozens of anacondas, wrapping around my legs and arms. I told myself no more dumb stuff before I walked in here and now look at me. This better not be how it ends for me. Living for the next hundred years stuck underwater by seaweed. I start walking backward pulling the seaweed tight. I can't break loose and I can't seem to pull them out of their roots. I see the rest of the seaweed forest start to lean in toward me.

I use my free hand to pull Bearpaw from its sheath and give a quick one-handed roundhouse swing with it. With a second swing I'm released and start to take a floating step back. "*Now you're going to get it,*" I think. I Paul Bunyan the nearby seaweed attackers with vengeance, then watch them float to the surface. Bearpaw leaves streaks of bubbles and shredded seaweed in its path. I take a moment to realize that I dodged another Game Over situation. If I would have been stuck here, the whole civilization would have ended, again. I look up and see the cut seaweed is being pushed toward the beach by the waves. I better walk back up to the beach so I could recover my seaweed harvest.

On my way back, I walk over to a coral-looking structure growing from the seafloor. It seems similar to a normal Earth dead coral except it appears to be a single standing structure. Usually coral carpets the seafloor, but this was like a towering white castle in the ocean protruding upward from a small footprint. I walk around it. Tap it with my knuckles. Does this thing have any more robot-killing aliens in it? It seems to be abandoned. I still have Bearpaw in my hand, so I give it a full underwater swing. A puff of white dust appears in the water clouding my vision, but I can see that I had cracked the coral castle. A few more hits and I am able to break off the whole structure, about the size of a canoe. I sheathe Bearpaw and pick up the coral castle, putting it over my shoulder. It is unusually light. Turning around, I walk back toward the beach.

As I walk out of the water, the coral castle gets much heavier. I can feel the water draining out of it. Once up on the beach, I toss it onto the ground as if I had just conquered an ancient mythological beast. I look over and see that all the cut seaweed has washed ashore. I walk over and examine my vegetable attacker. It looks like normal seaweed, just with a thicker stock and larger leaves. It also has tubular stems coming from it. I take the seaweed and drape it over tree branches by the beach to dry out.

I take a few moments to rethink what I'm doing. I need all these materials, but if I die in the process it will be all for nothing. This is a perma-death game here with no extra lives. Having a D-Clo backup does not do me any good here. I'm the only civilization-building robot on Prasares. I need to be more careful. I have a human incubating back at the M-TOG that I need to take care of.

COMMAND LOAD PLAY. I turn on my music player and start listening to "Safety Dance" by Men Without Hats to cheer me up. Doo doo *ding ding*, do do *ding ah ding,* Doo doo *ding ding*, do do *ding ah ding.* I can't help but do a few robot dance moves to the beeps and boops.

Back to work. For salt production I could boil seawater, but that would be a lot of work with cutting the wood and tending the fires. I'd rather let the sun do the work for me. I'll set up an evaporation pool where I can let seawater flow through a small canal, then close off the canal. The water would sit and evaporate leaving the salt for me to harvest. I'll need to build a watertight pool on the beach. Looking around I didn't see anything that would be good building materials to start with. I'll need to make my building materials up at the village and bring them down here to work on the evaporation pond. But for now, while I'm down at the sea, I should at least get some salt.

I cut a bunch of rugbynuts lengthwise into shallow, long bowls using Sting. Then I fill them with seawater on the beach. Nestling them into the sunny area of the sand should work well. In a few weeks, I should be able to scrape off a few packets worth of salt.

Looking around at the seaweed, coral castle, and salt rugbynuts, I can see that I'll have a lot of work to do. I grab a limestone pebble and one of the seaweed limbs to bring back to the Oracle for testing. I turn toward the path through the hills back to Remo, but I see something in the corner of my camera. I look over and see the dark orbs zooming out of the river into the sea. I see flying water over the dark humps like speeding torpedoes into the sea shooting out of the river.

"What the hell are you?" I say watching them head off into the sea. "I hope you don't kill me someday."

***

I've got about a month left before the goats are born. There is powdered formula on the M-TOG to get them started, then they'll switch over to hay growing in the field. I'll have a bit of salt for them, but not a whole salt lick. Plenty of water at the river and a cauldron to boil it. A nice barn to sleep in. The only thing I'm missing is a baby bottle. The powdered formula is in cans, not exactly something that would work as a baby bottle. Not to mention I don't have any rubber nipples. Rubber isn't something that could survive the five-thousand-year journey, even without air and water.

I need pottery to make baby bottles. And to make pottery, I need a kiln. I start harvesting clay from the river's edge to make the building blocks for the kiln. I have to dig down under the ground with Bearpaw at the river's edge to get to the good stuff. Using some cut wooden boards, I make brick molds that are rectangular framed shapes. A big handful is enough to stuff the mold with clay. With my palm I'm able to flatten out the clay into the mold. I tap the mold to release the wet brick. Repeating this process, I end up with a stack of wet clay bricks. I set the wet bricks next to a raging bonfire to dry out and harden. I turn them around to get all sides dried evenly. My finished dry bricks are not great, but they should work for a first kiln.

I don't need a big kiln and, frankly, making one big enough for me to walk in and out of won't be practical. I build up a small brick kiln that looks like two large doghouses connected end to end. I use wet clay as the mortar between the bricks. Once it dries it should hold it all together. One side is where the pottery is baked, the other is the firebox. Between the two chambers I leave a hole for the heat to go from the firebox to the pottery chamber. On the floor of the pottery chamber, I make a removable pallet made from a small aluminum panel from the M-TOG with its edges bent down on the left and right sides. I can put the pottery on top of it, but still have enough room to slip Bearpaw's blade under it like a pizza paddle. Laying on my stomach I use Bearpaw to move the pottery pallet in and out of the kiln. It works fine enough, but I'm sure I look like I'm working a miniature pizza oven. I start a fire in the firebox to test it and dry out the remaining wet clay mortar.

"I think this kiln would also work well as a meat smoker," I yell out to the Oracle.

"Sir, that would not be advisable," the Oracle replies with a lovely British women's tone that seems mildly uninterested in what I am doing, yet somewhat still upset by the voice change. "You are supposed to raise the goats, not smoke them."

I pause for a moment to keep myself from cracking up. "I think you're right, Oracle. I do think it will be several years before I'll need to work on my barbecue skills. You do such a good job to keep me in check," I say sarcastically back to the Oracle.

"It is my pleasure, sir," she responds with my comment flying right over her head.

While the kiln is seasoning, I go to work making baby bottles. Sitting with a pile of wet clay, I start shaping a classic baby bottle but quickly realize that it isn't going to work. What do I need? All I need is a cup that I can hold and a way of getting it into the kid's mouth without getting the formula all over the place. I end up shaping out a bowl and for the spout I make a short nose spout using a stick. It looks like an ugly teapot without a handle. The kiln is running hot now, so it can't hurt to give it a try. I take out the pottery pallet with Bearpaw. Set the ugly wet clay teapot on it and carefully move the pallet back inside the kiln.

While the prototype baby bottle is drying, I need to figure out the rubber nipple. Admittedly, I don't have much to work with. Ancient rubber nipples were actually made of leather, but I don't have any of that lying around. After some experimenting, I find that after boiling the seaweed tubes I had brought back with me they turn rubbery and elastic. After the teapot cools from the kiln, it is hardened and a much lighter color. If I dropped it, it would certainly break. But it should hold baby formula just fine. I take one of the boiled seaweed tubes and press it over the nozzle of the teapot. The elastic tube stretches to make a watertight seal. I had a great pliable tube, but it still isn't a rubber nipple. It lets too much milk out through its opening, as if I just attached a garden hose to a teapot.

I tie off the open end of the tube into a knot and then fold it back to make a bend. At the tip of the bend, I use Sting's blade tip to poke a tiny hole into it. I fill the teapot with water and tip it again. Just like a baby bottle, the water dribbles out. I squeeze the seaweed tube and the water comes out a little bit quicker from the hole. I don't think the seaweed nipple will last more than a few uses, and it will likely need to be rehydrated by boiling it. But it should do the job, and I've got plenty of seaweed monsters that I can kill to make more. Feeling accomplished, I look at myself. I am covered in orange clay and dirt from my pottery art class session. I'll need to wash myself in the river again.

***

Weeks pass. The goats should be ready to be born any day now. I walk over to the M-TOG and look at the incubation capsules. Three infant goats and one human floating in the fluid. Peaceful and quiet. A green light flashes over the male goat, then a countdown screen starts down from one hour.

"Well, buddy, looks like you'll be the first one," I say as I look at him through the capsule glass. He is a tiny cute goat bobbing up and down in the embryonic fluid inside the incubation chamber.

"I will call you...Floats McGoats."

***

I watch the countdown timer. Four...three...two...one. A ding sounds and another green light shines. I lift up the lever arm and carefully take out the incubation capsule. The bottom half of the capsule has Floats in it. The top is empty from where the food pellets were. I sit on the ground with the capsule held upright. I carefully unscrew the two pieces of the capsule and toss the empty top part aside. Looking down I can see Floats moving around in the fluid. I carefully turned it over and let Floats McGoats slide out into my hand. The embryonic fluid spills all over myself, but it doesn't matter.

"Bahhh," he cries while blinking his eyes.

Floats is black with strips of white with dark tan around his eyebrows. I have a rugbynut bucket nearby full of clean, warm water fresh from the cauldron next to me. I pour it over him to clean him off. I set him down on his legs on the ground. He wobbles, but stands up okay on his own.

"Bahhh," he cries out again.

I wish I had a towel or something to dry him off. He gives a shake and brushes off much of the water and starts to walk.

I mix up the baby formula, boil the seaweed, and fill the teapot. I try holding Floats like a baby on his back while I feed him the bottle, but he doesn't like it. He keeps squirming around trying to get out of my cradle of an arm. After trying a few things, I find he prefers to stand while I hunch over on one knee feeding him the bottle. A gargantuan Space Yeti tipping a cup to an infant goat. He drinks half of it and gives his lips a few smacks. "Bahhh!!" he blurts out again then turns his attention to see what is around him.

"Oracle, we've got a baby boy!" I cry out.

"You've got a baby *goat*, Nick. You should know your species by now," the Oracle says, correcting me.

The Oracle's bland banter doesn't faze me at all. I watch with amazement as Floats walks around sniffing at things as he goes. Eventually he comes back to me.

"Bahhh!!!" He looks back up at me and tells me what he wants.

"Sure, buddy, I'll give you some more milk. I can't tell you how glad I am that you are here. I was starting to go nuts talking to the giant coffee machine over there. I really need a friend to talk to."

Floats and I hang out until it starts to get dark. I had already harvested some of the hay and made a bed for him in the barn. I warm up some bricks by the fire and put them under the hay to keep him warm during the night. I sit him down on the hay bed and he looks up at me with his big eyes with alien flat rectangle pupils. I'm looking at the first interplanetary species.

Oh, I should turn on my Space Yeti face monitor so he can see my face. Inside the barn, there is a faint glow from my display. He sees me and I see him. Jerry told me they scanned my face to use in the LED monitor. I suppose I should check to make sure he didn't lie to me and kept ORIN's old face. Floats turns around, and then curls into a ball to lie down to go to sleep. I decide that I'll spend the night in the barn with him, but first I need to clean up the M-TOG area. I leave the barn, closing the door behind me.

Walking back to the M-TOG I see the two empty capsule pieces lying on the ground and the empty teapot.

"We did good, Oracle. We just birthed the first interplanetary species. Ever! That's a huge accomplishment. We'd be famous if anyone we knew was still alive. Either way, I'd call it a win for us. Good job!"

"Nick, as much as I would like to celebrate with you on this occasion, I must first inform you that the other two goats' timers have started."

"What? Really?! I just got the first one taken care of. Can't we stage them out better?" I say.

"Nick, the times are set for optimum gestation and maximum probability for peak conditions. We cannot control the times," the Oracle calmly explains to me.

I rush back into the M-TOG and see that one timer is down to thirty-two minutes and the other is at fifty-four minutes. It's now completely dark out. No moon, only the faint rings in the sky. I turn on my headlamps and start boiling more water.

***

When the sun rose, we had three goats. The one male, Floats McGoats, who was born the evening earlier. Then the two female goats that were born in the middle of the night. The first female goat I named Samus. She is light tan and white. The second female goat I named Peach. She has red-and-brown fur with patches of white. They're all happy and healthy. When you think of it, it's really a monumental scientific achievement here. Three successful interplanetary species births, all on the first try.

My only regret is having made only one baby bottle. During the middle of the night while Samus was feeding, Peach was bahhing herself hoarse at me. I kept switching back and forth, but I could never keep the two of them happy. Once I got them put to bed in the barn, I went ahead and built more teapots using the kiln. I didn't bother to go to sleep. After finishing the teapots, I realized that I don't have three arms to hold three teapots at the same time, so I made a wooden trough to hang off the inside of the barn fence. I put the teapots in the trough and they hung at the right angle and the correct height to replace me holding them.

When the goats woke up in the morning, they hopped out through the barn opening to the fence to find their breakfast. I had to replenish the milk teapots before they had their fill for the morning. After finishing their breakfast, they all smack their lips then explore their new fenced-in home.

"Oracle, we need to put in the request to the orbiter for the next batch of capsules. One human boy and two female goats. You can handle that, right?"

"Of course, I can handle it, sir. I am the Oracle of Remo. Your request is very good timing. The orbiter is in the optimum position to release the capsule transporter soon. The capsule transporter should arrive within a few hours. Where should we have it land?"

"One hundred meters south of the M-TOG. It's an open field out there. Also, please do a better job than you did with the Mars Hopper landing."

"Nick, you keep discussing the incident on Mars as if it was my fault. You should know that the failure analysis investigation concluded that it was ice buildup on the air speed sensor. Therefore, there was nothing I could do about it. Please note that I can only act on what I know. When the sensor is wrong, I am wrong."

"Yeah, that is what I'm afraid of." I wish I could change the Oracle's personality as easily as changing her voice. I'm getting the Kelly LeBrock voice, but not the Kelly LeBrock wit. At least I have Floats McGoats to talk to now. Something with a heartbeat has to be better.

Inside the orbiter, the capsule transporter deploys once above the correct location. The transporter is a very simple, small, slow-descent vehicle. It is designed to go as slow as possible during entry to reduce the frictional heat buildup since getting hot traveling through the planet's atmosphere defeats the purpose. Guiding propulsion carefully maneuvers the transporter and slows it down. Once inside the atmosphere, steerable parachutes deploy to navigate it to the landing site.

It would be hours before the capsule transporter would even be close. I head back over to the goats to see how they are doing. I see that I had left the gate open. I walk into the fenced area and into the barn. Samus and Peach are nestled on the hay bed. But Floats McGoats is gone.

"Ah, come on!" I shout. I rush out of the barn and fenced area, closing the gate behind me. I look around trying to find the little escape artist. I look up toward the mountains and see he's walking toward the upstream river's edge. I launch into a Space Yeti sprint after him. I quickly catch up to him and scoop him up. "Floats! You can't go wandering out here. If something were to happen to you, we'll all be in a bunch of trouble! I need you healthy and ready to mingle with the ladies, if you know what I mean."

"Bahhh!" he shouts back at me inside my hands. I carry Floats back to the barn and reunite him with Samus and Peach. They are already bouncing around in the fenced area. They meet us at the gate with an eagerness to play. I leave Floats with his friends, then walk back out the gate, making sure it's closed correctly. Then I walk around the other side to the barn door to double-check it's closed as well. Heading back toward the M-TOG, I look back at the goats. "Looks like I need to keep you guys on a tight leash, don't I?" Floats just gives me a blank rectangle-eyed stare, "Bahhh!" he says back.

After that mini-fiasco, I head back to the M-TOG to see how the Oracle is doing with the new stork delivery. I watch the progress of the capsule transporter on the M-TOG monitor. I don't say anything to the Oracle. She needs to have all her computer processing power focused on her mission. Everything is looking good. Hopefully none of the five-thousand-year-old equipment is faulty. The Oracle will need to make her first successful landing of her career. We can't have her burying the transporter into the field. I need that human boy on there. Civilization isn't going to work with only one girl.

I look away from the M-TOG up into the sky. I watch as the transporter comes into view through the white clouds. It is slowly heading toward us on a gentle glide. Its descent is frustratingly slow.

I hold my digital tongue to tell the Oracle to speed up. I know where that will lead toward. Finally, after painful anticipation, it lands with a light thump on the ground. The parachutes slowly float down over the top of the transporter covering it while my concerns relax. I peel back the parachutes and see the transporter. It is a simple cylinder with a domed, heat shield bottom. I open the top and it is just big enough to fit three incubation capsules. I pull them out one at a time and carry them back to the M-TOG to load into the empty incubator slots. After installing them all and pulling down the coffee-making levers, I look over at the first human embryo that is still growing in the fourth incubator slot. It has another three and half months to go. The thought of a human running around here hasn't sunk in yet. My mind is focused on the fact that there is still a lot of work I need to get done before she arrives.

I head back to the capsule transporter. I eye it as if it's a freshly fallen buffalo in the American prairie. So many useful parts that I can use. I won't let any of it go to waste. I take the parachute material and nylon rope and add it to the M-TOG collection of parachute material in the storage shed. I can see that the parachute material still has the MarsX logos on it. Jerry's and my start-up bought out unused equipment from the defunct MarsX, even the parachutes. I use the limited tools from the M-TOG to disassemble the capsule transporter. Anything that could be used as a spare part for the M-TOG is salvaged. Everything else gets disassembled and categorized. Steel parts, copper parts, parts that could be used as utensils. Parts that could be shaped into something else. I even got a big bowl from the domed heat shield on the bottom of the transporter. After I was done with it, there wasn't a screw or bolt left over. It all gets captured, categorized, and stored. It takes all day to dismember the capsule transporter while I take breaks feeding the goats.

It is dark when I finally finish with the transporter parts. I don't bother going to my house. I go straight to the barn. Looking in, I see that the three goats are huddled next to each other on the hay bed. I walk over to the goats and lay next to them. There isn't much for me in the house. Just an empty room with a dirt floor. As a Space Yeti, I don't need anything. I don't even need to lie down. I could do my low power sleep mode standing up just as easily as lying down. I give Floats a gentle pet on his head. I can only pet him with a few fingers of my giant Space Yeti hand. I turn off my face monitor and put my head down next to the goats. It is good to finally have living beings to be around. The Oracle is terrible company to be around. Without these goats I think I would start going crazy.

Chapter 11

Over the next months, the Remo village continued to grow. But I feel like a giant countdown clock hangs over my head with the impending human birth. So many things I need to complete before then. Floats McGoats, Samus, and Peach are doing well. They are gaining weight and getting bigger. The crops are also doing well. I completed the first harvest of the hay and wheat using Bearpaw as a sickle and storing the harvest in the storage shed. The goats enjoy watching me through the fence while I work. The bamboo is getting tall and in a few more months, I should be able to harvest it to create the water pipeline from the pond down to the river. The long days ended each night with me sleeping in the barn with the goats. Floats is particularly fond of me. Samus and Peach tend to be more interested in playing with each other. But Floats likes to be around me all the time. I can't let him roam freely when I am working. His adventure curiosity always takes him away from the village.

"Here you go, Floats, I made a present for you," I say while holding something behind my back. Floats gives me a look of intrigue and sniffs the air.

"Here you go, buddy! I made you a leash out of hemp rope. And what is the other end tied to, you might ask? Well, it's a big rock. Your pet rock! He'll keep you from running off while I'm working." I put the leash around Floats's neck. He sniffs the leash and tries to walk off only to be stopped by the rock. "See, Floats, your pet rock keeps you nearby. What are you going to name your pet rock?" I wait for Floats's response.

"Bahhh!!"

"Really? Well, I guess he is your pet rock. You can name him what you want. Stoney the pet rock, it is." I scoop up some orange mud on my fingertip and paint a smiley face on the rock.

"See, Floats, Stoney likes his name." I grab Stoney and rotate him to make it look like he agrees with me with a head nod. Floats gives me a concerned look.

I really need to talk to a human.

***

In the short time period before the first human is born, I continue completing the village production capabilities. It's good work to keep my mind occupied from the crippling loneliness I'm having. Right now, Floats is my only breathing friend in the whole universe. He's saving me from complete madness.

For the remaining work I set up a charcoal, soda ash, and lye production area near the storage building. For the charcoal I dig a large hole in the ground using Bearpaw and then start a fire in the bottom of it. Once the fire gets going, I pile a bunch more wood on top, then cover the wood pile with dirt, leaving the very top open and a small hole open near the bottom. This causes the fire to be oxygen-starved, burning slow and hot. After a period of time it will create the charcoal I need. While I'm waiting for the charcoal, I build a second storage building, this one bigger and better than the first. Every building iteration I do gets better. I also build wood boxes to store the charcoal and keep it dry. After I move all the cooled charcoal into their wood boxes and the boxes into the shed, I realize that I have a nice stockpile created. Floats gives me a nod of reaffirmation.

Soda ash is made by harvesting the seaweed and letting it dry. Burning the seaweed leaves a light-colored ash. I scrape out the soda ash and put it into empty rugbynut buckets. I'll need this soda ash when I start making cement. Lye is made by boiling the ashes left over from the campfire wood I was using to boil water. I store the lye mixture in some ceramic pots I had previously created. All this is extremely boring work that has taken me forever. But Floats has been by my side the whole time without any complaints.

"Floats, I've got to tell you, you're a much better companion than the Oracle to talk to. You don't give me a hard time about how I'm doing things. Pointing out how I'm doing it wrong. You just listen to me and hang out. You're an easy friend to be around, you know that?"

"Bahhh!"

"That's right, buddy. We're going to do this together. We're going to make the best civilization in the galaxy. It's time to get excited!"

Next to the kiln I build a smelter. My smelter is basically a firepit but used for melting ore. I build a crude bellow from parachute material and nylon rope from the capsule transporter. With two wood planks I am able to compress the bellow to heat up the fire to much higher temperatures than I would be capable of otherwise. Using the capsule transporter's heat shield as a crucible, I'm able to melt iron ore. I used crushed limestone and mixed it into the ore to help with the smelting process. Limestone helps to lower the temperature needed to extract the iron from the ore. After what seems like a ton of smelted ore, I am able to make only a small amount of iron. I would need a lot more ore if I am going to make anything of metal that would be useful.

For days, Floats, his pet rock, and I went up to the quarry area toward the mountains with a makeshift cart I had made. We'd fill up the cart with iron ore and bring it down to the smelter. I'd put Floats and his pet rock on top of the ore pile when we were coming back down to Remo village.

After getting ridiculously large piles of iron ore that took days to collect and smelting it all, I am able to build a sand cast mold of a mallet hammer. I start by first making the hammer out of clay and hardening it in the kiln. It is a large mallet with a short handle. Then

I build two boxes to hold the sand mold. Using the clay hammer template, I create the mold by sandwiching the clay hammer in between the two sand mold boxes. Then I carefully remove it. What I have left is a hammer mold. I pick up the heat shield crucible filled with molten iron using ceramic lifting handles. I carefully pour the molten iron into the sand mold in its inlet and watch it fill up the mold, waiting for molten iron to come out a second hole in the mold, a riser, to signal that it's full.

After the mold cools, I break open it and find a very rough-looking iron hammer. It doesn't look good, but it should be good enough to hit stuff with. I go on and make a pickax in a similar way. Floats doesn't seem too impressed with my blacksmithing abilities, but it is great hanging out with him. Floats is even a lot better than my colleagues on Mars. At least with Floats McGoats I don't need to save his life all the time. Or get so angry that I'd punch him in the face. Looking at Floats I realize again how it is just him and me in this universe. And the Oracle. But I don't think she counts.

***

After bated anticipation, the cotton harvest is finally ready. However, pulling the little cotton balls from the stems is ridiculously tedious. I can't get my massive Space Yeti hands to do the precise dissection well. I look over and see Floats munching down on my hard-earned cotton balls like they're cotton candy.

"Come on! Stop that!" I yell out as I pick up Floats and his pet rock to move them farther away from the pile. I drop them off at a safe distance. He does not look happy. I'll need to add building a cotton gin machine to the list of to-do items. After getting the entire cotton crop pulled and cleaned, I have three beach ball-sized mounds of cotton.

Building a spinning wheel will be the most intricate project I will have taken on so far. I need a spinning wheel to turn the cotton into yarn. After watching tons of YouTube videos and reading Wikipedia articles at the M-TOG, I think I can build one. But there are too many intricate parts in a spinning wheel for me to build it right now. I need to make tools. I need to cast parts. Maybe I can find some useful parts from the capsule transporter I scavenged. This will be the next big project, but it will take time. Too much time to have it done before the human baby is born.

***

It's been three months since Floats was born and the first human will be arriving in only a few weeks. Unfortunately, I don't have any cotton fabric. I don't even have yarn to knit. I do have plenty of parachute material lying around, though. I am able to make a quilt out of the parachute material sandwiching the harvested cotton balls as stuffing and nylon string tying the ends. I am able to make diapers with more parachute material. I use the three goats as diaper testers to make sure my diaper design would work okay. Three diaper-wearing goats on my alien planet civilization outpost. A good engineer tests their designs before production use. But this sight would make even Carl Sagan's ghost roll his eyes at me.

One thing I need but don't have is soap. I have lye, but I don't have animal fat. You need both lye and animal fat to make soap. I could get by using oil instead of fat, but I don't have that either. I look over at Floats.

"Bahhh!?"

"No, buddy, I'm not going to make you into soap."

The only animal I've seen so far is the lobster fish in the sea when I was battling the seaweed monsters. I don't know why but I am not seeing any land animals around. None. I don't understand what the deal is. I have seen flying birdlike animals, but they never get close enough for me to get a good look at them. I've seen the mystery dark orbs in the river, but I never get a good look at them to even understand what they are. Maybe they're animals. Maybe they're intelligent orbs of consciousness assessing their alien invader setting up shop in their backyard. If they have evil intent,

I'd hope that Sting would shine and let me know when they are near me. Maybe I'll call them Orcs so Sting will help me out.

I go back down to the sea to do some spearfishing and take my cart with me to bring back my catches. Before walking into the sea, I tie Sting to a long, rigid stick with a hemp rope tied to the end. I practice throwing it a few times on the beach, then proceed to walk into the sea. I do well to stay away from the seaweed this time. Walking along the seafloor, I come across a few lobster fish eating seaweed. The seaweed seems to not mind them, but I realize that the razor-sharp edges of the lobster fish are being used to cut the seaweed. I carefully sneak up on one of the fish, then launch Sting-on-a-stick.

"I got it!"

Holding on to the hemp rope end, the lobster fish thrashes and pulls with Sting lodged into its side. Luckily Sting holds on and I slowly tow the fish back up to the shore. Once on shore, I pull the rope until the fish comes with it. It is about the size of a tuna, but instead of normal fish skin, it has a hard multilayered orange-red armor shells with sharp blades protruding out the sides, top, and bottom. It is still flopping around on the beach. What should I do? I think a fisherman would cut the fish's head off in this situation. *The man who passes the sentence should swing the sword.* Ned Stark's words give me the courage to do what I needed to do. I lift Bearpaw above my head and strike down the lobster fish relieving him of his head. It's not a clean cut and the fish flops for a few more seconds before it passes. I feel nauseous. In my head, but not my stomach. I pick up the two pieces of fish and put them in the cart. Walking back up to the village I am happy that I got what I needed, but don't feel good killing the fish that way. That was the first time I have ever killed an animal.

Back at Remo village I get the cauldron fire going to start a boil. Tossing the lobster fish on the ground I take to cleaning it and cutting the meat into small pieces to put into the boiling cauldron. The lobster armor is so tough I have to rip it off by hand. The plan is to boil the meat to extract the oil, then pour off the top oil layer into ceramic pots. But after a quick check first with the Oracle's material identifier station. What I should end up with is fish oil for the soap. It won't smell good, but at least it's soap. It's a good thing I can't smell anything.

Chapter 12

Everything I've been working toward is going to culminate today. The M-TOG countdown has already started for the human girl. There has never been a birth on Mars. This is the first human to be born on another planet. This is the first human ever to be on a planet outside of our solar system. It is finally happening. Let's not screw anything up.

Learning my lesson with the goats, I make some towels out of hemp rope. I am able to make decent towels similar to burlap felt. Not great, but they should help soak up the water. I can't feel how rough the towels are. I try rubbing them against my hands while listening to determine if they would be sandpaper or not.

I watch the countdown timer. I turn on my facial display now so I don't forget about it later. Floats again is by my side lying next to his pet rock. Four...three...two...one...I can't wait. As soon as the timer goes to zero, I flip up the lever arm and take out the capsule. At the same spot that Floats and the other goats were born, I sit down with the capsule standing upright in my lap. I quickly unscrew the top and put it aside. I gently pour out the contents into my lap and out slides something I have never seen before. The bright brown eyes of a crying newborn baby looking up at me. In this instant, something has changed.

I am not holding a human baby. I'm holding a person. The first person on this planet. She'll grow up. Learn new things. Make mistakes. Find love. Have kids. Build a civilization. She has all of that to look forward to. But I have to make sure she sees it. There are a million things that will harm or kill her on this planet. If I slip, it will be the end of humanity. And the end of her.

"I'll name you Emma," I say, looking at her while she looks back at me for the first time.

After the first high wore off welcoming Emma into the world, I get her cleaned up, dried off, and wrapped in a parachute blanket. I have a teapot of formula milk ready to feed her. She seems to not mind the makeshift seaweed nipple and drinks the formula enthusiastically while staring at my face screen. She looks at me while she drinks. I have never held a baby before. I'm a planetary colonization engineer. Kids were never in my plans. But here I am. Babies get burped after they eat, right? I put Emma on my shoulder and carefully tap her back. I should probably read more information about babies from the M-TOG library.

After a few hours it is getting dark and starting to rain and getting cold. We move into my house where I had set up a bed of blankets. We lay down together, but she is shivering from the cold. I move Em by my chest. Instinctively it seems to be the right thing to do. She immediately stops shivering and settles down into the warmth. I lay motionless thinking about the moment. My thoughts move to what would be the next steps. What will tomorrow be and the following day. I'll need to be strategic to take care of Em, but also make sure the village is getting set up correctly. So much to do and now the clock is ticking even more aggressively.

While going through my to-do list in my mind, a thought came into my computer brain. Why is my chest warm? Oh yeah, it's just the HE-TEG embedded in me with its nuclear core. A sense of paralyzing panic sweeps through my thoughts. I stay still and try to not to panic or startle Em. I hope that the radiation barriers in my chest designed by the long-dead Earth engineers work properly and ensure that I don't kill off the first human on this planet.

I have only a hundred years of power from the HE-TEG starting from when I first landed on Prasares. After that point I'm nuclear waste that needs to be disposed of. My HE-TEG radiation shielding will eventually deteriorate over hundreds or thousands of years. Eventually my nuclear core will be exposed. If I'm not in a safe place at that point, I could end up giving radiation poisoning to the then grown civilization. I'll need to be sure to take matters into my own hands at that point. When it's time, I'll need to move myself to a final resting place. Maybe I'll crawl deep into a mountain cave. Or I'll find the deepest part of the ocean and sink to the bottom. Either way, I have a useful period then I'm a liability. A ticking time bomb.

***

Days and weeks go by with Emma. Some of it goes fast, other times are terrible. Em and I spend one hundred percent of our time together. I never leave her alone. I knew babies cried, but Em makes it real. Raising the goats was a breeze in comparison to Em. I am really struggling to figure out what she needs. I am a problem solver. That is what I do. But I can't solve what she wants and it's driving me nuts! While she cries, I turn down my microphones so I can't hear her and read through all the digital books and articles on infants I could find in the M-TOG file storage.

I am a good rocking machine when she needs to take a nap. My mechanical movements never get tired. She is so small compared to me. I can easily hold her in one hand. Changing diapers is a new experience for me. I always keep her diapers clean, checking every few minutes if she needs changing again. Her diapers are reusable, washable diapers. So, I spend a good amount of time cleaning them at the river downstream from the village.

I never get physically tired caring for Em, but mentally I am exhausted. I have to go into low power mode whenever she takes a nap. I set up my monitoring system to bring me back online when she starts crying again. Feed, burp, diaper, sleep, repeat.

Eventually we get into a reasonable routine and Em is finally sleeping better at night. I make a baby sling wrap that I can hold her up to my chest while I do light work around the village. After complaints from Floats, I take to keeping him and his pet rock around me too.

I can't do much but keep Em and the goats fed and taken care of. While feeding the goats, I get looks from them that seem to state their felt betrayal that I wasn't sleeping in the barn anymore and wasn't hanging out with them as much. Floats's stare is the hardest for me. He was my space sidekick for months. I miss hanging out with him too. I'm having a hard time connecting with Emma. Right now, she is just a screaming, eating machine that can't hold a conversation with me. I think I am in over my head.

After a month of this, we welcome two more female goats to the family. I name them Daisey and Gadget. It is a challenge birthing two goats while having Em with me. She is crying her eyes out while I am trying to unscrew the capsules and get the goats out, cleaned up, and fed. After birthing the two new goats I introduce them to the rest of the herd. Floats, Samus, and Peach are about ten months old now. Nearly fully grown. Floats now has horns. They accept the new infant goats into their family without question. I thank them then go deal with my own infant that is miserable.

I have the Oracle get three more female goats ordered from the Orbiter to put into the three empty slots in the M-TOG incubator. After the capsule transporter arrives, I load the new capsules into the M-TOG to start their incubation. I leave the new capsule transporter to be disassembled at a later time. With Em, that is work that can wait. Usually one male goat has about ten female goat companions. They'll need to be making milk for the human kids and making more goats quickly to support the village. I'll need the goats for wool, leather, and meat. Again, the thought of killing the goats doesn't sit well with me. I am not looking forward to that day.

To keep my mind off the goats' fate, I spend my days making a garden. It is easy work and I can keep Em comfortable in the baby sling and Floats happy with his pet rock near me. I plant kale and broccoli in the garden. Both are rich in vitamins K and C. Em wouldn't get these vitamins anywhere else. Without vitamin K, she wouldn't be able to form blood clots. Without vitamin C, Em would get scurvy. I also planted potatoes.

"Em, did you know that potatoes have all the nutrients a human needs to survive? It's the best type of food to have around. Just be sure not to have it be the only food you have around. Otherwise you'll end up like the long ancient civilization called the Irish. We'll see if we can make you some french fries someday."

Em looks at me and starts crying again.

***

On Em's four-month mark, we welcome Aden, the human boy into the world. At this point I'm an expert getting kids out of the incubator capsules, cleaned up, and fed right away. What I'm not an expert at is dealing with two screaming babies. Emma's first greeting to Aden is her screams...which prompts Aden to scream himself. Sitting on the ground, I'm holding one screaming kid, while another one is laying on her parachute blanket next to me. Screaming. Floats walks as far as away from us as his pet rock leash would let him.

Having two infants is a massive challenge. Twice the food, twice the diaper cleaning, twice the rocking. I only have two arms. Note to self: for the next interplanetary colonization project, be sure to have the Space Yeti design have more arms. I won't be able to put any more humans into the M-TOG incubators until these two are old enough to help me out. Until then it will just be goats.

***

Samus and Peach are now pregnant from Floats. I address Samus, Peach, and Floats, "Team, I'm glad you're doing your part to make this a successful colony. Your efforts won't be forgotten." I scratch Samus and Peach under their chins, then scratch Floats behind his ears and between his horns. "You're going to make me a proud, goat grampa!" Floats is happy to finally get more attention from me. I miss hanging out with him. When Emma and Aden get older we'll be able to do more together.

If I'm a grandpa to the goats, what am I to Emma and Aden? I can't be their dad. I'm going to need them to, umm, make their own kids someday. I can't have them both calling me Dad. I have fourteen more human embryos in the orbiter that will make fourteen more human kids. I can't have them all calling me Dad and then expect them to start their own families. Even worse, I can't have them call the Oracle Mom. That is even weirder.

"Oracle, help me out here. What should the human kids call me?"

"Nick, your name is Nick. That is what you asked me to call you."

"I know that, but what should be my title? On Earth kids have a mom and a dad. Em and Aden don't. I don't know how I'm going to explain that to them. Anyways, I can't be their dad and you can't be their mom. What are we to them?"

"Nick, all my suggestions are predicted to be rejected by you. I'm afraid I don't have an answer for you," the Oracle says with an oddly comforting tone of her English accent. Maybe she is starting to learn to not give me terrible advice. "Nick, while I have you, we need to talk about building the children's education syllabus and schedule. It was determined by the investors that education should start immediately."

"I'm a teacher! I'm *the* teacher! That's it! I'm Mr. Nick Burke, the Remo educator. The best teacher on Prasares! Thanks, Oracle!" As Teacher Nick Burke, I have a role. And certainly there has not been any problems with schoolkids getting busy with each other on Earth.

"Very good, Nick. If you are the teacher, what should I be called?" the Oracle asked.

"Well, of course, Oracle, you're the classroom computer! You've got the Oregon Trail game on you, right?" No response from her.

Chapter 13

Emma and Aden are both three years old now. Meanwhile, the goats have absolutely no problem procreating. I stop getting goat capsules from the orbiter after fourteen of them. Those fourteen goats made thirty-five more goats for a total of forty-nine goats. I built a second barn twice as big and a fenced-in area ten times as big. I also built a dividing wall in the barn and fenced area to separate the males from the females. I needed a way to control the baby goat-making otherwise things will get out of hand. In order to feed the goat herd, I set up serious crop fields with crop rotation.

Emma and Aden have been walking and talking for the last two years. Emma is very inquisitive to what I am doing. She's always wanting to be in the middle of what is going on, being around me, and asking questions. Aden is more interested to leave us to go explore. After getting tired of chasing down Aden when he has tried to make escapes, I end up giving Emma and Aden their own pet rocks with hemp ropes tied to their waists. Good thing I'm not their parent or the intergalactic child services would be all over me. It does the job. They are able to stay by my side and walk around, at least a little.

"Mr. Burke?" Emma says to me sitting down next to her pet rock. "When are we going to play?"

I stop stoking the fire for boiling water and look over at her and Aden. They both have faces of boredom. "Play with Aden, honey," I reply to her while turning back to the fire's needs.

"But I want to play with you. Can you give me a ride on your arm? I want a ride!"

I look over and see she is giving me her pouty face. Aden's interest perks up with the possibility of something exciting happening. They both walk toward me, stopping at the end of their leashes. Arms up, wanting a ride.

"Yeah okay, but just for a little bit, then I need to get back to work." I untie their waist ropes and pick them both up. I put Emma on my left shoulder and Aden on my right. They are so small. I don't remember kids being so small. They hold on to my helmet as I start walking around the village.

"Hold on tight. Don't fall off!" I yell at them as we carefully walk around.

Floats gives me an odd look as we walk past the barn. He has fully grown horns now and long white fur on his billy goat chin. He is still black with white stripes and he still has brown spots on his eyebrows, but they are bigger now. "Bahhh!" he yells at us as we shuffle by.

"Play the song!" they both shout at the same time. The kids have picked up that I liked to listen to music while I work. They know I am the only source of the music on all of Prasares and so treat me like a music-playing machine. But I can't resist, it's too much fun. COMMAND LOAD PLAY, Black Sabbath, "Iron Man". I start walking like a lumbering robot around the village stepping with the beat. Slow groaning guitar chords with Ozzy Osbourne's mellowdrone singing voice.

"Make it louder, Mr. Burke!" They both scream into my microphones. Stepping with the beat I am making deep footprints into the orange soil. The kids are hanging on to their slow giant while seeing the village from a viewpoint they can't see otherwise.

When the song is done, I carefully put them down.

"Come on, one more time," Emma cries, holding her arms up to me.

"I need to get back to work, Em. But we'll read later tonight." I tie her pet rock waist leash back on to her. Aden has already made a run for it when I wasn't looking. It only takes me a few steps and a quick swinging catch to sweep him up and bring him back. After tying Aden, I go deal with the boiling water at the fire. Emma sits down, pouting and leaning against her pet rock, while Aden is pulls with all his strength to move the boulder. I don't get it. I don't understand why they want to hang out with me so much. Emma in particular. She is like glue on me.

I have set up a top-notch goat milk production factory. We have a small holding pen where I milk the goats with ceramic buckets. It is tough for me to reach under the goats and milk them with my Space Yeti fingers, but I make do. We have so many goats, I don't need to worry about rationing and storing milk. But all the goats need to be milked regularly. I did make an attempt at making goat cheese. It seemed to be okay, but the kids wouldn't eat it. I couldn't taste it so I couldn't tell if it is good or not. Oddly enough they preferred the broccoli from the garden to my goat cheese. Kids. Go figure.

After I finish milking the goats, I come back to Emma and Aden still with their pet rocks. I find that they have gotten into some mud inside their leash area. They are covered head to toe in orange mud with both of them putting it on each other's faces.

"Well, that is one way to get used to the local microbes, isn't it? Hopefully there aren't super space bugs in there," I say looking down at them, fully knowing there are not any harmful microbes thanks to the Oracle's material testing abilities. They both give me a look of satisfied disobedience unaffected by my warning. "Let's get you guys washed."

I was able to build the water pipeline using the harvested bamboo without any problems. The water line runs from the small pond above the waterfall down to the village. I had set up a large circular ceramic-tiled tub sunk halfway into the ground with a tiled outer rim. Using the kiln, I was able to make the ceramic tiles. My tub is not going to win any home improvement awards, but it does the job. All the crevices are sealed with clay, then solidified with heat from a fire I used when I built the tub. The tub is located in the middle of the village serving as our central gathering place. Our watering hole. The bamboo water line from the uphill pond goes straight into the tub. Always flowing and feeding fresh water. There is a second, larger diameter bamboo line leaving the tub on the other side that goes back into the river downstream. This is the drain. I'm able to adjust the water level in the tub by moving the exit bamboo pipeline up and down on a sliding wooden wall. The tub always has fresh water and it is a lot more convenient than walking down to the river all the time.

"Mr. Burke, the soap is too stinky! I won't get in!" Emma says, crossing her arms and dipping her head. I see her scowling her eyes at me. I still haven't found another source of fat or oil to make soap other than the lobster fish. When I made soap just using the lobster fish oil, the kids wouldn't even get close to it. I've since added a sweet-smelling plant the Oracle helped me identify into the soap to mask the awful smell. But I had to put so much of the sweet plant into the soap to cover up the fishy smell, the kids now complain that the sweet smell is too much.

I don't bother negotiating with Emma. I pick her up and put her into the tub without any hesitation. Aden gets in on his own, lifting one little leg over the edge at a time. Before long the tub is full of suds and two upset kids. I use a hemp rope loofah to scrub them both clean. After I drain the sudsy water from the tub, I have them both stand next to the fresh water coming out of the bamboo pipe and fill a rugbynut bucket with water to dump on them to rinse off. Drying off still isn't ideal. There is nowhere near enough cotton to make towels. I'm still using the hemp rope burlap felt towels I used when the kids were born. I do my best to dry them off quickly before I hear more complaints.

I help the kids get their clothes back on. They both wear parachute nylon tunics with a nylon rope belt similar to what you'd imagine little Roman kids would wear. Except you can see the MarsX logo on them. Not enough cotton for towels and not enough cotton to make regular clothes either. I still need to make a decent spinning wheel and loom setup. It is too easy to use the parachute nylon from the capsule transporters. I at least don't let them run around barefoot. They are treated with the civility of having flip-flops made from wood and nylon rope.

I don't know that I could have lived like this as a kid, having been first accustomed to all the comforts of life back on Earth. I have to keep reminding myself that these kids have no idea how much easier their parents had it back on Earth. I realize again that these two kids' parents were probably billionaires. Some of the human embryos were supposed to be scientists, but they're probably mostly billionaire investors' kids. The change of lifestyle from parent to child is staggering.

"Mr. Burke, what is an Iron Man?" Emma asks, sitting down to eat a broccoli snack before bed.

"Well, I guess it would be a robot?" I answer.

"What is a robot?" Emma asks, not hesitating.

"Well, I'm a robot," I say back.

"You're not a man? What's man, then?"

"I used to be a man. Now I'm a robot. Aden will be a man someday and you'll be a woman."

"So, Aden will be a robot someday too?" Emma asks excitedly. Aden looks up from munching on his broccoli snack with a concerned face.

"No, Aden will stay a man. I am special. I'm sure I'll be the only robot on this planet for a long, long time. Probably thousands of years." I think about all the things that need to happen before the Prasares civilization would even come close to making robots like Earth. Materials, electronics, software, and all the people and knowledge to put it all together into a robot. I'll be disintegrated in a cavern or covered by layers of dead lobster fish at the ocean bottom by then. But there is so much I need to do. So much to make Remo a success. These kids have no idea. No idea how much I'm doing for them.

It's finally time for bed. In the house, we all have our own beds. The kids have parachute mats with cotton cushioning, and parachute blankets and pillows. I sleep on the floor. I could have just as easily gone into sleep mode standing up or sitting. But I decided long ago that I need to act like a human and sleep lying down so they would do the same. There is no need to waste any of the parachute material or cotton on myself for a bed. I did, however, make a bamboo floor inside the house to keep the dirt down.

"Mr. Burke, can we read the story again?" Emma asks excitedly. I had made our first book by making paper out of bamboo pulp, minced using Sting. It is labor intensive, but figuring out how to make paper will be one of the most important things I'll need to do. Emma and Aden crawl into my lap while I sit down on the cabin floor. I turn on my headlamps so we can see and grab the loose-leaf bamboo paper. It will be a while before I can make a bound book.

Emma immediately starts pointing at the first page and reading it.

"I...spy...a...goat!" Emma says while reading along with her finger over the charcoal text under a crude goat drawing. I can see that Aden is already falling asleep in my arm.

"And what is a goat, Emma?" I ask quietly.

"Floats McGoats!" she exclaims giggling. We shuffle the paper to see the second page.

"I...spy...a...rugg...rugby...rugby," she stutters.

"Nut," I impatiently interrupt her. "Come on, Em, you need to try harder here. This is important. Let's do another one. You know these, so let's get them right." Her face gets a bit dimmer while looking at the next page.

"I ...spy...a..ll...lllo...lobb..." Emma struggles.

"You know this one. We read this every night. You know this one," I say, knowing that we've read this book dozens of times by now. "It's the only book we have. Come on!" I say with fevering frustration.

"I...I...don't know it. Mr. Burke, help me!"

"It's lobster fish. Lobster fish! Heck, there is even a picture of a lobster fish on the page. How can you miss that?!" Emma looks surprised as if she's learned the word for the first time. That face triggers something in me.

"You know, Emma, you're going to need to start picking this stuff up if you're going to survive on Prasares. I'm not going to be around forever and this place will kill you if you don't shape up. I don't know what the Orcs are, but they're going to get you. You're the oldest and you'll need to take care of the village. What are you going to do if the Orcs get you?" The Orcs is what I started calling the dark orbs that go up and down the river. I still haven't been able to catch one to figure out what they are. But they've been good enough to be the boogeyman motivator to the kids. I don't hold back throwing the boogeyman threat at her.

Emma's eyes well up. She gets up out of my lap and gets under her blanket facing away from me. I shouldn't have said that. I can hear her sniffling under her blanket. Why do I say stupid stuff that I regret later? I put Aden into his bed and cover him with his blanket. I lay down on my side of the cabin looking up. I see the ceiling cracks have gotten bigger since when I first made the cabin three years ago. I still hear Emma sniffling. Maybe this is still a mistake. I think I am in over my head. I don't know how my dad did this himself. The cabin goes dark after I shut off my headlamps.

Chapter 14

Emma's tenth birthday is next week. We'll celebrate Aden's birthday in four months. I'd like to say that time has flown by, but it hasn't. I've been working nonstop since I haven't needed to be with the kids 24/7. I've been going without sleep lately. Sleep is good to get my mind refreshed but I've been able to power through without going into sleep mode lately. I feel I need to do everything possible to make sure the colony is set up for success.

Four years ago, I had the Oracle get another delivery from the orbiter. Two females and one male human embryo. Sophie, Ava, and Chase are four-year-old happy and healthy kids, and the newest citizens of Remo. We've stabilized at seventy-six goats by separating the males and females, only having them breed when we let them. I haven't brought myself to butcher any of them yet. I know I'll need to do it, but the kids have been getting by okay on lobster fish as their protein.

I've grown the village significantly over the past several years. More buildings and much more farmland. I built a second cabin that Emma and Aden are staying in by themselves. I'm assuming that someday when they're old enough they'll get married and start having children. Obviously to build the colony we'll need to start making babies the old-fashioned way eventually. Sophie, Ava, and Chase are staying in my cabin. It's cramped, but cozy.

I built a glass production shop next to the smelting area allow me to make glassware. Unfortunately, glassblowing is not working for me, given that I don't have lungs. I need a kid around to help me do the glassblowing. Aden has been the best at it so far, but even with him I can only instruct him so much to control his breathing while shaping the glass. I've been experimenting with using a bellow I've made out of parachute material to blow the air myself. I think if I can make the glass myself, I would be able to have more consistent bottles made as compared to what Aden can muster with his short attention span.

I even made a rough bacteria lab. I don't have a white coat or a sterile medical laboratory, but I was able to grow cultures of local microbes using rudimentary petri dishes I had made. I've been able to culture yeast and have been making bread for years now. However, I'm still working on making something close to penicillin. Luckily with the Oracle's help to identify plants, we've also got a fully stocked medicine shop full of glass bottles of every ailment solution you can think of. The kids have even been getting iodine mixed in with their salt. Making iodine was the hardest thing I've done so far. You need sulfuric acid and chlorine gas, not exactly stuff laying around on Prasares.

I've finally been able to raise our cotton production enough that we can use it to make clothes. With the kids helping with the spinning wheel and loom, we've been able to make cotton clothing for everyone. Granted, they're still tunics, but at least they're more comfortable than the parachute fabric, especially in the summertime. With the goat wool, we're able to make wool socks for everyone. The most intricate and labor-intensive things I've ever made are the spinning wheel and loom. There are so many moving parts that I had to intricately construct. I never let a kid operate them without me watching; the last thing I need is to have them break something. Even so, I need the kids to operate the spinning wheel and loom— my Space Yeti hands are way too big.

Over time I've found that boiled hemp rope made for better paper than the bamboo. I've been able to make reasonable sheets of paper. Now, we've got fully completed textbooks. Granted, they're still all handwritten. Building a printing press is still on the to-do list for me. One of the most important missions for the Oracle is to provide all the important Earth books to the new civilization, but the M-TOG doesn't have a printer. Every single book will need to be transcribed by hand. Which will take years. Maybe centuries. Having the Oracle be the center of Remo for a long time will be critical.

Once I got all the village essentials built, I finally started a pet project for myself. I built a brick-paved plaza in the center of the village. It has circular paver bricks I made in the kiln. I embedded the bricks into the ground, making three giant circles arranged edge to edge, one large triangle of three circles. The center is left with natural ground to support a large bonfire we light every night.

One circle pad has the main watering hole for the village. It's where we get our fresh water for everything we do. It has an incoming bamboo water pipeline and a separate waste water pipeline. Another circle pad is the main cooking firepit. The kids don't get to make s'mores, but they do like fresh-caught lobster fillets. And the third circle pad has the picnic table where we all eat together. I sit with the kids as they eat together, watching them grow up and learn how to be humans on this alien world.

Our plaza sits next to the M-TOG and my first house. As I look out at the village, I realize how much I've been able to accomplish. When I first landed the M-TOG here, it was an empty field. Now, it's a bona fide village.

The digital resource library in the M-TOG has been a lifesaver. I'm not a survivalist, or farmer, or carpenter, but there's enough information and videos available to learn those roles. Emma's and Aden's day jobs while I'm working are to watch over the younger kids and to do chores around Remo village, including feeding the goats. Usually Emma and Aden switch responsibilities each day. One day one looks after the human kids, the other day goats. With Emma and Aden doing these simpler chores I've been able to get more stuff done at the village.

It has been amazing how the kids have grown. Emma is tall now—taller than Aden. She's still glued on me and I don't understand why. She adores me, always asking questions, always wanting to learn. She could just as easily get the information she's wanting from the Oracle, but she always prefers talking to me. But Aden, he's on his own mission. He doesn't wait for me. He's figuring things out on his own, right or wrong. I haven't changed at all, except for my white Space Yeti suit continuing to become stained from the years of orange dirt and mud.

When the kids are not working, they are in school. I have built the best school curriculum on this planet. Most of the classes have been happening at the picnic table in the center of the village or at the M-TOG.

The first class is Production, where I'm teaching the kids how to run the village. Farming, smelting, cooking, everything. I give a lecture each day on different topics while they take notes on their hemp rope paper. The three youngest kids are barely able to write, but they still enjoy the class. It can't hurt to start them early. They get lots of hands-on practice.

I made each kid a garden hoe and have them grow small gardens by themselves. Unfortunately, they still don't make enough food not to all starve to death if I wasn't around. I've been cautious letting them do the more dangerous work, like working the smelter and kiln. The last thing I need is having any of the kids injured under my watch. Aden has been the only one that has been pushing through my hesitancy with letting them use the smelter. He has an unusual drive in him. I have to remind myself every so often that the kids are the offspring of billionaires and scientists. For all I know, some of them may be clones. I never did look at the logs to see who is who. I don't care. I didn't even name the kids what their parents wanted them named. They're all gone now. This is our planet.

The next class is Safety & Medical. We don't have any hospitals or doctors on Prasares. It's just us, and we're in a dangerous world. If we lost any humans, it would be an immense detriment to our civilization. So, I'm teaching the kids to handle cuts, broken bones, you name it. Really, I'm doing the class to keep them from bleeding out from an accident until I get to them to save them. I'm also teaching them all the contents of the medicine shop. They'll need to know all the different medicines I'm making for them. I've been making the kids take quizzes, tests, and write essays. Sophie has shown more interest in this class than all the others combined.

Next is Science & Exploration. We've gone on six off-village excursions so far. All of them have only been day trips. We can't go too far since we can't leave the goats on their own. The kids enjoy going to the beach the most. This has been Aden's favorite class by far.

Next is Math & Engineering. Emma and Aden are already doing calculus. The engineering work I'm teaching them is focused on construction and materials. It's still a bit too advanced for them right now, though that isn't a problem because I'm building everything around here anyways.

And last but not least is Reading & Writing. The young ones are doing the basics. The ABCs, writing their names, reading the children's books I wrote when Emma was younger. Emma and Aden have been transcribing books from the Oracle's database, mostly textbooks we need for the other classes. It's extremely boring work transcribing books onto hemp rope paper. Only Emma has taken an interest in it. Aden doesn't have the attention span, so I have to force him to get the work done. I've set Aden up to use the monitor at the M-TOG. As the monitor shows the text, Aden writes the text onto his paper. The M-TOG has only one monitor, so I sit across from Emma while I use my face monitor as a text display. She insisted that we sit together, leaving Aden with the M-TOG. She genuinely looks happy reading and writing down the text information. We stare at each other for hours. Aden would rather be building a fire in the smelter. After Emma had asked, I let her start to transcribe some of the literary classics. I may be a heartless robot, but even I wouldn't make someone transcribe algebra books without a break to read something else.

History is not in the curriculum. I wrestled with it but decided not to teach Earth's history to the kids. Instead I took to telling them the best things about Earth. How smart the earthlings were, how they were able to make me. The kids started calling the people of Earth "the Old Ones". I suppose they think their situation of being raised on an alien planet by a robot teacher is normal, because they don't know any better. Emma has started to ask more probing questions about the Old Ones after she started reading the literary classics.

Geography isn't in the curriculum either. I could have given them a full map of Prasares from the polar orbit surveys I made prior to landing on the planet, but the discovery of the unknown is something that drives humans. It's what drove me. If they already knew what was out there, would they bother exploring it?

Everything is going well at Remo village. I am really happy with myself. Everything is good except one thing: something or someone is eating the crops in my field in the middle of the night. I've had to build a fence around the fields and garden, which took me forever to build. I was perturbed building the fences and my foul mood was hot enough to cause the crops to burst into flames. Whatever it is, it keeps breaking through the fence. And I have to repair it. Whatever it is, I'm going to get it.

***

"Floats, you're doing a terrible job being the lookout for what is eating your food."

"Bahhh," he answers as I continue rebuilding the dismantled fence.

Floats McGoats is bigger now so he needs a bigger pet rock. It's a boulder the size of a beach ball, but it's still no problem for me to move around. I've continued keeping him near me while I work. Floats has been my space sidekick for a long time and more time to come. Floats is a mature goat at ten years old, most of the way through his expected fifteen- to eighteen-year lifespan.

I often keep the human kids within my sight tied to their own pet rocks when they're not being watched by Emma or Aden. I cut the ropes for the ten-year-old kids years ago. The young kids tend to complain while I work so I leave them out of hearing range so Floats and I could talk with each other.

"Floats, what do you think is doing this to our fence? There are no animals around here. No animals have ever bothered you or the other goats. I bet it's the Orcs that are doing this."

I've seen the Orcs numerous times, swimming up and down the river, but I've never seen them out of the river. Only as dark orb torpedoes swimming under the waterline. I don't know what they are. I don't know if they're even animals. Maybe they're sentient underwater balls of consciousness that are disinterested in us low-life alien intruders. Or maybe they're dumb space hogs that eat my crops. Pounding in another fence stake with Bearpaw I realize that I've become the angry farmer, but I don't care. My face screen must have a permanent scowl. I need to make sure this village is taken care of. And there is nothing on this planet that is going to keep me from doing that.

"Floats, do you think Emma and Aden are doing okay? Aden is great, but he seems to be not listening to me as much. He's still too interested to go exploring. At his age, he'll only get lost out there. Who knows what else is out there to harm him? Emma is okay to stay in the village, but that is maybe not a good thing. She's too attached to me. I'm not her father. I'm her teacher!" I hit the next fence stake too hard and I have to realign it. "Maybe that is the problem here. That they don't have parents. I'm doing the best I can to fill in. Floats, do you think I'm doing alright as a father figure? How have you handled it? You've got a bunch of kids now."

"Bahhh," Floats casually responds, then lies down to take a nap.

"Thanks, buddy."

Seriously though, we're not only into unknown interplanetary territory, we're also mentally and emotionally in uncharted territory for these kids. All I need is my new civilization being held together by emotionally-scarred people. I hope I'm doing okay for them. There is only so much a Space Yeti with a television monitor as a face can do for budding young minds. The Oracle isn't much of a mother figure either. Cold and vacant when they're expecting more warmth. She makes me look like the father of the millennium in comparison.

Unfortunately, there isn't much guidance for being a good father figure in the M-TOG digital resources. The only information I have to go on is what my own father did with me. I remember him giving me my space. If I wanted to talk to him, he'd talk with me. And when I didn't want to talk, he left me alone. Isn't that what a kid wants? My father did a good job with me. If he didn't, I wouldn't be here. He was the one that went against all good judgment to sign me up for a crackpot online service to stream your kid's life into the cloud to *maybe* make a digital clone of them someday. But here I am. A digital clone. A D-Clo. On an alien planet. Pounding in fence posts. Talking to a goat.

***

One night, with all the kids asleep, I stand perfectly still in the middle of the garden. Waiting. Watching. A silent sentinel waiting to find what is eating my crops. In my stillness I'm invisible. The sky is dark except for the faint rings in the sky. With no moonlight it's dark.

"Snap!" I hear, but I don't move. Adjusting my cameras, I see dark orbs approaching me, swaying side to side as they move. It's too dark to see them clearly but it's unmistakable that they are the dark orbs from the river. My computer brain searches in its image resources for an explanation of what they are, but it finds none. Six of them pass through the fence they broke and greedily start eating crops from the garden, inching closer to me.

Like a startling gun blast, I turn on my headlamps to shine directly at the orbs in front of me. I see twelve blinded, frozen eyes of the dark orbs looking back at me. Their shiny skin reflects the light at me. I fling out a hemp rope net on top of them and get five of the six orbs snarled while they yelp and holler. The sixth turns around and makes a run for the opening in the fence, bobbing and bouncing in a panic. I grab Bearpaw from my back scabbard and toss it like a javelin at the runaway dark orb. Its arc is perfect to hit its mark. *Thunk!* Bearpaw's blade buries into the ground right in front of the orb blocking the exit. The screaming orb turns around and runs right into my arms.

***

The next morning the kids and I finally see what the dark orbs are in the sunlight. What we've been calling Orcs are round, fat animals that look like dark beach balls with baby seal faces with innocent eyes. They have short squatty legs like a hippo. When they walk, they lumber side to side. But their large powerful tails presumably give them incredible speed in the water. Their skin is something I've never seen before, a hybrid of fur and scales, glistening dark gray that shines when the sun hits it at the right angle. Taking it all in I see that they are the true face of menacing evil. The kids and I are huddled around inspecting them.

"Mr. Burke! What are they?" Sophie asks.

"They're the Orcs! I finally caught them! They won't be bothering you anymore."

Sophie looks concerned. "But...but they're cute! I thought you said they are monsters that will eat us if we are bad. This one looks nice. You should let them go!"

"Yeah, that's not going to happen. Besides, we need to find local animals to domesticate. I don't think Orcs will be good for pulling plows, but they should make for good soap."

"Soap!" Sophie cries out. She leans in and smells one of the Orcs. "I don't think they smell like soap, Mr. Burke."

I look over at Emma. She has her arms crossed and for the first time is wearing a look of pre-teen disdain focused toward me.

"These are the Orcs? You gave me nightmares when I was a little kid over Orcs! You had me convinced that they were going to eat me in my sleep!" Emma storms off to the goat barn without letting me respond. The other kids quickly side with Emma and follow her to the barn, not wanting to spend any more time with the nightmare storyteller. As regret starts to well up in me, I shake it off. Now is not a time to brood. I have work to do.

After I finish interrogating our thieves, I start building a pen to hold them in. Knowing that the bamboo fencing I've been using isn't enough, I build the fencing out of logs instead. Floats helps me keep an eye on the Orcs while I work. By the end of the day I have the Orc pen done. I even dug a pool in the center for them to swim which I'll fill tomorrow.

As the sun sets, I release the Orcs into their new home. They waddle. They sniff. I toss some vegetables I pulled from the garden into a trough and they rush to it, eating happily At least I don't need to concern myself about what to feed Orcs. I grab a water trough from the goat yard and gift it to the Orcs.

I poke one of the Orcs with my finger while it eats. Their blubber should be good for lots of things. Cooking oil, soap, maybe even lamp oil. I could finally make the kids french fries. I feel for Sting sitting in its holster on the side of my thigh. One of the Orcs looks up at me with its disabling baby seal eyes. Its innocent look evaporates any thoughts I have of Sting tasting Orc blood. Someday soon, I'm going to need to get over the idea of having to kill animals. If I don't, the village is going to suffer.

Chapter 15

"Can we do rock band tonight, Mr. Burke?" Em asks. "Tomorrow is my birthday and it would be so much fun if we can play tonight!" The idea of having fun seems to have washed away Em's earlier upset mood about the Orcs.

The kids love, I mean *love* me playing music from my speakers. The fact that we don't have instruments or even electricity doesn't stop them from enjoying playing music. Rock band is what we call the kids air-guitaring and playing other makeshift instruments while I play music from my speakers. I have to oblige. Emma is talking with me again, which is a good sign. I should keep the positivity going with her. Plus, I am in a great mood having finally caught my garden-eating monsters. We're sitting around the bonfire in the middle of the village with firelight flickering against all the village buildings and the M-TOG behind us.

Em has a stick with a hemp rope shoulder strap for her lead guitar. Aden has several rugbynut buckets laid out into a drum kit on the ground and two sticks to hit them with. Sophie and Ava have their own stick guitars like Em, just smaller. Chase has one rugbynut bucket to beat on. Apparently, no one wants to be a bass player. When I play the music from my speakers, they put on the best rock show on the planet. And I am their audience.

They know all the headbanger songs that I like. AC/DC, Nirvana, Van Halen, Pearl Jam. Rock, punk, grunge, metal—we do it all. All the musicians were long dead before I was even born. But they were still around when my dad was a kid. He liked them, so I like them too. Now my kids like them. He did another thing to bring me up right. He introduced me to great music.

"Mr. Burke, play our favorite song!" Aden yells out.

"Right on!" COMMAND LOAD PLAY "Time Bomb" by Rancid. A pumping punk guitar riff plays out and the kids start to thrash with their wooden instruments. I love punk rock dancing in my Space Yeti body. I can't headbang given that I don't have a neck, but that just means I have to get my whole body into it. When the chorus kicks in, all the kids yell it out together.

I don't have a black coat. Or white shoes. No black hat or a Cadillac. But I am a time bomb. I loved the song as much as the kids, but it reminds me of the nuclear HE-TEG ticking time bomb in my chest. I know my end. But I need to make sure these kids are set up well to inherent Prasares before I go.

After a few more rounds of songs, the kids are finally tired out. We sit and talk to finish out the night.

"Something is wrong with my neck," Aden says. "It feels prickly on the back of my neck. I have shivers. What is that?"

"That's the chills you get when you hear mind-blowing music," I say.

"Mind-blowing?" Aden doesn't understand.

I clenched my hands into fists and held them to the side of my head. Then I shoot them out, fingers flying like an explosion from my head. "Mind-blowing," I say.

Aden and the kids are excited to learn the new phrase and start doing their own mind-blowing gestures to each other.

"Mr. Burke, what is *your* favorite band?" Em asks me.

"Wow," I say, caught off guard. When did the children start to ask such interesting questions? "I don't know if I can answer that. There is so much influential music in my life. I don't know if I can narrow it down to just one band. If I have to pick, I suppose it would be Pink Floyd. It's not just for their music. Their story is also important. The band during their height was led by two Old Ones, David Gilmour and Roger Waters. They both sang and wrote songs.

But they absolutely hated each other. Their music together was undeniably some of the best Earth had ever heard. They eventually broke up to form separate bands. Their music separate from each other was never as good as when they were together. That says something. I guess it says that sometimes you need to work through personnel dispute problems for the good of the end product."

"That's really interesting, Mr. Burke," Em says, smiling.

"Thanks, Em. I think that was the first meaningful adult conversation I've had since I've left Earth. Thank you, that means a lot to me."

The other kids look up at me with blank stares, having listened to my drunken college bar rant.

Em breaks awkward the silence. "Well I like the Old Ones named David and Roger. I'm going to name my first two sons after them."

"Uhh...please don't," I respond.

Em wraps her arms around my arm and rests her head against my shoulder. I don't feel like her father. I feel terrible that she doesn't really have parents. I suppose I'm the only parent she has. I think I'm finally really happy to have her in my life. She's not a burden anymore. She is finally someone I can talk to. I look down at her and see she has a smile on her face as she's starting to fall asleep.

***

The next morning, I do my usual rounds with the kids. Em is already up. She wants to get her chores done early since today is her tenth birthday. I find her at the water area cleaning tunics and socks.

"Did you feed the goats already?" I ask her.

"Yup, I woke up really early and fed them first thing," she says, glowing back at me while scrubbing clothes.

"Did you fill their water troughs?"

She stops scrubbing and looks up at me with a perturbed stare. "Of course I did." She turns back to her scrubbing, trying to get it done as fast as she can.

I go through the list in my head what else needs to get done. Looking around, I see the goat fence and see that the male goats' gate is wide open.

"Did you close the gate?!" My elevated tone sternly blocks Em from her work.

"I thought I did, maybe I didn't latch it all the way," she says as she looks back over to the gate.

Without responding to Em, I make a mad dash over to the gate. Looking in the male goat fenced area my vision algorithms count thirteen male goats. We are missing one male goat: Floats McGoats. He must have wandered out of the gate. In a panic I look in all directions and don't see him anywhere. I close the gate, double-check that it's secured, then head over to the human kids to get them to start searching for Floats.

"Aden, keep the little ones with you. We need to find Floats!" I yell at him.

"Floats!"

"Floats!!" We're all yelling out trying to find him. The kids are cupping their hands to their mouths to be as loud as possible. I find myself doing it as well out of instinct, though my speakers are plenty loud. We search the buildings and fields with increasing concern. It doesn't dawn on me to ask the Oracle if she had seen him until we'd been searching for two hours, walking past her multiple times.

"Nick, I did see a goat walk by the M-TOG," the Oracle says. "It was walking toward the waterfall west of here."

Of course he wandered off in that direction. He did the same thing when he was small. I run toward the waterfall, leaving the kids behind. Aden grabs the three young kids, keeping them back at the village. I look back and see Em coming after me, but she can't keep up.

At full sprint, I make it to the top of the falls next to the lake within a few minutes. In a panic I search around but I don't see him.

"Bahh...bahh...cough...bahhh." I hear him at the base of the falls. Looking down the cliff, I see Floats on a rocky shore at the bottom near where the falls meet the river. He is on his side and blood is spattered by his rear legs. He must have lost his footing at the top of the cliff and fell down to the base of the falls.

I quickly run along the perimeter of the cliff to get to a place I can navigate down to Floats. Finally, I get to him and fall to my knees to inspect him closely. His right rear leg is broken, the bone sticking out. Bleach white with red blood and pink tissue. Floats is in a panic. He's trying to get himself up, but can't.

"Bahh!!! Cough...cough..."

Every time he tries to get up, he ends up dragging his broken leg and getting more dirt into the wound. I put my hand on the back of his neck to try to calm him. My head fogs in anger. "Dammit, Emma, what the hell is wrong with you? This is your fault! You left the gate open!"

He's not going to survive. I don't think my medical supplies are enough to ward off infection. He's going to have a miserable death if I try to save him. I can't put him through that. I put my hand between his horns and rub his head. His rectangle pupils look at me. They're glazed in panic and fear. I haven't seen a look like that since Amy almost died on Mars. The same eyes of imminent death. I can't save him like I did with Amy. I need to put him down. Now.

I unsheathe Sting from the scabbard attached to my leg. I grab one of his horns, lifting up his head with my left hand and carefully line Sting to his throat behind his chin hair with my other hand. I don't know what I'm doing. I'm guessing this is how it's done.

"I'm so sorry, buddy. I'm going to miss you."

I quickly slash, cutting his throat. A wave of bright red blood comes out of his throat onto Sting and my hand. "Gurg...cough...gurgle..." I don't know what to do. I've never seen something like this before. I lean away but force myself to awkwardly pet his back to try to comfort him. His eyes are still looking at me. Blink. Blink again. After what seems like minutes, his eyes finally close. Then stillness. What is in front of me now is an inanimate thing. Floats isn't there anymore.

How could Emma do this?! My computer brain hazes with anger, then stops abruptly. I come back to and see that my computer crashed and rebooted. Only a second went by. What happened? Probably my D-Clo hit an out-of-boundary condition that it had never been trained to handle. When I was Organic Nick, I never killed anything. I realize this is the first time I've ever killed an animal. Anger is still rushing through me. I never should have left the responsibility of the goats to Emma.

I stand up to wipe Sting on my thigh. From the corner of my camera, I see Emma standing behind me. She had seen the whole thing. She is a silent, motionless, and shocked ten-year-old girl looking at a bloody Space Yeti standing over a goat carcass.

"Look what you did! Look at him! You did this!" I point at Floats's body as soon as I see her. "You're careless and this is what happens. You killed my friend! Don't you ever be careless again!" I scream at her. I tower over her as I stand next to her. "You hear me? *Do you hear me*?!"

She's cowering underneath me. She cracks and sprints back toward the village in a flood of tears. I still have Sting in my hand smeared in blood. I was waving it around when I was yelling at her.

I watch as she runs back toward the village. I shouldn't have done that. Why would I say that to her? I am such an idiot. This is me punching Owen in the face on Mars all over again. Why do I say this stuff without thinking? I realize again that I am a copy of Organic Nick. My D-Clo was trained to be just like him. Depressed and disappointed in myself, I pick up Floats's body. Blood keeps draining out of his throat onto the ground. His eyelids open a little, but there isn't any life in them anymore. Holding the body out in front of me, I walk back up to the village leaving a trail of blood behind me.

***

Aden and the kids run out to meet me near the fields. They stop once they see that I'm carrying Floats.

"What happened!?" Aden yells, wide-eyed. The young kids don't know how to process this. They have blank stares at Floats's body as I walk past them.

I don't answer. I walk straight toward the barn. I proceed like an emotionless robot. Once inside I grab some hemp rope and hang the body by the good back leg from the rafters to let the blood continue to drain from the neck out into a rugbynut bucket I put on the floor. The kids stare from the entrance of the barn but don't enter. I don't see Emma. I go through my motions in a cold, robotic manner trying not to think about Floats or what happened minutes earlier.

I stand by and watch Floats's body draining. I change the rugbynut buckets as they fill up with blood. I shouldn't have gotten so close to Floats. It's a goat. It was supposed to die and provide us with hide and meat. It's not a pet. But I needed him. He was someone I could talk to when I needed it the most. He was my friend.

I head back to the Oracle.

"Hello, Nick, what can I do for you?"

"I need instructional videos on carcass cleaning for removing hide and cutting meat from a goat."

"Happy to help. Here are one hundred and two videos on the subject," the Oracle says with the same tone as if I had asked her to give me videos on making knots in rope. The fact that the Oracle is a cold artificial intelligence hits me again. Floats was real and had real reactions to me. The Oracle is not my friend. She can't be when she can't even understand what I'm feeling right now.

After processing the videos, I stop by the storage shed and grab an M-TOG aluminum panel. I use alcohol to clean the surface before taking it back to the barn. I put the clean aluminum panel on the workbench and lay the goat carcass on top of it. Using Sting, I remove the head and set it aside. Then I carefully cut and remove the hide. I keep having a nauseating gag reflex, but nothing is happening. I don't have a throat. When the hide is removed, I hold it up and look at both sides. I go to the storage shed and come back with two buckets of salt I had harvested from the sea. I take two handfuls of salt and rub them into the flesh side of the hide. The salt will help dry out the hide and keep it from rotting. I then walk out of the barn and hang the hide, flesh side out, on the fence to dry. Aden and the kids are sitting and watching me. Not saying a word. Emma is still nowhere to be seen.

There is still a lot of work I need to do before I can start tanning to make leather. I still need to find tannin, a chemical found in Earth trees to allow for the tanning process to occur. For now, I'll dry the hide then figure out what to do later.

I go back to the storage shed and come back to the barn with a capsule transporter shell body wiped down with alcohol. And lots more salt. The shell body is similar to a 55-gallon drum without a lid. Back at the barn workbench I start dissecting cuts of meat from the carcass and placing them in the capsule with layers of salt in between the cuts of meat. The salt will preserve the meat since I don't have refrigeration. I fill up the shell body halfway when I'm done. I leave five cuts of meat out. The kids won't have lobster fish for dinner tonight. Instead they'll have their first taste of meat.

What is left on the workbench is a very bloody aluminum panel with bones, scrapes of flesh, and Floats's head. I leave the carcass and I leave the barn walking out past the fields toward the falls. Once past the fields I stop. I pull out Bearpaw from my back scabbard and start digging. It only takes a few minutes for me to dig a grave. I fling Bearpaw's blade into the dirt pile, sticking it with the handle propped upward. I return to the barn and walk out carrying the aluminum panel with all the goat pieces on it. Walking past Aden and the kids I say the first words since putting Floats down, "Come with me." They get up with stiff legs and follow me to the grave. Waves of emotions hit me as we walk in our funeral procession. It hits me again and again that I'll never be able to talk to Floats again. I need to cry but I can't. I haven't been to a funeral since my dad's. I was a pallbearer for my dad too. I feel like I am burying my dad over again. Guilt floods over me.

I set the panel next to the grave and start to carefully put the pieces of Floats McGoats into the grave. I lay out the pieces as best I can to make them seem comfortable. Nothing is crowded. Nothing is overlapped. The kids quietly watch, staying their distance back. Finally, I put Floats's head facing up at the head of the grave. His eyes are closed.

"We need to give thanks to Floats," I say to the kids, waving them to come closer in an awkward, stuttering voice. They all peer into the grave seeing Floats.

"Floats was a good goat. But he is a goat. Goats make our food and hide for us." My voice chokes up and my mind fogs. I continue, "The goats were provided to us so that we can survive. Floats gave his life for us. We need to give him our thanks." Aden is tearing up, but the young kids look confused. I grab a handful of the dark orange soil from the dirt pile and toss it into the grave. "Thank you, Floats McGoats," I say. "Now your turn. You need to pay your respects."

One by one each kid grabs a handful of dirt with their little hands and throws it into the grave saying, "Thank you, Floats McGoats." Aden is full-on crying now, sniffling and wiping his eyes. I'm sad but can't cry. My D-Clo copy of Organic Nick is struggling to handle what is going on. Organic Nick would be balling his eyes out right now, but I can't. After the kids say their words, I fill in the grave using Bearpaw while the kids watch on. I take my time while gently filling in the grave. The kids eventually sit down and watch as Floats disappears.

After filling in the grave, it hits me. Why I am so driven to make a successful colony. My dad died and gave me the chance to live on with my D-Clo. I need to repay the debt to him. He needs to live on forever in the form of a colony I build for him. His memory ingrained into an ever-living civilization. His way to live on.

***

After the funeral ceremony, I wade into river until the water gets to my waist. I wash the blood off me, then clean Sting of the dry, crusted red blood by rubbing my fingers over it. Red ribbons in the river flow from me going down stream. I'm clean, but my once bright white suite has become darker and more orange from the years. My suit has changed a lot since when I first landed on Prasares.

I check in with Emma and find her in her house. Peering through her cracked open door, I see she is bundled up on her bed in isolation facing away. I watch her breathing for a moment, then decide it would be best to leave her alone.

Later that night I take the extra goat steaks and cook them at the firepit.

"I like this! What is this?" Sophie, the youngest girl says, while chewing happily at the picnic table at the center of the village.

"It's salted goat meat and a baked potato," I say. Sophie keeps eating without responding, while kicking her legs that are hovering over the ground since she is too short sitting on the picnic booth seat.

"Why aren't you eating anything, Mr. Burke?" Ava asks, the second youngest girl.

"He doesn't need to eat," Aden interrupts, his voice burdened by the day's events. "He is a robot. He's not like us." Ava quietly turns back to her meal, sorry that she asked.

After dinner I make sure to get all the kids into bed. I walk with Aden to his house he shares with Emma. Before Aden opens the door, he looks back at me. "You should leave her alone. You've said enough to her today." Then he walks through and closes the door behind him. In the brief moment the door is open, I can see that Emma is still huddled under her blanket.

Chapter 16

Weeks turn into months. Months into years. Decades pass in what seemed like a blink of an eye. Every day I make the village stronger. Every day I keep everyone alive. Today is Emma's thirtieth birthday. It is a big adult milestone to become thirty. But we're not doing anything special for it. She is spending her day taking care of the two kids she had, naturally, with her husband Chase. I always thought that Emma and Aden would be getting married to each other, but I suppose after all those years together they felt too much like brother and sister. Emma and Chase got married six years ago and now have a five-year-old daughter named Joan and a three-year-old son named Roger. They had lost their third child at birth and haven't tried for more since then. Aden married Ava about a year ago and have one son named Maynard. Though I obviously let them name their own kids, I wasn't a fan of them naming their kids after their favorite Old Ones musicians.

The Oracle also gave birth to the remaining eleven embryos that were stored in the orbiter over the years. The Oracle kids range in age from five to twenty-one. The oldest one, Luke, is already engaged to Sophie. The rest of the Oracle kids are being jointly raised by Emma, Aden, and myself. In total the village has nineteen humans and ninety-three goats.

The Remo village has continued to grow. I built more dedicated housing and storage sheds. Our food production has drastically increased over the years with all the older kids working in the fields.

We've set up an area to raise domesticated Orcs. They have become our staple source of fat for oil and soap. Their unique hides have been good for making water-resistant tarps but haven't been comfortable to wear as clothing; everyone still prefers the cotton tunics. We've also been using the goat hides to make leather shoes, belts, and pants. It took a while to find a source of tannin for the tanning process. It ended up that the hemp rope, when crushed and boiled, produced the tannin we needed. Tanning is a very labor-intensive program taking several people preparing the hides, tanning them in a clay vat I had made, letting them dry, then manually working the stiffness out of them. Floats was the first animal I killed, but since then Sting and I have butchered countless goats and Orcs without blinking an eye.

The whole village is working well. The kids are eating like royalty with all the goat and Orc meat. I've even been making french fries with the potatoes from the garden and the Orc fat melted into frying oil. I don't bother to tell them what french in french fries means. They like them no matter what I call them.

The Orcs have been a success in finding a local animal to domesticate. They've become our version of pigs. They're good for food and fat. Okay hides, but not the best. But they're not able to pull plows in the fields. We still need to find a larger animal to be our beast of burden for pulling plows and carts.

Breeding the Orcs had been a mystery. Years ago, when we had captured Orcs, they wouldn't breed in captivity. It wasn't until a few broke out of their pen and I followed where they went. They headed to the river and swam up toward the mountain range, only leaving the river to sidetrack around the waterfall. When I caught up to them at the mountain base, I followed their tracks until I found them in a cave in the mountainside. Inside the cave was steam bellowing out of hot spring water pools.

I found the Orcs giving birth in the hot pools, but they were not giving birth to live pups like mammals. Instead they laid soft-shelled eggs about the size of softballs with the half-developed pup inside. The eggs stayed in the hot pool until they finally hatched. I found that the soft shells allowed for nutrients to enter the shell from the hot pool. Both male and female Orcs would add more nutrients to the hot pools by throwing up half-digested food. What you'll do for your kids, I guess. Nevertheless, once I figured out how to breed the Orcs, we would herd them like cattle up to the base of the mountain and leave them to do their business knowing that they wouldn't leave their pups. We would come back to the cave after about thirty days to herd the adults back to the village and carry the newly born Orc pups in a cart while their parents anxiously watched us. All told, our village has sixty-three Orcs now.

***

We've hit a point in the farm where we need a larger animal to plow the fields. The amount of grain needed to feed the goats and Orcs has started to surpass what we can handle plowing the fields on our own. I've done countless excursions exploring away from the village, but I haven't found a suitable animal. In fact, I haven't found any land animals at all. Only flying, bird-like animals that I haven't been able to catch. They always stay their distance away from us. I wouldn't consider Orcs to be land animals. They're more of a hybrid animal of the sea and land. I'll need to make the farthest excursions I've ever done in hopes of finding our next animal to domesticate.

When Emma finds out about my excursion plans, she confronts me.

"Why do you have to go? I don't understand. We're fine as we are. We don't need anything else," Emma sternly asks, looking up at me.

Emma is relentless. She is no longer the young girl I remember. Since we lost Floats, she hasn't been the same with me. On that day, we both changed. I still have guilt on how I treated Emma. But I also miss Floats. After that day I hadn't had anyone to really talk to. Emma treated me more as a facility manager than a friend. I can't blame her. But I still need to make sure Remo is a success. Even if she hates me.

"And why do you have to take Aden with you?"

"He's the oldest that can go while you take care of the village," I answer while packing provisions for the trip, knowing she doesn't like my answer. "Do you want to go?" I say, stopping and looking back at her, knowing the answer already. I can see the light of my face monitor shining in her staring eyes as she pauses. After a second, she shakes her head no and turns around walking away from the discussion.

I had been planning this trip for months. I built backpacks out of leather for Aden and me. Now, they're stocked with the Remo equivalent of an Earth backpacker's gear, even including mats and blankets for Aden. My pack is full of food and cookware.

Aden and I leave at first light, hiking first toward the sea. Our journey will head north along the sea. If there are land animals, they'll need fresh water. There are more rivers coming from the mountain range to the sea. Maybe we're at the wrong river and need to find another one to catch our beasts of burden refreshing themselves with cool river water.

Aden and I don't make it to the beach before we hear, "Hey, we're coming with you!" I look back and see Sophie and her fiancé Luke holding hands as they run toward us, arms full with their bed mats and blankets. "We want to come with you!"

"Does Emma know you left?" I ask.

"Uhh...no," Sophie says, glancing over her shoulder, "we decided to go without telling her. We really want to go exploring with you. We're dying to get out of the village, even if it's for a few days."

"Besides," Luke adds, "we are adults. We are in our twenties. We can do what we want. We don't need to ask for anyone's approval."

I can't argue with that logic. But Emma is going to kill me when we get back. But I don't know if she can hate me any more than she already does. I pull down some hemp rope and help Sophie and Luke make makeshift backpacks by rolling up their blanket inside their bed mat and tying it into a roll with arm straps. I'll need to hunt for food for them, but that shouldn't be much trouble. There are plenty of lobster fish in the sea. Besides, we'll only be out for a few days, a week tops.

"Here, put on your backpacks and let's get going," I say handing the packs to Sophie and Luke. "I need you to keep up the pace with me. Don't slow me down."

***

After five days, we've come across four more rivers coming down from the mountain and two more clear meadows similar to where we built Remo, but no animals. I don't understand how this area can be so vibrant with vegetation, but so devoid of land animals.

Walking along the beach, we weave between a forested area and green mossy ground cover butting up against the orange sand beach. Sting is serving me well as a machete cutting our way through the tougher areas. The kids are exhausted. My Space Yeti body doesn't get tired; I didn't seem to keep that in mind when setting our hiking pace. Once it gets dark, we stop to set up camp for the night. Tucked up by the trees, the kids lay out their mats and I start a fire on the beach for dinner.

Looking at their exhausted faces I know our trip needs to end. "This will be our last night heading out. We're going to start heading back to the village tomorrow. I'm sorry, but we're not finding what we're looking for here. Once we get back to the village, we'll rest for a while then head out again going south. I know I'll find what we're needing for soon. I'll need to make sure we find our working animal for the survival of the colony."

The group doesn't say anything back. But the looks they give me are assurance that they believe I can succeed for them. And comfort knowing they are finally going home. They quietly eat their dinner while the firelight flickers on their faces. The view we have during dinner makes the situation more bearable. Looking out at the sea, we can see the faint glowing ring in the night sky, the waves lapping up on the dark orange sand beach. COMMAND LOAD

PLAY Pink Floyd's album *The Dark Side of the Moon*. We quietly listen to music while tending to the fire. Luke and Sophie eventually disappear to their beds. Aden and I continue to listen to more music and stare out to the sea.

Aden breaks the silence. "Don't worry, Mr. Burke, I know you'll find our beasts. We're counting on you. My grandkids will build a statue for you for all you've done for us someday." Aden has grown up, but his drive for exploration hasn't stopped. He had begged me for months to go on this trip. Even though we are coming up empty-handed I can tell he is still happy coming along. He's now twenty-nine years old. He seems…so familiar. Like someone I knew on Earth. But I can't put my finger on it. He's certainly the offspring of someone famous on Earth. Maybe that's where I recognize him.

I look up at Aden as he stands up to head to bed. My face monitor lights up his face.

"Don't stay up too late, Mr. Burke. You can relax tonight," Aden says tapping my shoulder as he heads up to his bed mat to go to sleep for the night. I decide to sleep on the beach next to the fire. When I don't go into sleep mode, I find my mood is unpleasant. Sleep mode helps clear my computer brain. I'm not looking forward to the defeat march back to the village in the morning. Let alone dealing with a terribly upset Emma. I really regret losing her. She should have been my best friend, but I ruined it. I don't know if I'll be able to repair my relationship with her. Maybe I'm still in over my head. Lying back looking at the sky, I go into sleep mode.

***

My vibration monitor interrupt wakes me into a startle, but I can't see anything. My helmet cameras are covered with something. I can't move my hands or feet either. "What the hell is going on here?!" I yell out while thrashing around, trying to get loose but unable.

SEED

I hear a sound. *"Burr...urptt...upt...upt."* It sounds like a horn playing a short musical pattern. *"Bruppt...brupt,"* a second horn answers.

"What is going on here?" I yell out again. I can hear hands patting around me. They're doing something with me. I hear a rope being tied around my feet.

"Burpft...brupft...brupft!!" I hear a horn shout out. Then I start sliding on the beach. I'm being dragged along the ground.

"Aden! Aden! Can you hear me?!" I shout out.

"Mr. Burke, we're here."

"What is going on?! I can't see anything!" I shout out as I hear the beach sand sliding past me.

"I don't know," Aden replied. "Sophie and Luke are here, but we all have bags over our heads. We can't see anything either. Our hands are tied. I think someone has captured us. They keep poking me in the side with a stick and it hurts! They're making us walk out on the beach."

I can hear Aden's voice following me as I'm still being pulled out on the beach. I can hear the waves becoming louder. "What are you going to do, aliens? Try to drown me in the sea? Good luck with that!" The pulling pace doesn't slow down. I can hear Aden comforting the others in between the horn blows. I don't know what is pulling me. I can hear panting. It's pulling me with a paced gait, not a steady pull.

I can't believe there is intelligent life on this planet! During the polar orbits, we didn't find any artificial light. Maybe they hadn't gotten that technology yet. Maybe we really have been captured by the alien natives. This is not good. "You better not harm us. I will mess you up!" I can't let the kids get killed. I can't get killed. If they severely damage me, I become a nuclear dirty bomb ready to kill off the local life. I need to get the kids back to the village. I need to make sure the village survives. That is why I'm here. This trip was a bad idea.

Thump...thumppp... I can hear now that my body is being pulled up on wooden planks. They're putting us on a boat. They must have

133

seen our fire on the beach and stopped to kidnap us. Once my body gets pulled fully onto the deck of the boat, I can hear Aden, Sophie, and Luke being walked past me. Based on the sounds of feet, I can hear six pairs of feet plus the kids. Also, whatever is pulling me has four feet...and it is heavy.

I hear a loud wooden thump and metal crackle like a gate closing. They must have pulled me up on a foldout ramp of the boat and they just closed it. I can now hear grunting and horn blows of aliens outside of the boat pushing it off from the beach. The boat starts to glide once we get off the sand and I hear at least four more pairs of feet crawl back onto the boat dripping water. The waves gently move the boat up and down as we head out to sea. I hear fabric unrolling, which must be a sail. *"Brupft...brupft...brupft...."* I hear the horn start a cadence and something splashing into the water. They are paddling us out to sea.

***

Aden, Sophie, and Luke feel their way to find me on the deck of the boat. They huddle against me. We've gathered that we're all unharmed, but no one knows what these aliens look like or what they want with us.

"Sophie," I say as quietly as possible. "You're close to my head, right?"

"Yeah, I think so," she says.

"Okay. Stay calm. I need you to carefully grab the bag that is over my head and slowly pull it off. I'll raise my head so it should come off easily. Just move slowly so they don't notice. Once the bag is off, I can see what is going on and I'll figure out how to get us out of here. I'll keep my face monitor turned off so they don't notice me."

Sophie does what I ask. As the bag is being pulled off, I can see the night sky again. I lean upward to see better. The kids are beside me. Their heads are covered with burlap bags tied at their necks.

Their wrists are bound together with hemp rope. My arms and legs are bound multiple times with thick twisted hemp rope cable.

Looking forward, I see two humanoid figures standing at the front of the boat and the other eight rowing while facing away from me. The two seem to be talking to each other. The perimeter of the boat has torches, making the deck of the boat well lit. They're the size of humans but covered in furs, feathers, and painted leather head to feet. Their faces are covered by wooden masks. One is facing away from me, but I could see most of the face of the second alien. The mask has brass horns sticking out like tusks. Those must have been the horns I heard. That must be how they're communicating with each other.

Beside them is something I've never seen before. It is huge. It looks like a giant silver fox. But its fur is like the Orc fur, shiny and scale-like. It must be another hybrid land and sea animal like the Orcs. The beast is lying down with its eyes closed, no different than a dog next to its master. It must have been what pulled me up onto the boat. It's the beast of burden I'm looking for. It can certainly pull a plow if it can pull me over the beach and into a boat. While looking in awe at the beast, I see its eyes flash open. It shoots up into the air and in one pounce, its front paws land on my chest slamming me back down into the deck. The deck boards crack under its hit. I can hear the kids shuffle backward away in terrified screams. All I can see is snarling teeth bearing down on me. Its two paws are the width of my chest. I can see its tail waving in the air. It isn't a fox's tail. Instead it is like the Orcs'. A tail for water travel. Its saliva is dripping down on me until I hear footsteps coming over toward me.

"*Burrpft...Burrppfft...burrpffft!*" I hear the aliens' horn howl. The beast looks back at its master, then jumps over the ledge of the boat into the water. I slowly lean back up into a sitting position. The alien leader walks up to me. Its mask is intricately carved and painted with feathers emanating out like a headdress. Its horn tusks are dented and burnished from years of use. It looks at me for a moment. I can't see anything through the eye holes. Just darkness. Behind it I can see that all the other aliens had stopped what they were doing and were looking back at me. Ten masks quietly watching. The alien leader brings its gloved hand up to its mask, moving it up off his face onto the top of its head. I see a human face look back at me.

He says, "Mr. Burke. We've been looking for you for a long time. It is time to see Emma and pay for what you've done." A loud splash bursts from the sea followed by a loud thump of rattling deck boards. The beast had jumped back onto the deck of the boat from the sea, then shook itself dry.

Chapter 17

It was two days before the boat started back toward land. I don't know how far we've traveled, but I was able to see the mountain range to my left so we must have been traveling north along the shore. Our kidnappers fed the kids okay but left them in their hemp rope restraints. It wasn't until the end of our trip that the leader finally came close enough that I could talk with him.

"What is your name and where are you taking us?" I ask.

"You don't remember me?" the leader says. "I suppose not. I was young when you left. I'm Lemmy, son of Ozzy."

Ozzy!? Lemmy?!

"Where are we going?!" I ask leaning forward, but still bound, unable to move much.

"You know where we're going. I should be the one asking the questions. Where did you take these Remons? Where are the rest of them? There should be more. No matter, I suppose Emma will sort it out when we get home."

I look over at the kids. They had already had their hoods removed and their hands untied to eat. They are busy eagerly eating food from bowls. I can see over the boat's ledge that we are nearing the land. I see more of the beasts swimming out toward the boat. The monster that dragged me up onto the boat is standing at attention looking at the oncoming beasts. I get a good look at it. It must be seven meters long with its tail and three meters tall while standing upright. Taller than me. I can tell it is evolved for swimming. It looks like a Water Fox.

"Hey, Lemmy, what do you call those things?" I ask, motioning to his beast.

"You must have really messed up your head. You don't remember?! They are Water Foxes, of course."

Of course. That sounds like what I'd name them.

"My Water Fox is named Gibson. He's been my sidekick through lots of adventures. More to come I suppose."

Two approaching Water Foxes swim toward the boat, their ears folded backward like shark fins above the water. Two of Lemmy's men toss out hemp ropes to the Water Foxes and tie them to the rear of the boat where the ramp gate is located. The two Water Foxes grab the ropes and start swimming toward the left to turn the boat around and be tugged backward toward the shore. Once we hit the shore, Lemmy's men open the ramp gate letting it fall to the beach.

"Mr. Burke, I assume you'd rather walk than be dragged back to Emma. Although I'd prefer to drag you. But I do love my Water Foxes more than I hate you right now. So, will you walk?" Lemmy waits for my response while his Water Fox, Gibson, stares down at me.

I nod yes and he cuts my bound feet with a rusty blade pulled from his side scabbard. He leaves my hands bound.

"Hold on!" Lemmy says to me before I get up. "You don't need these anymore." He pulls Sting from its scabbard and hangs it from his belt as his new prize sword. He then walks around to my head and pulls on Bearpaw. I lean down to help him get a better grip. Once he pulls it outward far enough, it is too heavy for him to hold any longer and it drops to the deck with a thump. Three other men come to help pick it up. It took all three of them to carry Bearpaw off the boat. I stand up. All of Lemmy's men finally see how tall I am for the first time. They all look upward at me. The Water Foxes still look down at me.

"Guys, we need to go with them. They won't hurt us," I say to Aden, Sophie, and Luke. We all calmly walk off the boat onto the orange sand beach. We head back up into the trees through a carved path. Water Foxes flank my sides making sure I don't do anything stupid. After an hour of walking we make it through the woods into an opening.

"Welcome back to Remo, Mr. Burke," Lemmy says, holding out his hand.

This is not the Remo I know. I don't see a village. What is ahead of us is a city.

As we walk toward the city, I realize how much bigger it is than my village. It must have about a thousand residents. We pass what seems to be never-ending fields of crops before we enter the city's edge. Water Foxes are pulling plows in the fields. *Well, I found the beast of burden of Prasares finally.* The crops in the fields look terrible though. I don't know what is going on there.

I can hear Aden, Sophie, and Luke talking among themselves behind me. *I thought we were the only ones. He told us we were alone on this planet. What is this? Did he lie to us? Why are they treating us like prisoners?*

As we enter the city, we see more of Lemmy's Remons. Farmers, laborers, families, kids. All human. Walking by, we catch their attention. Several alert their neighbors in perfect English. Their kids stare in awe at me. It's as if they are seeing a ghost. Lemmy's marching group grows as the townsfolk start to follow us toward the city center. Many of them still carry their farm implements, which oddly are old and rusty.

Getting close to the city center there are stone buildings and stone roads. It begins to look more like a Roman city than a colonial village. But I can see some of the buildings around us are crumbling. Some have even fallen down. We make it to a small clearing area between the buildings. It is the same brick plaza I had made using circle bricks back at my Remo. The south Remo. This North Remo brick plaza is nearly the exact same, but this one has vegetation overgrowth covering much of it. Then I notice something that looks out of place off to the side. It looks like a burned-out metallic shed. Portions of molten aluminum dripped over charred panels. It is an

M-TOG! Looking closer I see M-TOG 839 stenciled on the panel. My M-TOG was 486.

"Jerry!" I yell out, startling the Water Foxes. "That snake! That cheat! He lied to me!" A crowd of people gathers around looking concerned. My business partner Jerry! He told me the M-TOG number didn't mean anything. He told me they didn't have enough funding to make the M-TOG bigger. He told me we didn't have enough money to have more supplies and more embryos. That snake lied to me! That wasn't the case at all!

He made copies of me. And made multiple M-TOGs. That lying bastard. To increase his percentage of successful colonies he must have made hundreds, maybe thousands of me and M-TOGs and fired us out into the galaxy. He was a sower of seeds. *Dammit, Jerry!* A rage fog builds in my mind. He should have told me! Why would he lie to me like this? Thinking for another moment it dawns on me that I was so adamant about one large M-TOG maybe Jerry felt it was easier just to go around me. That rat!

"Keep moving!" Lemmy shouts at me, walking back from the front of the crowd of people ahead of me.

I take a few steps forward then stop again. "Wait, why is the M-TOG burnt to the ground?" I ask Lemmy.

Lemmy turns around. "The Oracle was punished for not telling us where you disappeared to. The Oracle knows everything, but she would not tell us where you were. She had to be punished. We put her to the fire. So Sing the Old Ones."

***

At the city center is a large stone temple building reminiscent of Roman architecture with large steps leading up to the entrance. The parade of people that we accumulated during the march accompanied me into the building. We walk into a large open area with a tall ceiling inside the building. Toward the back of the room is a classic throne, but it is empty. Lemmy has his Water Foxes accompany me to the center of the room. The three Water Foxes lie down in a circle around me, dividing me from the streams of people coming into the building. I look over and see Aden, Sophie, and Luke standing near the wall of the room flanked by Lemmy's men. My Remons look nervous and confused. The North Remons look at my own Remons with fascinated intrigue. If you didn't know any better, you would assume they are all from the same place.

Standing in the middle of the Water Fox circle I look above the throne to see a story. There is a painted mural showing three scenes. The first scene is a bright white space suit man with two short human people standing beside him. Wavy lines emanate from the space helmet. The humans have their hands to their heads with fingers pointed outward. The second scene has the same tall space suit man, but his suit is a dirty light orange. Multiple humans are standing around him. They all have their hands to their head with fingers out. The wavy lines emanating from the space helmet are larger than the first scene. The last scene has the space suit man running. His suit is very dark orange now. In his arms are two babies. Ahead of him are adults carrying more babies. There are no wavy lines in this scene.

The room quiets as an old woman walks in. She is wearing an intricate, brightly colored tunic. It sways as she shuffles her feet alongside her walking stick. Her skin is weathered and wrinkled, her silver hair unkempt. She calmly walks to the stone throne and takes her time to sit down. I amuse myself thinking she looks like a silver-haired version of Yoda.

She breaks the silence in the room. "Mr. Burke, you have finally come home."

My face monitor must have shown confusion. "I'm sorry, but who are you and what are you talking about?" I say. The room erupts in chatter from the audience.

"Mr. Burke, I don't know where your travels took you, but they must have caused you to lose your memory. I am Emma."

She isn't my Emma. She doesn't look anything like her. Even with the age difference. The face, the hair, the body structure is completely different. She is a different person. A different Emma.

"You're not my Emma," I say.

"No, you are right. I am not your Emma. I am your Emma's granddaughter. I am named after her. Your Emma has been laid to rest at the field's edge long ago. Mr. Burke, I have one question for you. After all that has happened, I trust you will grant me the favor of answering my one question. Why did you leave us?"

"I'm sorry, Emma. You're not my Emma and I'm not your Nick Burke. It seems that there were multiple versions of me launched from Earth to start multiple colonies. Each one of me thought I was the only one. I'm guessing we were sent to different planets since there were so many habitable planet candidates. But the first planet I traveled to wasn't habitable by humans, so I diverted to this planet. It seems this planet already had me on it—I mean another copy of me. Based on the size of your colony, I estimate I arrived about a hundred and fifty years after your Nick Burke landed and brought your grandmother into this world. Does that make sense?"

The crowd stays quiet.

"Mr. Burke, I don't know why you lie to me now. You said yourself that you are the only robot on this planet and would be the only robot for a thousand years. You are Mr. Burke. There is only one Mr. Burke. Where did you take our people? How did you convince them to leave us? You left in the early morning when I was just a young girl. You left and didn't tell anyone. You left with our people and supplies. You left like a thief."

Looking back up at the mural I realize she was talking about the third scene. "I don't know what you are talking about. That wasn't me. That Nick Burke on the wall isn't me. Look at its suit. It's dark, covered by decades of dirt. My suit isn't that dark. It's much lighter."

Emma turns in her throne, looking back at the mural. "Yes, but that one looks like you." She points at the middle scene. "You must have made a new soap to wash yourself."

"Tell me, Mr. Burke, where are the rest of the Remons you took?! By this time there should be dozens of them. You only brought back three of them. You must bring back who you've kidnapped. Mr. Burke, you don't know how much of a failure you've been to this colony. Not only have you betrayed us by kidnapping our people, you have left the rest of us to die. Since you've left, we've had nothing but failure. Our crops failed. Our tools rusted. Our people grew ill and we're unable to cure them. During the great illness many Remons died. I watched my mother die from your disease you brought on us. I promised myself that when we found you, we would make you pay for what you did. When you left, you left us to suffer. This betrayal is unforgivable. So Sing the Old Ones."

What the hell did I do? I mean, not me, but the other Nick Burke. What did he do? Why would he kidnap people? It doesn't seem like he kidnapped people, but rather they left voluntarily. On the mural the adults are running in front of him. He must have convinced them to leave somehow. But why? Why would he abandon the colony? His purpose is to make sure the colony is successful. That is my purpose. I can't imagine why he would leave it to let it fall into this terrible condition. Why would he do it? He is an exact copy of me, so why would I do it?

"Take him to the prison until I decide what to do with him," Emma says to Lemmy. Lemmy lets out a blow from his horned mask and the Water Foxes stand up. There is no reason to fight them. I walk out of the temple with my hands still bound, flanked by Lemmy and his Water Foxes. I look over to Aden, Sophie, and Luke. Their faces tell me they are as disappointed in me just as much as their North Remon brethren.

***

The prison is a small stone building with a rusty iron gate. Lemmy opens it with a key he pulled from his pocket. I stare at the entrance. We both know the door is too small for me. "Crawl in," Lemmy commands.

I obediently drop to my knees and shuffle into the prison. The width of the door is too narrow for me to fit so I have to shuffle in on my side. Lemmy closes the gate and tells two of his men to keep watch with the Water Foxes to make sure I don't escape. I rearrange inside the prison cell to a seated position. I could break out of this prison as easily as standing up. But what good would it do me? Where would I go? I'm here for one reason: to make a successful human colony on this planet. And I failed at that. I can't believe it. And I can't leave them. But I don't know what to do. Emma isn't listening to me.

Days pass by. I continue to think and brood in my small prison cell. Lemmy visits once a day to check in on his men and on me. Depression clouds my thoughts. An empty path lay ahead of me now knowing that I failed in my mission. Guilt of letting down my father flows over me. Not only did I abandon them, but they are struggling without me. Why would that happen? I put together the most comprehensive strategy and program possible. It was designed for success. The crops. The materials. The education. All of it was perfect. I don't understand why things went wrong. This is Mars all over again. Destined to fail. I couldn't make a successful civilization on Mars. I couldn't do it here either. I was wrong to think that this planet would be different. This whole endeavor is a mistake.

The next time Lemmy visits, I am able to stop him before he leaves. "Lemmy, what happened after I left Remo? Why where there so many problems?"

"Mr. Burke, I was very young when you left us. My memory doesn't stretch back that far." He stands straight, staring at me with uncaring eyes. "But my parents told me the story many times. When you were here, Remo was great. Every year there were new inventions. You seemed to have an unending source of ideas to make our lives better. You built our first stone buildings, then showed the craftsmen how to follow your designs. You even led the construction of Emma's temple. Even the prison you're sitting in was designed and built by you. You pushed us hard. Driving us to keep up. We tried our best. You gave us a reliable water source and added a waterwheel to it. We used it for crushing grain and eventually you added a new invention called a generator to it to make electricity. Before you left you had made electric lighting in the streets at night.

"There were always new chemicals coming out of your lab. If anyone got sick, they only needed to come to you for medicine. Every year it was getting better. You even stopped sleeping so you could work through the night as well. You worked very hard, but you also enjoyed celebrating by playing the Old Ones music. That made us very happy. The city worshiped you. You were the only one that could make the Old Ones sing. You were everyone's hero." His face grows dark. "But after you left, things had changed. The Old Ones music stopped. No one had practice designing things. We could remake the things you gave us designs for, but when we ran into problems, we didn't have you there to help us. A great sickness swept through the city when I was a young boy. Many people died. We never figured out how to cure the illness. A few died trying different chemicals in hopes it would cure them. Emma took all the children out of the school to have everyone in Remo focused on the fields to make sure we had plenty of food. But even with everyone working the farm, the crops began to fail over the years. We kept trying what you had told us, but it wasn't working anymore. You weren't there to help us."

Lemmy's words make it finally dawn on me. I've failed them in the most basic way. I gave them the things they needed to live, but I didn't give them the skills they needed to grow without me. The education system I had set up didn't have problem solving in it. It was all prescribed information intended for them to follow like obedient robots. But life doesn't work like that. There are always new problems that people will need to solve. I solved all the problems for them. When I left, they didn't know how to do that on their own. I completely failed to prepare them for life without me. I wasn't thinking about them after I'm gone.

"Mr. Burke, it is time to go," Lemmy says, breaking me out of my thoughts. He opens the prison cell gate, grasping Sting's hilt as it hangs brightly from his belt.

***

Outside the prison cell is a large cart with a Water Fox pulling it. It's Gibson, Lemmy's Water Fox that helped kidnap me from the beach. "Get in," Lemmy instructs me.

Without much thought I climb into the cart. My computer is still processing what I had done. What the other Nick Burke had done. But since he is a copy of me, he is me. And his sins are my sins. At the current downhill condition of the colony, it will certainly fail. They are one drought, plague, or natural disaster away from extinction. My village and my Emma are the exact same as the North Remons. I didn't prepare them for surviving without me either. Here in North Remo, I am looking at the future of my kids in my Remo.

When I sit down in the cart, Lemmy's men begin wrapping me with hemp cables, tying me down to the cart. Loop after loop. When they are done, my arms are hidden behind all the hemp cable holding me down to the cart.

"I don't know why you are tying me down. I'm going with you willingly."

Lemmy doesn't respond.

Then Gibson picks up the hemp rope tied to the front of the cart and starts pulling. We leave the prison and head back toward the city center. We pass the North Remon onlookers along the side of the road. We approach Emma's temple in the city center, but we don't stop. A bit confused, I realize that the temple is not our destination.

Riding along, I see an old, weathered stone statue of a goat. I read the inscription "*Floats McGoats, The First Goat of Remo and true friend. Here he lies after dying of natural causes after seventeen years on Prasares.*" The other Nick must have named his first goat Floats McGoats as well. But he didn't have to put him down. His Floats McGoats lived his full life. The cart continues on while I am still trying my best to look back at the statue of Floats. It is good to see my friend again, even if he isn't my goat.

In the distance ahead of us, I can see black smoke billowing out to the sky. We continue to progress through the city streets until we turn into the plaza where the Oracle was slain. Next to the destroyed M-TOG are two crudely constructed elevated wooden platforms with massive stacks of burning logs on top of them. Two twin burning towers. The top platforms holding the burning log piles are hinged and held up by two hemp ropes anchored to the ground per tower. If the hemp ropes are cut, the burning log piles would be dumped into the space between the two towers. The entire plaza area is packed with North Remons. The entire city must be here.

Gibson pulls the cart about fifty meters away from the towers, then drops the rope. It seems to hate the burning fires and shuns its eyes away from the flame with its tail between its legs as it walks around the towers.

"Mr. Burke!" Emma yells, gaining the attention of the crowd. "You are found guilty of kidnapping, abandoning us, and lying to us. Your fate is the same as the Oracle. You are sentenced to die by fire!" A wave of cheer comes from the crowd of people. Their excitement to see me die is deafening.

I yell back in protest. "What, wait?! You can't do this! You don't understand. I have a HE-TEG in my chest. If you burn me, I'll release nuclear waste. You're all going to die! Don't you understand? You'll get sick and die from nuclear poisoning!"

"More lies!" Emma yells, raising her arms to the crowd. "Start the ceremony. So Sings the Old Ones!"

One of Lemmy's men ties extra hemp rope to the cart rope Gibson was pulling using a double fisherman's knot. The lengthened hemp rope is thrown between the two towers. I can see through the towers that the rope end is grabbed by another one of Lemmy's men, then carried over to Gibson waiting on the other side to pull the rope. They're going to pull me into the space between the towers and dump the burning logs on top of me. I won't stand a chance once they dump the burning logs on top of me. The amount of burning wood is too much, especially since I'm tied down onto this cart. I'll burn and the HE-TEG nuclear source will be released. All of North Remo will become a nuclear waste zone killing everyone here. I feel my computer brain trying to fight through the panic towards a solution. I try to stand up, but the hemp cables are too strong. I start rocking the cart side to side, but I can't break free or tip it over.

"Start the pull!" Emma exclaims, pointing toward a long row of drummers. I look to see dozens of drums they've made using wood and leather. Drums of varying size. Large and small. Masked Remons with large drumsticks stand over each drum. Their masks have the same horn tusks that Lemmy's group wore when they kidnapped me. Their blank stares give me a simulated chill in my computer. Lemmy gives his Water Fox the command to start pulling using his own horned mask. Then in unison the drumline begins.

Boom...boom! Bah...bah...bah...bah...ba...ba...baa...baa...
Boom...boom! Bah...bah...bah...bah...ba...ba...baa...baa...

Loud thundering booms come from the drums followed by systematic blows from the horned mask. The cart slowly begins to move toward the burning towers. This can't be happening. They can't do this to me. They have got to stop.

Boom...boom! Bah...bah...bah...bah...ba...ba...baa...baa...
Boom...boom! Bah...bah...bah...bah...ba...ba...baa...baa...

As the cart lurches forward my panic is sidestepped by awe in the drumline. Their musical precision is impressive. It's as if they've been playing it for years. As if it is a religious chant.

Boom...boom! Bah...bah...bah...bah...ba...ba...baa...baa...
Boom...boom! Bah...bah...bah...bah...ba...ba...baa...baa...

Wait. Hold on. I know this song. Are they really playing this classic? I listen to the drum line one more time, and it hits me. The wavy lines on the temple mural. I know what the lines are! COMMAND LOAD PLAY, Start 00:51 AC/DC, "Thunderstruck".

Boom...boom!

My speakers in my helmet sync up with the drumline playing the song. My speakers at full volume fill the air with Brian Johnson's voice, Angus Young's guitar, and Malcom Young's genius. I look towards Emma. Does she remember? The nights of rock band and air guitars with the other Nick Burke. He had to have done rock band with his Remons because I did it with mine. I can see in her eyes that the precision guitar riff with the booming Remon drums are causing her to dig deep into her memories. The Remons are so religious about the Old Ones music. It must be like hearing a long-lost god.

Emma looks up at me. Her eyes stare at me in confusion, wonder, and finally fear. I think I'm hitting a chord with her. She starts waiving her hands demanding the execution to stop, but the crowd cannot hear her over the thundering drums and chants for my death. The cart continues to roll towards the burning towers. Taking matters into her own hands, she drops her cane and starts pulling on one of the anchored hemp ropes holding up the burning logs. She is trying to drop the logs before I get to the towers. I can see her panic realizing her mistake calling for my execution but unable to stop it. The cart has rolled so close to the towers that I can see the burning embers falling in front of me.

WHACK!! I look up to see Lemmy standing over Emma with Sting in his hands and the anchored hemp rope cut. Emma stands back with a smile to let Lemmy finish the job. Lemmy gives a quick blow with his horned mask to stop Gibson, but it's not loud enough over the drums. Gibson is still pulling me to my death. One more rope needs to be cut before I am saved.

"I haven't heard this song since I was a little girl!" Emma shouts at me while tearing up listening to the roaring airborne electricity coming from my speakers. The crowd starts to take notice, but they are not sure if this is part of the execution ceremony or not.

WHACK!! Lemmy doesn't wait any longer. He slices the second rope to stop the execution.

Sound from the drums…

Beating in their ears…

The roar of the song…

Cuts ropes apart…

I've been…*thunderstruck*!!

The giant pile of burning logs from the tower come crashing down in a thundering boom right in front of me. The Remon drums finally stop when they see that I am not under the pile. Only my speakers playing music fill the air. For the first time, many of the

Remons are clearly hearing an electric guitar from the Old Ones. I see looks of confusion and intrigue.

Emma walks up to me with her eye welling up. "Mr. Burke, I haven't had tingles on the back of my neck since I was a little girl. This song was a favorite of my mother. Old Ones music has returned to Remo. We cannot let the music die. Lemmy, please release him from that cart. Mr. Burke, we need to talk about your future. Please come with me."

Chapter 18

"Emma, I have failed you and I am sorry," I say kneeling to Emma back in the temple. She is sitting on her throne again, listening patiently. "I'm not your Nick Burke. There are two Nick Burkes. And I don't know where your Nick Burke is. I don't know where he took your people. But I can tell you that there is another Remo. A different Remo that I built, south of here. There are sixteen Remons there waiting for me to return. My Emma is one of them. And they need my help. They need your help. I can't take back what your Nick Burke did. What I did. But I can help make it right now. Please let me help."

Emma gives me a cautious but positive look. "Mr. Burke, you have given me something I haven't had in a long time. The true joy of music. Not since my childhood have I heard the Old Ones music. The music from my Nick Burke. It reminds me of our days having rock band concerts by the bonfire. That was truly a highlight of my life. This world is not easy. But those times when we had music made it much more bearable. Unfortunately, I am one of only a few here at Remo that is old enough to have heard the Old Ones music. I must make sure my Remons do not lose the Old Ones music like I lost it. Mr. Burke, I ask for your help. Help us fix our city. Help us grow crops. Help us become healthy. And help us have music." Emma stands and walks toward me using her walking stick.

"I will do my best," I answer back to her.

"That is all you can do," she says, putting her hand on my shoulder.

"I need to go back to my Remo and bring my people to you. We will be better off having everyone in one location. Let me go to them," I ask.

"Lemmy will go with you. Aden will stay with us. You have my permission to go, but you do not have my trust yet. You need to earn that back," she says, stepping back while overlapping her hands over her cane.

I look over to Aden. He nods his head yes in agreement.

I stand up and say, "I understand. Thank you." Looking down at the old woman, her head looks ached looking up at me. I give her a smile and say, "I'll be back."

***

Lemmy's best men load supplies for the journey back to South Remo into the same boat we rode on when we were abducted. Lemmy enlists an additional ten cargo sailboats accompany us to transfer the goats, Orcs, and supplies back to North Remo. Sophie and Luke load into the boat with excitement to be heading home. But I can see they are also uneasy about leaving Aden behind. Aden watches on the shore, giving us a wave goodbye. Lemmy closes the ramp gate after watching Gibson make his way onto the boat. His men toss out two ropes toward the sea. Two Water Foxes already floating in the water snatch up the ropes and begin to pull us out to sea. Once away from the shore, the Water Foxes drop their ropes and swim back to shore while Lemmy's men pull the ropes back into the boat. The boat's sail drops and we head south.

"Mr. Burke, how did you know that song would save your life?" Lemmy asks after he stabilized the boat and set its course.

"I guess I didn't. I didn't know what else to do. When I heard the drums and the horns, it hit me what song it was. I guess I couldn't help myself playing along. Luckily for me it worked out."

Lemmy gives me a smile. "Aye, you are lucky. Your fate would have been the same as the traitor Oracle. Mr. Burke, I have a confession to make. It is unfortunate, but I was the one that killed the Oracle. She would not tell us where you had gone. We stacked firewood around her for hours before lighting her on fire. She never said a word, not even a scream for help. I also must confess that I don't believe your story about two Remos. And it doesn't make sense that there are two of you. That seems too far-fetched to be true. Too convenient. Maybe you made it up to get out of being burned alive. Maybe we're sailing on a wild-goose chase to try to find this fictional Remo of yours."

"Do you even know what a goose is?" I ask Lemmy.

Lemmy pauses, trying to remember. "I don't know. It was something my father used to say. Maybe it is an Old Ones saying he learned from you. Even if we do find a village, it's probably the village of people you kidnapped from Remo and started a new colony with. I suppose we will find out soon enough."

***

The journey takes two days by sea. We sail parallel to the beach, far enough away that the waves are not noticeable. We find the South Remo landing site by looking for the salt ponds on the beach near the river. We land the boats on the shore and drop the ramp gates. Lemmy's men anchor the boats to the beach with wooden spikes to keep them from floating away. All these years and Lemmy never found us. He had been doing reconnaissance to find me for most of his adult life. South Remo must have been too far inland for him to see us. The salt ponds are small. You would miss them if you're not looking for them. The only reason he found us when we were exploring was the campfire we had on the beach. Had it not been for that campfire, we could have gone years or decades before finding each other.

"It's this way." I point into the woods heading toward the mountain range.

Our train of people walking through the forest path included all of Lemmy's men, Lemmy himself, and his Water Fox, Gibson. Walking behind me, Sophie and Luke get increasingly excited as we near our village. The hike in familiar territory is comforting.

We hike through the woods until we make it to the clearing. The experience is eerily similar to when Lemmy abducted me and marched me into North Remo. But this trek is to my tiny South Remo village. We walk up to the edge of the village without anyone seeing us. Finally, one of the young kids see us. "He's back!" I see all the familiar faces coming out behind the buildings and from the fields heading toward us. The kids rush in first to stare at the monolithic Water Fox standing taller than me. Gibson lays down when he sees the kids.

My Emma comes running around the corner to see me standing towering within a group of happy people welcoming me back home. Without pause, she pushes through the crowd and walks straight up to me. "What the hell do you think you're doing!?" she yells. "You left us! You didn't tell us you were going to be gone that long. We thought you left us!" She looks at the large group behind us and seethes. "Where are Sophie and Luke? They disappeared the day you left. We thought you left us and took them with you! What the hell is wrong with you?!"

Sophie and Luke poke their heads out from behind me. "Hey, Emma, we're right here. We're okay. It's crazy what happened! We have so much we tell you!"

Emma diffuses for a moment with the sight of Sophie and Luke safe and unharmed, but she reignites when she looks back at me. "And what the hell is this thing?" She points to Gibson, who is lying on the ground getting pet by the kids. Gibson, now being called to attention, stands up and towers over everyone in the crowd, including myself. Emma doesn't step back. She still stares at Gibson without a millimeter of fear in her. Once Gibson stands up, he looks down at her with his head twisting to the side.

"Where is Aden?" Ava says rushing into the crowd. "Where is my husband?! Why have you been gone so long? Who are these people you brought back! I thought we were the only ones here. You told us we were the only ones!"

I kneel down to catch her in my arms. "He is safe and doing ok. We have a lot of explaining to do. Let's go sit down," I say to Emma and Ava, shepherding them back toward the picnic table for a long discussion.

While explaining everything that has happened over the past several days, I watch Lemmy and his men inspect the M-TOG. Their faces look like they are seeing a ghost of someone they murdered. Lemmy thought I was lying, but the truth is pointing back at him as he walks around and around the M-TOG.

***

After all the fanfare of our return and explaining what happened, I finally get a moment with Emma near the bonfire. After my near-death experience, I need to make amends with Emma.

"I'm really sorry, Emma. I treated you poorly when you were growing up. I wanted the best for you, but how I was doing it was not right." I feel emotion welling through me. "I thought what I was doing was making you a strong, knowledgeable person, but I see now that I was missing many key things to set you up right. I've had a lot of time to think about it and I'm going to be different now. I need to be different." I pause, feeling the same overload coming on as many years ago. "I'm sorry about how Floats McGoats died. It wasn't your fault. You can't control what a goat does. You were just a kid. How I treated you was unfair. If nothing else I say means much to you, I do want you to know that I'm very proud of you and I love you very much."

I can see her eyes welling up. She hugs me without a word. The first hug I've gotten from her since she was a little girl, back before her tenth birthday. I hug her back. I remember the night she was born. When I held her to my chest to keep her warm. I knew I wasn't her father, but I feel like her father at this moment. I need to make things right with her. I need to make sure Emma and the rest of the group are taken care of and have happy lives.

"Mr. Burke, sorry to interrupt," Lemmy says solemnly as he joins Emma and me. "Mr. Burke, I need to apologize to you. I can see now that you were telling the truth. I'm sorry that I almost killed you in the fire. It would have been a massive mistake. Please let me know what I can do to make it up to you."

"Lemmy, don't beat yourself up. We can let go of the past now. But there is something you can do to help. In fact, both you and Emma can help. I need your help to move everyone and everything we have from South Remo to North Remo."

Emma sharpens again. "You're kidding me, right? We're just going to pick up and leave? This is my home. We can't abandon our homes and move!"

I pause, letting Emma take a breath. "North Remo has large stone buildings. One of them is a library. They have schools. They have laboratories. But they need our help, Emma." Gesturing to Lemmy, I continue, "They've fallen on a difficult time due to not using those facilities and institutions correctly. We need to help them. We are the only people on this planet that can help them. Please, trust me. It's the right thing to do. And no, I won't move you. You will need to decide for yourself. I've been making too many decisions for you. Please sleep on it tonight and let me know in the morning."

***

The next morning, I make Lemmy and his men breakfast. A familiar meal. Goat sausage, hash browns, and Orc milk. Lemmy tells me it reminds him of his father's cooking. As we are enjoying ourselves discussing the differences between the two Remos, I see Emma walk up to us with her two children, Joan and Roger.

"I want to ask one thing of you, Mr. Burke." Emma stands confidently looking at me. "I want you to tell me that moving my children to North Remo is the right thing to do."

I think about it for a moment. Although North Remo has its problems, it has strength in numbers. It can weather a catastrophic event, like a natural disaster better than nineteen people in South Remo. Statistically the smaller South Remo is at a higher risk. Not to mention that assimilation would be much easier now than later. If South Remo stayed independent, someday North Remo might be looking to replace their Oracle. Maybe by force. I won't be around forever, so I need to see this merger happen now. I've never lied to Emma and I'm not going to lie to her now.

"Yes, Emma, it is the right thing to do for your children." I hope she can see in my face monitor eyes that I'm still telling her the truth.

"Okay, then. We are fine to move," Emma says looking at her children then turns to me to ask, "What are your plans, Mr. Burke?"

My plans? I know exactly how to move the village. What to take. What to leave. How to transport everything down to the beach and load onto the ships. But I can't do that. That is what the old Nick would do. And the other Nick would do. That mindset I had is what is causing the problems. I need to not do all the work myself, otherwise the colony won't be able to survive on its own. I need to be a teacher, not a doer. I need to change and they need to start figuring it out on their own. And it starts now.

"It's not my plans that matter. It's your plans we need to talk about. Both you and Lemmy here. We know that we need to move to North Remo. How do you both think we should do it?"

Emma and Lemmy look at each other, taken off guard from the question. Emma responds first. "I…I think we need to start with the people. I mean, talk to them first. Let them know why we need to move. Let them know where we are moving. Calm their concerns. If they are fine with the move, everything will go better. Wouldn't it, Mr. Burke?"

I am surprised by Emma's response. It's good. And it is something I wouldn't have thought of. I would have told everyone in the village what we're doing and go do it. I like Emma's suggestion. "Yes, Emma, it would make everything go better. That's a great idea. You should lead this effort to talk to everyone in the village and get them okay with the move. What are your thoughts on the livestock?"

Emma glows with each question I give her. "We'll need to shepherd the goats and Orcs to the shore. If we take them in manageable groups, we should be okay. We do similar moves when we migrate the goats to the fields and the Orcs to mountains for birthing. But we'll need to figure out how to feed them on the boat ride. I'll need Lemmy's help with that."

I turn to Lemmy. "What are your thoughts?"

Lemmy rubs his chin for a moment. "Aye, feeding the livestock on the boats shouldn't be a problem. But moving all the dry goods is another story. We should build more carts and take them with us. When we arrive at the North Remo beach, we can use them to help carry the material into the city."

"That sounds good, Lemmy, but what about the M-TOG?" I ask.

Lemmy looks over at the nearly unblemished M-TOG lander housing his second chance with the Oracle. After scratching his chin for a moment, he responds, "I don't think we'll be able to move it this trip, Mr. Burke. But maybe on a different trip. Is that what you think?"

I nod. Yes, moving the M-TOG will be a massive undertaking. We have plenty of time so we can wait until we've moved everything else to North Remo.

"I'd like to handle talking to the villagers about packing up their belongings," Emma says.

Lemmy smiles. "Aye, and I'll handle making the carts with my men. We should be able to leave within a few days."

Chapter 19

The move is difficult and takes several days. The urge to jump in and give the answers is ever present, but I hold firm as best I can. I try to only ask them questions to help them think about the problems instead of giving the answers. Lemmy is focused on moving all the dry goods to the boats first. He has built six wagons and has tied them together in a row to make a small train to be pulled by Gibson. Lemmy and his men load up all the dry goods on the carts to begin the journey. Grain, medical supplies, materials, tools, and household items.

We depart toward the boats. But before the train makes it to the decline toward the beach, I ask Lemmy to stop. "Let's talk about the next several steps before we proceed, Lemmy. What are the problems you're going to run into before you make it to the boats?"

Lemmy scratches his chin. "Well, Mr. Burke, we're starting to go downhill and the carts are moving easier. Too easy. I suspect that before long, when we get to that steep section down there, they'll roll on their own. Maybe too fast for Gibson to control." Gibson turns to look at Lemmy and cocks his head sideways.

"Very good," I say. "What do you think we should do?"

Lemmy scratches his chin again. "Well, what if we put Gibson at the rear of the wagon train and he could slowly walk the train of carts down the hill. He could pull back as needed to keep the wagons from going too fast. I could steer the first wagon to make sure we are heading in the right direction."

Yeah, that sounds like a terrible idea. I stop myself before saying something I'd regret. Pausing for a moment I continue, "Sounds interesting, Lemmy. Do you have any other ideas?" I say hoping he's got a better idea in him.

"Hmm…well I suppose, we're not too far from the beach at this point that we couldn't just take one cart down at a time with Gibson. We would need to take six trips though, so it would take longer. But it would be much safer. If the long train got away from Gibson, we would have a wreck on our hands. Even worse, Gibson could get hurt. I think we should just take one cart down at a time. It wouldn't take that much time."

I smile at him. "Sounds like a good plan, Lemmy. Once you get into the woods, what other problems do you think you'll run into?"

Lemmy looks down to the woods that are between him and his destination of the boats. "We'll need to take the carts through the dense woods. We can use the same path we took when we came up here, but I'm not sure that the path is wide enough for the carts. We should double-check that the path is okay. We can cut down any trees or branches that are in the way."

"Sounds like a great idea!"

Lemmy looks at his spear stick. He lays it in front of the first cart and asks for Sting from my scabbard. He uses Sting to scribe on his stick how wide the cart is. "I'll use this to measure the width of the path." Lemmy explains. He gets up and starts walking toward the woods to begin his path surveying.

"Lemmy, one more thing. What should we do with the carts before we leave?" I say, looking at the wheels of the carts. He better get this one or I'm going to do it for him.

Lemmy jumps into action and grabs rocks nearby and puts them under the wheels as chocks to keep the carts from rolling downhill while he is away. "Sorry, Mr. Burke. In my excitement I almost forgot."

"Looks good, great job! It's too bad we didn't bring more Water Foxes with us or moving all these carts down to the beach would go quicker."

Lemmy puffed up with a bit of pride figuring out his plan. "Aye, it would make the move go faster. But we want the Orcs and goats to make it all the way to their new home. If we had any more Water Foxes with us, we would end up with fat Water Foxes by the time we got home."

While Lemmy and his men inspect the path through the forest, I return to the village to find Emma. She's prepping the villagers to start moving groups of goats down to the boats. "Emma, how are things going? What is your plan to move the livestock?"

Emma wipes her brow and turns to me. "Mr. Burke, we're close to start taking the first group of goats. We have ninety-three goats total. We're going to move them down to the boats in six groups, one group at a time. We'll only have fifteen to sixteen goats in a group. Chase will be at the front of the group and I'll be at the rear. Sophie, Luke, and the older kids will be on the sides making sure none of the goats stray away. Once we get them onto the boats, we'll get them fed and watered while we return to the village to get the next group."

"Sounds good, Emma. How about the Orcs?"

"We have seventy-six Orcs. We'll move them in a similar way, by taking them in similar sized groups."

"How long do you think this will all take?" I ask Emma, though I already know the answer from my calculations.

She takes a moment to think about it. "Well, we will have six groups of goats and five groups of Orcs. So, we'll have eleven round trips to make. It takes about an hour to walk to the beach from here. I guess it would be twenty-two hours, then. That seems like a long time."

I find myself growing perturbed. Emma should have thought this out more before I asked. I hold my tongue. "Okay, Emma, let's talk about this a little and work it out. Do you think you'll be able to walk to the beach as fast as you usually do when you're trying to shepherd livestock?" She shakes her head no. "How much time do you think it will take to load them onto the boats? That will take time too. What do you think we should do?"

Emma thinks for a moment. She looks at her villagers, then looks at the couple of Lemmy's men that stayed back from clearing the forest path. Emma goes and sits down at the picnic table with hemp paper and a charcoal pencil. After a few minutes, she comes back to me to lay out her plan.

"Okay, Mr. Burke, I think I have it. Let me know your thoughts. I think I'll need six people to move each group of animals. I think the maximum number of animals we can move in a group is twenty—more than I originally thought. Lemmy should be able to spare twelve of his men to help me. Then we can move three groups at a time. Each trip should take," she pauses to check her calculations, "an hour and a half down to the beach. Fifteen minutes to load the animals, a fifteen-minute break for us, then an hour to walk back to the village. That's a three-hour round trip. We'll need to move five groups of goats and four groups of Orcs for a total of nine groups. With three groups being transported at the same time, that should take us nine hours total. That is much more reasonable than twenty-two hours. If we start in the morning, we should be able to set sail by early afternoon."

It's a good plan. It's maybe not exactly how I would do it, but I think it will get the job done. "Good job, Emma, I think that would work out great. I recommend you coordinate with Lemmy tonight at dinner. He should be finished with moving the dry goods by dinner tonight. Hopefully, we can do the final move tomorrow and set sail to go to our new home."

***

"Mr. Burke, what are you cooking for us tonight?" Lemmy asks, looking accomplished as he walks back into the village with his men and Gibson. "We've gotten all the carts moved down to the boats. Everything is loaded up. We've even set up food and water troughs on the boats for the livestock. It's been a hell of a long day though. Even when we cleared out a few trees from the path, we got the first cart stuck a few times. We tried different things and eventually got it down to the beach okay. Gibson here, he did most of the hard work." He pats Gibson, who curled into a comfortable position on the outer edge of the circle plaza using the picnic table as a shield from the bonfire.

Emma walks up to Lemmy and me ready to talk details of tomorrow's last move. I decide to excuse myself and let them work out the details on their own. I feel it is easier to prevent myself meddling in their plans if I am somewhere else.

I scoop up the two little Oracle-born kids, Alex and Evelyn, that are sharing my house with me. We head home to go to bed early.

"Ah, come on, Mr. Burke! We want to stay up later!" Alex protests while Evelyn is already getting droopy-eyed in my arms.

"We've got a big day tomorrow. We should rest well tonight." I help Alex and Evelyn into their pajamas and settle in for bed. Evelyn is already asleep before she finishes putting the blanket over herself. Alex crawls into my lap with a book to read.

"Mr. Burke, I want to read before I go to bed. Can't we read for a while?" The book is one of the first I had ever made. It is made out of bamboo pulp before I figured out that hemp rope is a better paper source. Over the years, it has been heavily used and worn. Alex crawls into my lap and I turn on my headlamps.

"I...spy...a...goat!" Alex says while reading along with his finger over the charcoal text under a crude goat drawing. Alex quickly flips to the next page.

"I...spy...a...rugby...a...rugby," he stutters. I want to jump in. I can't help it. But I wait for it, and finally, "rugbynut!" Alex screams. Evelyn groans from the noise in the cabin.

"Good job, buddy! Keep going."

"I...spy...a...ll...lllo...lobb..." Alex struggles. "I...I...don't know this one Mr. Burke, help me!"

"Think about it, Alex. What does the picture look like? You like to eat this with Orc cheese. Do you remember?"

"Lobster fish!" he exclaims. I can see Alex covering his smile with his hands with pure joy, then he lets out a yawn. I tuck him into bed, then lie down myself. Staring up at the ceiling I see the same cracks that have been there for the past thirty years. I feel good. Maybe this isn't a mistake. Maybe we can actually do this. I fall into sleep mode feeling optimistic for tomorrow.

***

Early the next morning, Emma and Lemmy begin the livestock move. Just how Emma planned, they move three groups at a time. Starting with the goats, they walk the animals down to the beach, load them onto the boats, give them food and water, then head back up to the village to get the next group. All the boats are stationed on the beach with their back gates down ready to be loaded in. When a boat is filled, the back gate is closed. I keep an eye on everything down at the boats, only stepping in when there is no one else to do so.

Emma's livestock moving team is the first to move Orcs. I see her emerge from the forest with the small herd of Orcs as Lemmy is finishing loading his group of goats. She has a smile on her face as she is walking at the rear watching the Orcs following their noses along the path being flanked on the sides and front by Chase and others.

When the Orcs reach the beach, all their heads shoot up at the same time looking out to the sea. I can see in their eyes; they are going to make an escape run into the sea. All twenty Orcs sprint in different directions toward the freedom of the sea. Groans and squeals erupt as their little legs sprint and their large tails thrust them through the sandy beach. Within a moment they all have gotten to the water. I throw Bearpaw ahead of one of them to try to stop it from escaping. Bearpaw lands directly ahead of the Orc, but it bounces off the lodged ax, then rolls sideways to continue its escape into the water. Within seconds we see twenty dark orbs speeding outward into the sea.

This is a mistake. I should have led this move. Emma isn't ready. I clench my fist and look at Emma. She is in shock at what had happened. I think of Owen on Mars. I think of when Floats died.

Clenching my fist, I decide to wait a few seconds before saying anything. After a few seconds, I wait more. Once my clouded head clears, I unclench my fist and finally speak.

"Well, that didn't go as expected. Emma, this is not the end of the world. But what did we learn here?"

She's opens her mouth to speak but comes up empty. She was expecting a massive blowup from me. She staggers in her response. "Well, I guess I didn't think about what would happen when the Orcs saw water. It makes sense now. We'll need to do something different for the next group. I'm really sorry. I realize that losing Orcs isn't a good thing," Emma says calmly.

I look at Lemmy and he is oddly calm. He smiles and then pulls his horned mask from his pack and puts it on. *Brumpft....Brumpf!!* Gibson leaps up and rushes to Lemmy's side. Lemmy gives another two short blows and points to the fleeing Orcs. Gibson slicks his ears back and dives into the water at full speed. I see a speeding submarine catching up to the black orbs.

Lemmy gives us another smile. "Don't worry. Gibson will have them all back in about twenty minutes. Our Water Foxes are masters of many things. Shepherding Orcs is only one of their skills."

Huh, well there you go. Not a big deal at all. I look at Emma and she has a relieved smile. I am really glad I didn't blow up. Not only would it not have helped, but it would have left Emma double upset knowing that all the Orcs are coming back anyways. For once I didn't do something I regretted.

"Emma, what is your plan? What are we going to do differently next time?" Emma looks around at the situation, then gives her thoughts. "I think we need to build a fence. A fence that would restrict any access to the ocean. We should build it between the boats, and up to the path entry point. That way the Orcs have nowhere to go other than into the boats."

Chase chimes in. "Maybe we can cover up gaps in the fence with large leaves. It seemed when the Orcs saw the water, that's when they sprinted to the sea."

"Aye, we've also used food as a lure as well with the Orcs," Lemmy says. "We've used that trick before to help keep them focused. If you lay out food right, they'll walk right into the boats for you."

I give them all a smile, "Yes, those sound like great ideas. I'll help you build the fence so we keep to the schedule. If we all work on it together, we should have it done within an hour." I pull Bearpaw out of the sand and head up to the forest with the team to start cutting wood.

***

The team is able to move the rest of the Orcs without any troubles. Gibson keeps a close eye when they move the remaining Orcs into the boats. His mouth waters watching the Orcs waddle into the boats. It is clear that the Water Foxes must be on the top of the food chain around here.

While everyone is securing the cargo on the boats and preparing to depart, I head back up to the village to take one last walk through it. I don't know how to feel leaving it behind. I've been here thirty years, building it from scratch. Each cut log. Each fire kiln brick. I walk through the first cabin I built. It's where Emma and I slept her first night on this planet. Walking through the village, I can see that the storage shed has been emptied. Everyone's belongings have been removed. All the livestock is gone. The barns are empty. The village is eerily quiet. I decide to walk out to Floats's grave by the edge of the wheat field. It's covered now by the green moss with only a stone monument showing the location. It's engraved "*Floats McGoats, The First Goat of Remo and true friend. Here he lies after dying before his time.*" I miss Floats. But I feel worse about how I treated Emma about his death. It wasn't her fault.

I need to say one last goodbye before leaving the village. "Oracle, I'm leaving on a trip but we will be back to get you."

"Sir, thank you. Do you need any directions on where you are going?" The Oracle asks in her annoyingly helpful tone.

SEED

"Uh, no. We're good. You'll just need to make sure not to burn the place down while we're gone. As it turns out, an M-TOG is pretty flammable."

"Mr. Burke?" I turn around and see Emma standing behind me. "We need to go. Lemmy says we need to set sail soon before the waves get too rough." Emma and I walk together along the path down to the beach.

"Emma, I'm proud of you. You did a great job with the move. Even when you ran into problems. But you solved those problems. I'm glad that you stepped up and became a great leader for the village."

Em looks up at me and gives me a smile. "Well, thanks for not being a jerk." And she gives me a punch in my arm. I could barely feel her punch, but I get the message.

Once we get to the beach, we do a headcount to make sure we are not leaving anyone behind. The South Remons load up while Lemmy's men and Gibson help push each boat off the beach one at a time. The sight is impressive. Ten cargo sailboats loaded with goats, Orcs, food, and supplies. We have everything, except the Oracle. Making the move to North Remo has me excited. I built South Remo. But technically I built North Remo too. Now it's time to build the real colony. The colony that will last longer than myself.

I jump into the lead boat with Lemmy. He turns and studies me for a moment. "Mr. Burke, I feel sorry for doubting you. There is another Remo. There is another Oracle. My Mr. Burke deceived me. But you are not him. I won't doubt you again."

I give him a smile in return. Finally, I gained his trust. "Lemmy, have you ever listened to the music you're named after? Or for that matter, the music your father Ozzy is named for?" He shakes his head no. "Well, then. We've got a good music playlist to listen to for the ride home." COMMAND LOAD PLAY Motörhead, "Ace of Spades".

167

Chapter 20

It is two days before we reach the North Remo shore. Everyone is already exhausted from the move and the two-day blistering ride on the boats. When we arrive, the beach is empty except for a few fishermen. Lemmy puts on his horned mask and gives another series of horn blows. We see dozens of Water Foxes poke their heads out of the water from a nearby cove. They immediately swim out to tow us to shore. Lemmy, Em, and I caucus on the beach before opening any of the boat gates.

"What is the plan, team?" I ask.

Before anyone could respond, Ava and her son, Maynard, jump out of their boat. "We need to see Aden. We need to make sure he's okay!"

Lemmy stops her before she starts up the path on her own. "Hold on now. I can send one of my men to run up to the city with you. He will take you to Aden. He can also have people come down to help with the move to ease the burden off us. He can let the ranchers know to prepare for the new livestock." Ava and her son hurry into the woods with their guide.

Em regains everyone's attention. "We need to take care of the rest of the villagers. We're exhausted from the trip. We all need a bath and fresh meal. We are in no shape to move everything up to our new home."

"Aye," Lemmy agrees. "My men will take care of moving all your supplies. I recommend you gather the personal belongings you can carry and take a walk up the city to gain some rest. I would be happy to take you myself."

"Thank you, Lemmy," I interrupt. "But I know the way. I will take them to Emma—your Emma. She'll be able to care for them."

The remaining South Remons and I make the walk up to North Remo. It is refreshing to make the walk without being a hemp rope-bound prisoner like last time. Once we make it past the forest, the South Remons can finally see how big North Remo is. Everyone is amazed at the size of their fields. They are in awe of their buildings. The fact that their fields and buildings are failing seems to be overshadowed by their staggering size.

We continue to walk toward the city center where Emma is located. North Remons start to take notice and watch us proceed into town. They are not celebrating our return. Instead they are staring in intrigue. I suppose they still don't know what to think of me. After a long walk into the city, we make it to the center city plaza. Sophie and Luke point out the circle bricks of the plaza to the rest of South Remons.

When we come upon the burned wreckage of M-TOG 839, Em walks around it, inspects it "Did Lemmy do this? How could he do that to an Oracle?"

"There was a misunderstanding," I explain, "Lemmy didn't mean to do it."

"Are these people really our friends?" Em says, looking at me with concern. The area starts to fill up with more people watching us. "Why are they just staring at us? Didn't they think you were their savior?"

"Watch this," I say to Emma with a smile on my face. "I know how to cheer them up and have them welcome us." COMMAND LOAD PLAY Aerosmith's "Back in the Saddle." The North Remons' ears perk up as the song intro begins to fill the air. The city center plaza fills with more people hearing the music.

"I'm baaackk!!!"

Smiles race across everyone's faces hearing the Old Ones music again. The pumping guitar riffs give my people a boost of energy to keep walking to Emma's temple. The crowd of excited North Remons follow us. Everyone is doing their best to be within earshot of the music from my head speakers.

We march up the temple stairs again. This time with energy and hope instead of uncertainty and dread. Inside the temple, the older Emma is already waiting alongside Aden, Ava, and their son. I kneel down on one knee and address her. "I have returned and have brought my villagers with me. They are weary from their trip and require food, bath, and rest. Can you help them, Emma?"

"Mr. Burke, you have stuck to your word. I am pleased and grateful that you have returned to us. Of course, we will help your villagers. They are now part of our city now. They are now Remons."

Em steps up beside me. "Emma, I must introduce myself. I am Emma, from South Remo. You can call me Em. I am happy to finally meet you," she says, holding out her hand.

"I see." The short, silver-haired Emma studies the youthful Em, squinting her eyes. "My child, please come closer so I can see you better." Emma delicately takes Em's hand and studies her eyes. "My grandmother had the same nickname, Em. We lost her ages ago, but I am glad you are here now. So Sing the Old Ones."

Watching the two of them, it strikes me that they are completely two different people. They don't look anything alike. Em is tall, dark hair, with brown eyes. Emma is short, silvered-haired, and with green eyes. The only thing they share is their name. I hope this integration goes smoothly.

***

Lemmy leads the South Remons to their new homes. A short walk away from Emma's temple is a group of unoccupied wooden houses surrounding a failed wheat field. All the families take to their own houses. Emma and Chase. Aden and Ava. Sophie and Luke. Although the houses are run-down from years of neglect, they are still an improvement to the log cabins back in South Remo. These houses at least have hinged front doors and glass windows.

"Alex. Evelyn." I kneel down to address them while the families were heading into their own homes. "I think it would best if you start staying the night with Emma and Chase."

"Yeaahhhh!!!!" they both scream. "Sleepover at Joan and Roger's house!" they both yell as they run to Emma. Wow, I thought there would be at least a little bit of resistance.

Em smirks as she shows Alex and Evelyn into their new house. "We will see you tomorrow, Mr. Burke. We're so exhausted, we're just going to roll out our mats and go to bed. Thank you for getting us here."

None of the houses are big enough for me to easily get in and out of, but there is a barn at the edge of the field. After giving it a quick walkaround inspection, I start cleaning out the inside. I find a straw broom hanging off the wall from hooks. I borrow the broom and take my time cleaning the floor and knocking down the cobwebs. I set the broom down in the corner, then do something I have never done before. I unsheathe Bearpaw and hang it on the hooks that once held the broom. I then unstrap Bearpaw's scabbard and hang it on another one of the hooks. Then I untie Sting's scabbard and hang Sting in its sheath off the other broom hook. It's the first time I've taken off the sheaths since I put them on thirty years ago. I look at my chest and leg where the sheath straps had held themselves to my body, still shown by white stripes surrounded by decades of dirt-stained Space Yeti skin.

I find a place to sit down and go into low power mode. Before I power down, I take one last look at the interior of the barn. The other Nick Burke must have built this barn. It is odd to think that I built this, but I didn't build it. I'm not physically tired at all, but I am mentally tired. I can use a good sleep mode mental refresh.

***

After a night to refresh, we meet in the temple again over lunch. Emma with Lemmy. Em with Aden. And myself. We need to discuss the next steps.

"We all have the same goals," I say. "We want to succeed. We want to prosper. We want to have happy lives. We'll need to work together to achieve that. We will not spend time passing blame. Instead we need to discuss what are the problems and ideas for solutions. Emma, you know better than anyone what Remo needs. Please let us know your thoughts."

"Thank you, Mr. Burke. We have suffered food shortages, crumbling buildings, and disease. Our population has slowly shrunk since you've left us...I mean, since the other Mr. Burke left us." Emma takes another glance at the mural inside the temple, which prompts everyone else to look at the mural also.

"Okay, good." I thank her. "What are the root causes of those problems?"

Lemmy interrupts, "Isn't it clear? When you left, that's when all the problems happened. We need you to fix it and keep the place working, right?"

"I can do that," I say. "But what will happen when I die? I don't live forever. My HE-TEG power will eventually run out. Then what? We need to think about things differently. We need to think about how to prepare when I'm no longer here."

Lemmy rubs his chin thinking about the situation. Emma puts her hand on Lemmy's shoulder. "Mr. Burke is right. We need to be able to live without him. If we go back to the way things were, we would fall back into the same issue we're in now. We can't allow that to happen. So, what do we do?"

Em begins to speak, "I think we need to focus on our people. We need to teach them. We need to figure things out on our own. It's not enough to have them memorize Mr. Burke's teachings. We need to become problem solvers, researchers, and innovators."

"I believe you are correct," Emma says. "It appears to be a mistake when I closed the school to have everyone focus on tending the fields. That did help for a short while, but we can see that it is a losing strategy now. Unfortunately, the schools have been closed for so long that we won't be able to get our teachers back. We'll need a whole new teaching staff."

Lemmy stiffens. "We can't have everyone go to school. Who will tend the fields and the livestock? I'm sorry, but we still need to keep the city running."

"I don't think that is what Emma meant," Aden says. "I think we should focus on the children's education in the schoolroom. For the adults, we should focus on hands-on education. The kind that they use in their daily lives while they are still doing their jobs. The city will still run. Everyone will be learning."

Lemmy looks calmed at Aden's response, but replies, "Aye, but who will be the teacher to the students?" Everyone looks at each other, then finally focus on me.

"I will not teach your students," I say with my arms crossed. "Instead I will teach your teachers. The best way to learn is to teach. I recommend that Em be the lead schoolteacher. Lemmy and Aden should be hands-on teachers. Under your guidance, I think Remo will build a great education system. Through that education system, you will build a great civilization. One that will last a millennium."

The group nods in agreement.

"Before we break, I want us to write our goal and our plan on how we are going to accomplish it on the temple wall. When we see the inscription, it will help us remember." We deliberate for several minutes and eventually paint the following on the temple wall. *Happy, Healthy, and Prosperous by Inquisitive Learning.* Not the best slogan, but I think it gets the point across. We don't chisel it into the stone walls so we always have an opportunity to change it. At some point, I'm sure they will. It will be a good reminder whenever we're in this temple what our goal is. I look up at the mural behind the throne. The three scenes with the last one of me running away. I'll need to see this Remo through to ensure it becomes a self-sustaining civilization. This is my last chance to turn it around. Perhaps if we make it, they'll paint over that ugly third mural scene.

***

Em and I walk to the Remo library after the temple meeting to see what books North Remo has that we can teach with. We enter the library in a pleasantly-large door sized for a Space Yeti. What we find inside is beautifully bound paper books filling row after row of bookcases. Textbooks ranging from grade school to college level. Math, biology, engineering. Not to mention all of Earth's literary classics had been created too. It must have taken decades to make all these books.

Em's face brightens. "Mr. Burke, this is fantastic! I've never seen so many books before in my life. Our village's small bookshelf pales in comparison, this is amazing!"

"We should talk about what classes you are going to teach, Em. Have you thought about what you want to do?"

Em's bright face started to fade. "I...I don't know. It's such a huge undertaking. I don't even know where to start." I can feel her tense up a little. I built the entire education system in South Remo and presumably I built the entire education system in North Remo too. I can do it again now. But that is not what I want. I want the new education system to be owned by Em. If I lay it all out for her, she won't feel it's her design. And when things get tough with it, she won't dig in to protect her design.

"Well, let's start by reviewing the South Remo curriculum. Do you remember all the subjects?" I calmly ask.

"Of course, I do. Production, Safety & Medical, Science & Exploration, Math & Engineering, and finally Reading & Writing. We had only thirteen students in South Remo. North Remo has over three hundred students varying from entry level to young adults. How can we teach them all?"

"Let me give you some tips on how the Old Ones used to do it. They would split up the students by age so they could keep each group a reasonable size and be able to teach a curriculum that was appropriate for the age. Do you think something similar would work for Remo?"

Em pauses, thinking about the idea. "Yes, I think that would work great! At South Remo, we had children start attending school when they were four years old and they stopped when they were sixteen. If we split up the three hundred students into twelve groups based on age, that is twenty-five children per group. That seems reasonable. But I don't have twelve teachers. I don't see how this is going to work."

"Let's remember that North Remo hasn't had an education system for at least two decades. So that means that all the kids are blank slates. When you were attending school in South Remo, how hard do you think it would have been if you started taking biology classes without learning how to read first? What that means is the older students need to learn the basics too. What do you think we could do given that case?"

Em pauses to think again. "What if we doubled the class sizes to fifty people. That would be six different classes. If one teacher does two classes in one day, that would mean I would need three teachers. Who can be the other two teachers?"

"Don't look at me," I say, and Em turns away, her brow fixed in thought. "Who do you think would be best?"

"Well, Chase would be really good, but if I'm going to be teaching all day, he'll need to be watching over our kids. Aden will be tied up with his own hands-on teaching so Ava will also be tending to her kids. But she only has Maynard. Maybe I can convince Chase to look after Maynard with the other kids during the day. Yeah, I think that will work. I need one more. All I have left is Sophie and Luke. I'd better talk to them and see which one would want to do it. I don't want to presume. But we'll need more teachers in the future. We won't be able to sustain with only three teachers."

"Teaching the teachers is my job. I'll pick a few of the brightest of North Remo to sharpen up for you. I'll do night classes for the adults to find more capable teachers. I think within a few years we should be set up with enough teachers. Also, the curriculum doesn't need to be fully finished at the start. Since everyone is starting from a blank slate, you'll just need to worry about the fundamentals. In the coming years though we'll want to grow the curriculum as the kids grow. When they graduate at sixteen, I'll set up a university to focus on making them teachers and advanced trades like doctors and engineers." My enthusiastic plan seems to cool her excitement. "I...uh...I mean, don't get me wrong. You will be involved in all of it. I'll only be taking the lead on teaching the teachers until your program is up to speed. Together I think we'll be able to do amazing things. What are your thoughts on the initial curriculum?"

Em smiles and ponders the question. "We certainly need reading and writing. That will be key. I can easily make beginner and intermediate courses for that. We should do beginners and intermediate classes for math, reading, and writing. The other courses we did at South Remo don't seem to be such a priority. But we would want to add them into the curriculum as we grow."

"I would recommend you keep the South Remo Safety & Medical class. It wouldn't need to be a long class. But I do think it would help everyone. North Remo is just as dangerous as South Remo. Also, I recommend you figure out a way to fit in teaching the children to be inquisitive. To solve problems on their own. They should really know the scientific method."

Em looks puzzled. "Mr. Burke, I don't think you talked about a scientific method back in South Remo."

Of course I didn't. Back then, I was too focused on getting things done correctly quickly. There wasn't time then to teach how to figure it out on your own. Now I need to make the time.

"Well, that was a mistake I made. The scientific method is very important. You'll want to write down the steps. First, you need to identify the problem. Next, you find all the information you can about the problem and learn what is already known about it. Then, you will build your hypothesis."

Em looks puzzled again looking up from her hemp rope paper notepad. "What is a hypothesis?" she asks.

I really botched teaching the kids, didn't I? This is terrible.

"A hypothesis is your guess to what is happening with the problem. But it is not a wild guess. It's your best guess using all the information you've learned."

Em returns to writing feverishly.

"Next, you need to test your hypothesis. This can be done many ways. Sometimes it is doing a physical test. Or sometimes it is just trying out what you think is right and seeing what happens. The next step is analyzing what your test found out. You will want to review the results and make a conclusion. The last step is determining if you are right or wrong. Sometimes your hypothesis is correct. But sometimes it is wrong. If it is wrong, that's okay. You'll go back and make a new hypothesis and start over. If you are right, you need to share the information with others so that they know how to solve the problem too."

Em glows with excitement. "This is fantastic, Mr. Burke! I think maybe I'll make my own scientific method tests in building the curriculum. It will be great to figure out what works and what doesn't! I think within two weeks we can have the curriculum designed and the classrooms set up."

"Mr. Burke, we should also include music in the curriculum. Music is so important. Everyone should be learning it. I'll speak with Ava, Sophie, and Luke to get the help now." Em starts to walk out of the library, then pauses at the doorway. "Mr. Burke, I don't suppose that you would be willing to review my curriculum plan, would you?"

"Absolutely! I'm always available to bounce any ideas you want off me."

Em and I leave the library to go inspect the schoolhouses. Leaving the library, we attract a small crowd of children wanting to get a glimpse of the giant Space Yeti.

A young adolescent boy with a brave face approaches me. "You're Mr. Burke, right? I've never seen you before. You're really tall! You have Old Ones music in your head, don't you? My grandma told me the Old Ones made happy music for us. We want to hear it!"

I kneel down to get closer to the boy. "What is your name, kid?" He steps back, a bit intimidated by me.

"Eddie. My name is Eddie!" he says, trying to stand tall, his chest puffed out.

"That is a great name, Eddie. Let me play you some music of the Old One guitarist you are named after." COMMAND LOAD PLAY Van Halen, "Hot for Teacher". While the irregular double kick drum intro starts, I began shaking as if something has gone haywire in my Space Yeti body. The kids all cautiously step back wondering if something has gone wrong. Did they just break Mr. Burke? My robot shakes turn into a rhythmic, full-body headbang with my air guitar starting its intro solo. I stand back up while surgically fingerpicking my air guitar. Once up, I let the air guitar rip and now the kids know the Old Ones are for real. The song kicks into gear into a driving riff and I can't help myself from doing an air-guitar shuffle toward the schoolhouses. The crowd of kids start following us, jumping and screaming, wanting to hear every beat. I can hear Em behind me.

"Real subtle, Mr. Burke."

Chapter 21

After a day with Em helping with her education program, I set out to meet up with Aden and Lemmy. I find the two of them standing in a desolate-looking wheat field with a ring of gruff-looking farmers standing around them.

"There you are, Mr. Burke," Lemmy says, looking out to the field. "We've been growing wheat in this field for decades. Shouldn't we be getting it right at least some of the time?" He raises a hand, feigning a grab at some of the half-grown stalks. "Look at this wheat! It looks terrible. Aye, you can still harvest it, but we can't get much grain out of it like we used to when I was a boy."

Looking at the field, I can tell right away that they have depleted the nitrogen in the soil because they haven't been rotating their crops. I could test the soil and confirm if Lemmy hadn't torched the Oracle.

Lemmy startles me from my thoughts. "Well? Mr. Burke, we need you to fix this! When you left, the crops all failed!"

"I know you are frustrated. We will get this figured out and get the crops growing again. What are all the different crops you are currently growing?"

"Well, there is wheat and alfalfa. Soybeans and corn. Potatoes, kale, and broccoli. Cotton for our clothing. The other Mr. Burke also found us a Prasares plant to eat. He called it Carrot Roots, whatever that means."

I look to Aden. "Do you remember what we did in South Remo? How we planted the fields? What did we do once we harvested? What did we plant in each field?"

"Yeah, Mr. Burke, I see what you're saying. We didn't plant the same crop on the same field. We would change it. Sometimes we also left the field bare and let the goats graze on it for a while. I think you called that leaving the field fallow."

"That's right, Aden. Do you know why we did that?"

Aden shakes his head no. Of course he doesn't know. I didn't bother to tell anyone.

"The practice is called crop rotation. It was first discovered by the Old Ones. There are crops that take nitrogen out of the soil, like wheat and corn. And there are crops that help put nitrogen back into the soil, like alfalfa and soybeans. Also, when you let the goats graze a fallow field after an alfalfa or soybeans crop, it gives the soil time to absorb the nitrogen from their remaining roots. Having the goats on the field give it an added boost of nutrients from their manure. Aden, what do you think we should do with this field we are standing in?"

Aden thinks for a moment. "No wheat, right?" I nod yes, then he continues, "If alfalfa puts nitrogen back into the soil and the wheat needs nitrogen, shouldn't we plant alfalfa then?" I nod again.

"The wheat fields are very nitrogen depleted. What else could you do to put more nitrogen into the fields?" I ask.

Aden answers, "We can't let the goats into the field when we're growing alfalfa. They would just eat it. That defeats the purpose, Mr. Burke."

"Aye, if manure is what you need, we have plenty in the goat feeding lot," Lemmy interjects. "We are constantly shoveling it out of the way into piles off to the side. We have too much as it is. We can load it up on carts and spread it over the fields before we plant the alfalfa crop."

"That sounds like a great plan, Lemmy," I say. They will finally get a good yield if they fertilize with goat manure and plant alfalfa on the wheat fields. They can do the same thing planting soybeans

SEED

on the corn fields. They will be able to do the opposite by planting wheat on the alfalfa fields and corn on the soybean fields. "I recommend you set up test fields and try out different crop rotation methods. Talk with Em. She can tell you about the scientific method."

Lemmy and the farmers do not look too enthused to be pitching manure. But they seem to be satisfied with a path forward. I look at the farmers. Worn. Tired. They have brought their sickles with them to cut the wheat. They look like they are a hundred years old. Rusty and falling apart.

"Why haven't you been making any new tools?" I ask the men.

"There haven't been any new tools since you left." The oldest of the farmers says. He has a bristled white beard highlighted by his tanned skin from his time in the fields. "The smiths gave up working the smelters and furnace not soon after you ran away. You best go look at the sorry state you left them in." His years saw the best and worst of me. Earning his trust back will take time.

***

I take a walk by myself to the blacksmith center located near the river. When I arrive, I can see that it is my dream built into reality. I had done a wonderful job designing it. It is a large stone building with three large iron ore smelters and a smaller one for copper. Next to them stood a ceramic ladle for steelmaking about the size of a washing machine. There are six forging stations with anvils circled around one large forge furnace.

When I walk in, I can see that everything is cold. No flame has been lit in years. A burly old man with a long, braided silver beard grabs my hand before I can pick up an anvil hammer to inspect it.

"You decided to come back, did yah?"

I experience more resistance getting my hand back than expect. I turn around to see a mammoth Remon. Much shorter than me, but arms that would make me work in an arm-wrestling contest.

"We didn't expect to ever see the likes of you around here again. Whatcha want, Night Thief?" Two more blacksmith men come out hearing the noise we're making.

"I'm here to help. Look, I'm sorry for what I did. It was a mistake. But let's not waste time on the past. What is your name?"

"You've had too much smoke in your head if you don't remember me. I'm Peter. I work the steel. These men here, they're Remo's finest blacksmiths."

"How is the steelmaking going today?" I say in the dark, cold foundry.

"You always were too smart for your own good, Night Thief. Aye, but you are right. We haven't been able to make steel since you left. You always used to blast the furnace yourself. You designed it, so you knew how to operate it best. I always watched. But you moved faster than I could keep up. I don't even know what all this stuff does. What is this thing? It looks like a sword with a tail. You kept stabbing the molten iron with it. But when I tried, nothing happened. We kept getting pig iron. Eventually we gave up. The furnaces haven't been lit in years. Nowadays we do what we can to repair tools."

I take a walk around the ladle. It is a simple but ingenious system. Ceramic troughs transfer the molten iron from the smelter into the ladle. The iron ore has too much carbon in it. To make steel you need to take most of the carbon out. To do this you inject oxygen into the molten iron. The oxygen bonds with the carbon and gasses out as carbon monoxide and carbon dioxide. Getting the oxygen into the molten iron is the hard part. Once you've decarburized iron into steel, the ladle tips to pour into molds.

I take a look at what Peter the steelworker had called a sword with a tail. It was actually a water-cooled oxygen lance. It's a long tube that pumps oxygen through the ceramic-protected tube. Inside the ceramic armor are ports for water to help keep everything cool while it's inside the molten iron. You use it as a lance to stab the molten iron to mix in the oxygen. I trace back the flexible tubes to their sources. The water tube and the oxygen tube are both going into their own respective pumps. I had made mechanical pumps! Each pump has a set of gears and chains connecting to a drive axle that leads out of the building. I look out the window to see the drive axle connected to a wagon wheel in the river. The wagon wheel is turning in the river, but the axle is not. I see that there is a mechanical clutch that needs to be engaged to turn the pumps on. I trace the oxygen tube away from the pump to a ball valve. Past the ball valve, I see a tube running outside. I head outside to investigate, with Peter and his men following behind.

We walk outside and see an out of place sight. "Your underwater garden is still here. But nothing grows. I don't know why you'd ever want this seaweed up here. It's bad enough in the ocean. We lost another Water Fox last year to the seaweed in the cove. Nasty stuff. But it's all dead now here. Good riddance. Your glass covering the underwater garden has already been pilfered for better uses."

I see what I did. I was trying to produce pure oxygen. I had dug an Olympic-sized pool into the ground, but much deeper. It looks about ten meters deep. I can see channels dug to let water in from the river to fill the pond. A broken frame that used to hold glass panes still hovers over the pond. The glass cap was used to capture the oxygen generated by the seaweed. Pure oxygen for steelmaking. I think I aimed too high on this one. Too complex. Seaweed won't grow in the fresh water from the river. I must have been trying to raise the salinity manually. I'm not surprised it didn't work.

"Night Thief, do we need your stinkin' seaweed to make steel?" Peter gruffs.

"No. We can use air instead. It will be good steel, but not the best possible." I follow the oxygen tube back to the pump and grab for Sting to cut the tube. I awkwardly grab my thigh realizing I took Sting off and left it in the barn. "Peter, I need your help. We need to cut this tube to allow air to get into the pump. We will be using regular air instead of pure oxygen."

Peter smirked, pulling a large set of pliers from his belt. He uses the pliers to grasp a spring clamp holding the tube to the pump inlet.

With a small tug, he removes the tube without damaging it. "That do for ya, Night Thief?"

I could almost feel my face monitor cheeks get flushed in embarrassment. "Uh…yeah, that's great Peter. I remember how to make steel. And I'm going to show you how to make it yourself. Let's get to work."

"Aye, the Old Ones will sing tonight. Men! Grab the Orc oil! Douse the furnace firewood and light them ablaze!"

Peter pulls a lever engaging the main axle clutch. All of a sudden, large bellows start expanding and contracting, pumping air into the furnace fires. The men start shoveling iron ore and limestone into the smelters.

Peter approaches me during the excited commotion in the foundry. "Aye, Night Thief, may we listen to the Old Ones music while we work? Working the smelters needs the right music to motivate the men. What do you say?" Peter gives me the first smile I've seen since I met him.

"Sure, any requests?" I ask.

"Aye, I need the music that warms my bones, stiffens my back, and hardens my arms while I work. Aye, you called it Pantera when I was a young lad."

I had to laugh a little bit, feeling like a heavy metal jukebox. "You got it, buddy." COMMAND LOAD PLAY Pantera's album, *Vulgar Display of Power*.

"Aye, that is the sweetness in my ears. Men! We work through the night while the Old Ones sing!"

***

By the morning, we had refined a good yield of steel. I had walked Peter through the entire process. Taking my time and explaining everything. Over the coming days, his men should be able to make new steel farm tools. We all depart the warm foundry when the sun rises. I decide to walk to the medical facility and find out what condition it's in.

I find that a small stone building infirmary has been constructed. I walk in through another Space Yeti-sized door to find Sophie and others inspecting the racks of medicine.

Sophie finally sees me and approaches in excitement. "Mr. Burke! It's wonderful to see you this morning. We need your help. Luke has decided to help Emma as a teacher. I still want to help so I decided we should work with the medical supplies. Look at all these bottles! There are way more than what we had in South Remo. What do you suppose we should do first?"

All the walls of the infirmary are lined with shelves brimming with bottles of different sizes. Holding all sorts of liquids, twigs, leaves, and berries. I am sure that the other Nick had done an exhaustive search of medicine, checking everything he could with the Oracle. I pick up one bottle and read its label, Cooling Balm.

"Sophie, please look around and see if you can find a record book listing all the medicine." If I had assembled this stockpile of medicine, I certainly would have made an inventory log.

"Mr. Burke, do you mean this?" A young Remon woman named Debbie raises up a book she must have found on a shelf. "I can't read it, is it what you are looking for?"

"Debbie, can I see that?" Sophie asks, taking the book from the young woman and inspecting it.

"Yes, Mr. Burke, this looks to be the book you are wanting," Sophie says, holding out the book to me to take.

"Very good. You should keep it, Sophie. Let's talk about what we should do. You have an inventory book of medicine, but it is probably out-of-date. All the medicine we have is on the shelves. What are your thoughts?"

Sophie flips open the book and starts skimming. "This book is two parts. The first is a listing of all the different medicines, then it references later pages for each of them." Sophie flips to a later page. "Ahh, they are descriptions of all the medicines here. Each medicine has a description of what it is."

I'm surprised the other Nick bothered to even write this stuff down. He certainly had it all memorized in his computer. Maybe if

I were in his shoes, I'd make a book to use in case of emergency if I wasn't near the infirmary. "Sophie, does the book have an index of symptoms and what medicine to use?"

Sophie flips through the book toward the end. "Yes, at the end it has all sorts of symptoms listed with corresponding medicines and page numbers."

"Very good, Sophie. I think the book is a reference of all the medicines, what they do, and what medicines should be used for what symptoms. What do you think we should now?"

"Huh...well, the book is dusty. It looks like it hasn't been used in a while. Maybe we should check to see if we have all the medicine this book says we should have."

"That's a great idea, Sophie! I recommend you make a log document. List out all the medicines and determine how much you have of each."

Sophie looks at the other Remons in the infirmary with excitement. It will take them a few days, but they should easily be able to complete the task. I am concerned about not having the Oracle here. It is going to be difficult without the material identifier station capabilities of the Oracle.

"Sophie, after you complete the inventory of the medicine, what do you think you should do next?"

Sophie thinks for a moment. "Emma was telling me about the great library with all the books. Maybe there are books that would help us."

"That's a good idea, Sophie. What other ideas do you have?"

"Well, Debbie here mentioned that her son is not feeling well. Maybe we should let the city know that people can come here to get help. We should take a few days to get everything organized, but we should start helping people as soon as possible. Don't you think, Mr. Burke?"

"Yes, I think that is a great idea. Once you take care of the sickest, you may want to consider making medical records of everyone in the city. Having that information can be unbelievably valuable. It will be up to all of you to make sure the city is healthy."

Sophie looks concerned with the prospect of such a daunting responsibility.

"Don't worry, I'm not going anywhere. I'll be here to help if you need it."

Chapter 22

Today is Em's fortieth birthday. It's been ten years since we merged the two Remos and the change has been amazing. Em is the headmaster of the Remo school program. There were some stumbles, but she has built a fantastic program. Ninety percent of Remo can read now, with only a few holdouts that are old in their ways. She's built a twelve-year program with some kids that have excelled so quick they graduated early and have moved on to the university.

One of the night courses I started was for building construction. Many of the town's laborers attended and enjoyed the hands-on work we did—constructing new buildings in the city. We built additional schoolhouses for the influx of children, a separate university building where I taught, and an add-on to the library. We demoed the crumbling buildings and replaced them with new. Over the past ten years, the city population doubled to approximately two thousand people. To house all of them, we've been building nonstop over the past several years. In the entire ten-year period, I never picked up a hammer. I never used my shovel. But I was there supporting them and giving guidance.

Aden and Lemmy did a fantastic job fixing the crop yields. Once they started rotating the crops, they had ample food for the growing city. Peter and his men kept the foundry warm producing new tools for all the farm labor. With the aid of some of the older students, new farm tools were being developed and built by Peter's men.

Sophie leads the infirmary, which has now grown to be more like a hospital. She has taken on some of the students that have graduated to focus more in the medical field. Interestingly enough, Sophie had many unanticipated benefits from her program. She built the first census the city has ever had. Even the old Nick Burke never did that. She has also been a pioneer in statistics. Keeping track of everyone's health information prompted her to organize and study the data. Sophie has had some of the greatest struggles out of anyone. Much of her work is limited by not having the Oracle. Her team takes weekly boat trips to South Remo with various plants and materials to be analyzed. She has a small team stationed there to handwrite all the medical books that the Oracle can provide. We will need to move the Oracle up to North Remo.

"Mr. Burke, do you think we are ready?" Emma asks. That silver-haired gem is still spry as ever and never missed a beat since I've been here. I meet with her weekly in her temple to give her status updates on our progress and discuss strategy for the city's growth.

"I do, Emma. We are ready to move the Oracle here. But it will take time. Maybe years. We only have one Oracle, so we need to do it right." I look up at the murals in the temple. Still unchanged. The last scene still has me as the Night Thief. "Once we have the Oracle back in Remo, it will help us be complete. I want to do right by bringing back the Oracle." Emma nods in agreement. Hopefully when we get the Oracle up here, they'll finally change that mural.

On my way back to my barn, I stop by Em's house to wish her a happy birthday. Since moving to North Remo, Em has finally become my friend again. We talk for hours with her asking me my thoughts on her curriculum. But what she doesn't know is I desperately need her. She is one of the few true friends I have. I need to make sure I protect our relationship. Protect it from myself. After saying our goodbyes, I head back to my barn. I haven't bothered to do anything with it. It only needs to keep the rain off me when I go into low power mode. I sit down and look up at the wall. Bearpaw and Sting still hang on their hooks. I haven't touched them since I put them on the wall. They're covered in thick dust now.

***

After getting Emma's blessing, I opened a new university class called "The M-TOG Transfer Project". A small team of Em's brightest students showed up, including my old roommates Alex and Evelyn, and Aden's son, Maynard, all now grown up in their teenage years. Additionally, a few of Peter's sharpest blacksmiths decided to join. I held a special enrollment meeting to make sure they really wanted to be a part of it.

I address the eager class of eighteen students, "This is going to be a difficult class. There is only one test. And you must pass it. We need to move the M-TOG with the Oracle in it from South Remo to here. It may take months. It may take years. But once done, it will be the biggest achievement you will have done so far."

Two familiar faces walk into the classroom. "Aye, we couldn't let you move the Oracle without us, could we?" Lemmy boasts with Aden by his side.

"We're here to take your course too, Mr. Burke," Aden adds. "We want to help." Aden's familiar face hits me again. Where have I seen that face on Earth before?

The next day we take the entire class sailing to South Remo. I believe that the first day of the class should be looking at the M-TOG. Many of the students have never seen it before. It's not worthwhile trying to talk about it in the classroom when we can look at it directly.

Once we arrive at South Remo, we settle in to spend a few days on-site. The village has been turned into more of an off-site camp, where visitors would spend only a few days at a time. No livestock, but plenty of food and supplies, with sleeping quarters for everyone. No one wants to wait after dropping off their belongings at their sleeping quarters. They want to start work.

"This here is a 400 Class Transporter Lander designed and built by the Old Ones. It's the most technologically advanced thing on this planet. More so than myself. It is named M-TOG 486. Does anyone remember what M-TOG stands for?"

An eager hand jumps up from Evelyn before anyone else could think about the question. "Mr. Burke, M-TOG stands for Machine Transport for Organic Growth. It's the motto that brought you here and helped set up Remo."

"That's right!" I say standing in front of the class with the M-TOG behind me. "And inside the M-TOG is the smartest entity on the planet. The Oracle. She knows many things from the Old Ones, and she can tell you a lot about your planet. There is only one Oracle on this planet so we must take the utmost care moving her," I say looking at Lemmy. "I will let the Oracle herself tell you about her. Oracle, please read off the 400 Class Transporter Lander Summary Sheet."

"Nick, it would be my pleasure," a familiar and comforting British woman's accent says. "The 400 Class Transporter Lander has a tare weight of 3,608 kilograms. Its major dimensions are 4.23 meters wide, 4.23 meters long, and 3.87 meters tall when in its landing position. It is constructed of 6061 aluminum alloy for structure and paneling..."

I can hear Alex behind me talking to Evelyn. "If the Oracle is so smart, why does she mispronounce aluminum?"

"I think that is enough, Oracle, thanks for the background," I jump in and say. "I'd like us to discuss ideas on how to move the M-TOG from here all the way home without damaging it. We need to discuss every step. What are some of your ideas?"

Everyone stays silent until Evelyn answers, "3,608 kilograms seems very heavy. There is a weight scale back at the grain storage facility in Remo. It weighs the carts that bring in the grain from harvest. The heaviest the highest the scale goes to is 1000 kilograms. 3,608 is much higher! Mr. Burke, do we need to move all of the M-TOG?"

"Wow, that is a great question, Evelyn. I wasn't thinking about that. Technically we don't. The Oracle uses the main computer, but also utilizes the auxiliary computers. We also need all the material identifier station and power system. We can definitely remove the embryo incubator equipment and the launch seat I rode in on. Disassembling the structure of the M-TOG would be challenging though. We would likely cut wires that are harnessed into the beams. We don't have the right tools to fix it. So, we would be able to reduce the weight in a few places, but it would be only by a few hundred kilograms. Not really enough to make it worth our while. It would probably be best that we don't disassemble anything to prevent mistakenly breaking anything. If we break it, we may not ever be able to fix it. But that was a really good question, Evelyn. Keep'em coming."

Aden jumps in. "I assume we will sail the M-TOG back home. We would need to build a bigger boat to carry that large and heavy of a load. But we would still need to get the M-TOG to the beach. How are we going to do that?"

"Aye, we built carts before when we moved supplies from South Remo years ago. Maybe we can build a large cart this time to move the M-TOG?" Lemmy says. "But the path through the forest is much too narrow. We would be cutting trees forever. Plus, the ground in the forest is too uneven for a large cart. We would have to dig a road through the forest. It could be done, but it would be difficult work. Not to mention that building a road that large here at South Remo would be a waste. If we are going to build a large road to the beach it should be back home at North Remo where we could reuse it for decades."

Not dismayed by her earlier comment, Evelyn answers again, "What if we use the river? Cutting a path through the trees there wouldn't be that difficult. We could float the M-TOG downriver to the beach. The river is certainly wide enough."

"Aye, that is a fine idea," Lemmy exclaims. "We won't be able to use the North Remo river to bring it up the city. Going upriver would be too difficult. But building a wide road at North Remo from the beach to the city would be worthwhile. We could pull the large cart with the M-TOG all the way up to the city safely. Afterward, we could then easily move goods to and from the beach. I would be fully in favor of that."

I'm impressed how well the class is thinking. "These are great ideas. So what we have is move the M-TOG to the river, transfer the M-TOG downriver on a raft, load the M-TOG on a freight ship, then off-load the M-TOG onto a large cart and tow it up the city on a new road."

Aden finally gives us his thoughts. "That is a lot of handoffs of moving the M-TOG from one thing to a different thing. I count five. One: from the South Remo ground to whatever we are going to use to move the M-TOG to the river's edge. Two: from that device onto the river raft. Three: from the raft to the boat. Four: from the boat to the cart. Five: from the cart to the North Remo ground. That seems like a lot. Why don't we just load up the M-TOG onto the cart here in South Remo, then move it all—the cart and the M-TOG—together. The only difficult moves would be moving the M-TOG on and off the cart. What are your thoughts on that?"

"I think that is a great idea, Aden," I say, smiling. "So, I think we have it. We need to build the cart, the raft, the boat, and the road. We need four volunteers to lead the teams that will build each item, and one person to oversee the whole project."

"You are not going to be the one that oversees the whole project?" Aden asks. I shake my head no. "Well, then. I guess I'll do it." There are no objections from the group.

Evelyn offers to lead the raft since it was her idea. Lemmy can't wait to have a new ship in his fleet so he offers to lead the boat. Alex offers to lead the road, and one of Peter's blacksmiths named Trent offers to lead the cart construction. There we have it. We have the team leaders.

Lemmy jumps up rubbing his hands together. "Alright then, let's get this M-TOG moved."

"Hang on," I say. "There is one more thing. Before you move this M-TOG, you need to build a copy of it. The same weight. The same size. And successfully move it from South Remo to North Remo undamaged. Only then can you move the real M-TOG. And we'll need a leader for building the M-TOG copy group."

Maynard, who has been silent the whole day, raises his hand "I'll do it, Mr. Burke." Aden pats his son on the shoulder for taking on the responsibility.

***

During the boat ride back home, the class breaks up into the four different working groups. Even during the trip home, each leader leads meetings within their group and Aden leads the full group meetings. Once we get home, the class spends another week in the library hashing out their designs. I spend time with all of them, helping them out as best I could without giving them the answers. I have to bite my tongue a lot. I keep reminding myself that I'm not developing the M-TOG move, I'm developing problem solvers.

"Evelyn, how is the raft design coming along?" I ask sitting down to join her group.

"Mr. Burke, please take a look at these drawings. It uses tree trunks tied with hemp rope to make the base and sides. It has a ramp to roll the cart up into it."

"That looks promising. Say, one thing the Old Ones did to test out designs like this was making scaled models and testing them in the water. You might want to try that out."

She nods excitedly.

Trent the blacksmith has also completed the drawings for the cart. It is a scaled-up version of grain carts used in Remo. "This is good, Trent, but let me give you some recommendations. You will want the M-TOG to be as low as possible. If it is too high in the air, it will have a high center of gravity. That means it will tip over easily. The lower you can have the M-TOG ride on the cart the better. But keep in mind that you do not want small wheels. The bigger the diameter of the wheels, the easier the cart will roll. Keep in mind that wider wheels are good. Less likely they will sink into the ground. Think about your design more and see what you come up with. Also, you'll want to work with the foundry to build these." I hand Trent a book on ball bearings.

Lemmy clears off the table next to me and lays out his drawings for his freight ship. "Aye, look at this beauty. Twice as wide and three times as long as our regular ship. We will park the M-TOG right behind the mast here. When we're done moving your M-TOG I'm going to have a lot of fun with his ship. So Sing the Old Ones." It is a good-looking ship. Lemmy's years with his own fleet gave him plenty of experience. But I do see one problem.

"That does look like a fantastic ship, Lemmy. Let me ask. How are you planning to secure the cart when you are out on the ocean? If the cart shifted, it could cause the whole boat to tip. Maybe even capsize?"

Lemmy ponders the question. "Aye, we can use wheel chocks, just like we did in South Remo. It kept those carts from rolling down the hill. We can add plenty of hemp cables for good measure too." I nod knowing he's thinking about a good solution.

I find Aden leaving the library and join him. "Aden, I wanted to catch up with you and Maynard. Do you know where he is?"

"I'm heading to him now. Care to join me? This project is exciting, but admittedly it is difficult keeping all five groups on the same page. Any suggestions, Mr. Burke?"

"Be sure to have information shared between the groups. In fact, one of the bits of information I think is important is something I need to speak with Maynard about." We find Maynard and his team weighing logs on the grain scale.

"Hey, Dad. Mr. Burke. We're weighing out the wood M-TOG parts so that we can match the weight."

I'm impressed. "That is fantastic! But Maynard, one thing I want to talk about with you is not only matching the size and weight, but also the center of gravity. See, center of gravity is the point..."

Maynard interrupts me. "I know what the center of gravity is, Mr. Burke. Emma taught us that long ago in our physics class." I stand silent but impressed.

"That's great, Maynard. How are you planning to figure out the M-TOG center of gravity and verify your copy has the same CG?" I have finally stumped Maynard.

"I hadn't thought that far ahead yet," he responds. Figuring out the CG height of the M-TOG isn't trivial. Normally you would lift one side of it and measure the weight difference side to side. Using the height difference you lifted it, and the weight difference, you could calculate the CG height. But doing this with the M-TOG would be tricky. We would have to build something to lift the M-TOG, not to mention scales to take to South Remo. All that, plus the risk of dropping the M-TOG and damaging it. I'll need to think about this more before I give Maynard more guidance.

"Hey, Mr. Burke!" Maynard interrupts my thoughts. "Can't I just go ask the Oracle? Shouldn't she know the CG height of the M-TOG?"

He's right.

I am impressed with this kid. "It's worth a try, Maynard," I respond.

"Okay, Mr. Burke. When I get the CG height, I'll confirm it by lifting up my copy on one side and weighing the other side with this grain scale. A little bit of math, and I'll know the CG height."

I look to Aden. "You have yourself a very smart kid." Aden gives me a smile in return. "Aden, do you know where Alex is? I haven't seen him all day."

"He's walking the path that they are going to cut in the road. He's recruited some of the farmers to help since they've done most of the road building around here. I'm expecting him to be back tonight. In a few days, I'm planning to walk the proposed path with him to make sure it will work out okay."

I say goodbye to Aden and Maynard to make one more visit before the end of the day. I walk over to the foundry to find Peter.

"Men, see who's come. The Night Thief is back again," Peter jokes with me.

"Why are you still calling me that? By this point, shouldn't you know that I'm not a thief?" I ask.

"Aye, I do. But it is too much fun to give you a hard time. Maybe if you bring something back to the village, I'll stop calling you a thief. I think a new Oracle would do. What do you say?"

I give him a grimace with my face monitor.

"So, what will it be, Night Thief?" Peter already knew that when I stop by the foundry now it's to ask for him to build things for me. I should stop by without business in mind one of these days.

"We're going to need a lot of tools to move the M-TOG. Saws of all sizes, chisels, drills with drill bits, hammers with nails, planes, and clamps. Do you think you can make them?"

Peter strokes his long-braided silver beard for a moment. "Aye, we can do it. If you get us the designs from the library. And you give us some more of the Old Ones sweet songs while we work."

Chapter 23

Months pass by as the teams toil with their work. So many projects where Bearpaw and Sting would have helped. It is excruciating to leave them hanging on the barn wall. Everything would go quicker if I could dust them off and get to work myself. But I held myself back, never picking up a tool.

The team fabricates their equipment parts in North Remo and transports them to South Remo for assembly. Trent completes the cart first. Steel ball bearings and all. His cart has four large wheels and a smooth deck. After completing the cart, his team moves on to make skids to slide under the M-TOG to pick it up slightly off the ground and slide it onto the cart. We'll need to dig near the M-TOG so that the cart deck is at the same height as the feet of the M-TOG. That way the skids can slide straight from the ground onto the cart deck.

Evelyn's group finishes the raft next. It isn't perfect, but I want to let her find her way with it. It is a simple square raft made of logs and hemp rope. It has a deployable ramp on the side to allow the cart to roll onto the raft.

Maynard also completes the wood M-TOG copy made from logs and hemp rope. He first assembles it in North Remo to confirm the weight and CG height, then disassembles and transports it to South Remo for reassembly. To achieve the correct weight and CG height, he has to load the interior of the wood M-TOG with a large pile of rocks. I find Maynard and his dad, Aden, next to the completed wood M-TOG that he had reassembled next to the real M-TOG.

"Maynard, I have a gift for your wood M-TOG." I lift a glass bottle. Inside the bottle at the top are small round dried soybean seeds and below them are a series of pathways inside the bottle before they can fall to the bottom of the bottle. I give it a slight jostle and a seed falls to the bottom of the bottle. Then I tip the bottle slightly sideways, and another seed falls down. I attach the bottle firmly to the side of the wood M-TOG using hemp rope. "This is the test." I look to Maynard. "You need to get the wood M-TOG to North Remo without any more seeds falling down."

The road and the freight ship are still under construction at North Remo. Aden estimates it will take several more months before they are ready. Given that the rest of the team are waiting, Aden asks Trent, Evelyn, and Maynard to practice the move down the river. They had done the calculations that, with a team of Water Foxes, they could pull the raft upriver with the cart inside. They could do the same with the wood M-TOG, but only if they removed the rocks.

Next to the wood M-TOG, the team digs down beside it so that the cart deck is the same height as the M-TOG feet. The dug-out depression looks similar to a loading dock. Trent moves the cart into place with the help of two Water Foxes, then secures it with wheel chocks. Then his team slides the skids under the wood M-TOG. To lift the M-TOG, Trent's men use a long steel pole as a lever arm to raise the M-TOG slightly so that a space block can be put between the skid and the underside of the M-TOG. They repeat the process three more times to set all four corners on the M-TOG. Next Trent's men tie down the M-TOG's feet to the skid using hemp cable to keep the M-TOG and skids locked in together.

After the wood M-TOG is secured on the skids, Trent has a team of Water Foxes line up like a sled dog team. He's fashioned harnesses for all of them that connect large hemp cables to the skids. Trent puts on a horned mask similar to Lemmy's and lets out a screaming horn blast. The Water Foxes pull, digging their paws into the ground as the skids slowly slide onto the cart. Creaks and groans are heard as the cart takes on the weight of the M-TOG. Once it is slid into place on the cart, Trent's men secure the M-TOG to the cart with more hemp cables, then attach his sled dog team to now pull the cart.

Trent and his team had previously cleared the way to the river, having cleared out trees and cut a gentle downward slope to the river's edge. His route to the river is the same I had made over forty years ago when I pulled groups of logs from the river's edge when I first landed on Prasares.

Trent removes the wheel chocks, then gives another horn blast to have his Water Fox team pull the cart toward the river. Trent had added an ingenious braking system that clamps down on the wheel treads when he pulls a lever. Trent rides on the front of the cart, watching from an elevated position while his teammates lead the Water Foxes at a walking speed. As the cart enters the portion of the road that had to be cut into the ground, the wheels start to sink slightly into the ground. Getter closer to the river, the dirt road becomes mud, making it more difficult for the wheels to move. Finally, when the Water Foxes arrive at the river's edge, I inspect the soybean bottle. Not a single seed had fallen during the trip. Now for the difficult part of loading it onto the raft.

Evelyn's team had secured the raft using hemp cables tied to nearby trees. This is needed to not only keep the raft from drifting downriver, but also to keep it secure when the cart rolls onto it. Trent's team disconnects the Water Foxes and has them swim to the other side of the river. One Water Fox pulls a long hemp cable to the other side. Once there, they reattach them and hook up the long hemp cable. They are now ready to pull the cart onto the raft from the opposite side of the river. Trent gives another loud horn blast directing the Water Foxes to pull.

Slowly the cart moves forward. When the first set of wheels moves onto the raft, the raft instantly tips downward under the weight until it bottoms out on the riverbed. With the cart and M-TOG tipped, I can see soybean seeds making their way to the bottom of the bottle. The Water Foxes continue to pull now at an even greater effort to pull the cart up onto the tipped raft with the rear wheels sunk into the mud.

The Water Foxes hunch down, digging their paws into the muddy ground to slowly move the cart forward. Panting and groaning. Finally, the cart makes it to the end of the raft where the cart's front wheels hit a bumper that keeps them from going any farther. Trent's men disconnect the Water Foxes from their harnesses and treat them to a bounty of Orc tails for their reward. Evelyn's team then secured the cart onto the raft with wheel chocks and hemp cable.

The cart and M-TOG are secured to the raft, but the whole raft is bobbing side to side in a concerning way. The whole assembly is too top-heavy. I don't think it will capsize in the river, but it is something we need to keep an eye on. Two of Evelyn's team members load onto the raft with long bamboo poles to steer the raft down the river. The rest of the team walk along the river as they slowly negotiate toward the center of it.

I can see the job of steering the raft is a bit much for only two Remons with bamboo sticks, but I keep quiet. We continue to walk along the riverbed, watching them carefully as they negotiate downriver. As we continue, I notice that our walking speed is increasing. Evelyn's face is still excited and glowing finally seeing her creation working. The raft speed continues to increase that now we are jogging to keep up.

"Slow down!!" I yell out.

The two Remons stab their bamboo poles into the oncoming water to use the riverbed to slow them down, but the weight of the raft and its cargo is too much.

Evelyn is now running beside me looking concerned. I can see the river delta opening up to the sea ahead of us. The raft is going way too fast. We can no longer keep up with it. One Remon aggressively stabs his bamboo stick into the water. It grabs the riverbed, but the jolt causes him to lose his grip and the stick falls into the river. The second Remon stabs his bamboo stick in a last attempt to slow the raft. The stick grabs on the riverbed, but the raft rolls over the stick snapping it in half.

"Jump!!" I yell. "You need to jump off!"

The two Remons jump off the rear of the raft into the river.

We continue to run after the unsteered raft. We see it slam into a boulder on the side of the river. When it bounces off, we see that the whole raft is leaning to one side with Maynard's rocks spilling out of the wood M-TOG.

"Mr. Burke, what is going to happen?" Evelyn yells.

"Don't worry. It will float out into the sea and the waves will bring it back to the shore. We will be able to recover it, no problem," I assure her. We continue to watch the leaning raft speeding into the river delta. The raft turns to have the dipped end going forward. The nose-down end dips farther from oncoming waves from the sea. Finally, catastrophe strikes. The dipped end clips a hidden boulder in the shallow river delta bottom. The boulder doesn't move, but the raft tips forward violently ejecting the M-TOG and cart into the sea. At the excessive speed the raft is moving down the river, the collision is reminiscent of two freight trains colliding.

The team reaches the beach out of breath. We find broken logs and tangles of hemp rope swaying in the waves. Months of hard work destroyed in seconds. Evelyn, Trent, Maynard, and Aden are all in shock. I look at my hands. Neither of them is clenched. I'm not even mad. This is new for me. But I really should be the one building this stuff. They're too inexperienced and they might get hurt. I mimic taking a few breaths. Finally, I break the silence. "Well that was a learning experience. At least no one got hurt. I don't think we need to count how many soybean seeds fell. Let's take a seat on the beach and talk about it."

***

"It's all your fault Evelyn. Your raft was terrible! You don't know what you are doing!" Trent lays into her with his frustrations.

Evelyn snaps back, "It would have been fine if Maynard's M-TOG didn't shift its weight. A big pile of rocks inside the M-TOG? Of course that's going to shift!"

I jump in before Maynard retaliates, "Hang on now. None of us are perfect. Everyone can make improvements. Aden, please take the lead to discuss what you think went wrong." I hope he doesn't blame one of the students. That would be the worst thing to do right now. That is what old Nick would have done.

Aden looks somber. "It was my fault. I'm the leader and this failure is on me. I should have better communicated information between the three of you. It's clear when the raft, cart, and M-TOG were all together, they didn't act like we thought."

I give Aden a big smile and pat him on the shoulder. Aden continues, "But I think we can do better next time. Mr. Burke, I think we need your help. Will you stop sitting on the sideline and start helping us?"

I pause for a moment. I could help. I want to help. And they would get the M-TOG to North Remo with me helping. But moving the M-TOG is a short-term task. Me performing that task defeats the purpose. My task is to develop these Remons to be able to solve the next problems on their own when I'm gone. "I am really sorry, but you need to do this on your own," I say.

Aden somberly accepts my rejection then addresses the team, "I'd like us all to talk about what we want to do differently next time. Trent, can you please start."

I take a seat off to the side and let Aden lead the team.

Trent lets out a breath as he collects his thoughts. "We were having problems with the wheels. They were sinking into the mud too much. It was becoming difficult to pull. We should put crushed rock or wood planks on that section of the road. The cart also had lots of problems getting onto the raft. As soon as the first axle got onto the raft, the whole cart tipped."

"What do you think would happen if you increased the number of axles on the cart?" Aden asks.

Trent thought about the question for a moment. "If I increased the axles from two to four, it would make it easier to get onto the raft. When the first axle gets onto the raft, it would have the three other axles back on the ground to keep the cart upright. It would also decrease the weight on each wheel—cut it in half. The wheels should dig into the ground less. Yes, I think that is what I'll do."

Evelyn jumps in as Aden opens his mouth to thank Trent. "Trent, I'd like to talk to you about figuring out a better way to secure the raft to keep it from moving around when the cart is loaded on it."

Trent nods with a smile.

"Also, I have ideas on how to improve the raft." She holds up her hands like a raft, mimicking the shape and size of it. "I think the raft deck had too small of a footprint. If we make it wider, it should be more stable. Maybe we could even add stabilizing logs far out away from the raft to keep it from bobbing side to side so much."

"I think those are great ideas," Aden adds. "What are your thoughts on keeping the raft from going too fast?"

"Trent's Water Foxes did a great job pulling the cart. Maybe we can use the same harnesses attached to the raft to have them swim upriver, slowing down the raft?"

"We can do that, but the Water Foxes will need rest after pulling the cart," Aden says. "But that shouldn't be an issue. The cart can stay on the parked raft until we are ready to go down the river. Any other ideas, Evelyn?"

"We should go inspect the delta where the raft capsized. Maybe we need to dredge the delta to make sure we have plenty of room," Evelyn adds.

Aden nods in agreement. "Maynard, how about you? What are your thoughts?" Aden asks his son.

"We still need to put extra weight in the wood M-TOG, but we need to make sure it doesn't move around. I think it would help to divide the inside of the M-TOG into smaller compartments before filling it with rocks. That way the rocks won't be able to move around as much and cause the wood M-TOG to tilt."

"Very good, Maynard, that is a great idea," Aden says, standing with his hands pressed together. "Alright then. I think we have great plans here. Let's get to work!" Aden says helping everyone up onto their feet from the beach. They walk back up the river while the debris of the wood M-TOG crash still floats out in the surf. I stay seated for an extra moment realizing that I hadn't said a word to help them. Good job, Nick.

Chapter 24

The team returned to North Remo to reassess their designs at the library. Weeks pass as they refine their designs following the failure they incurred. I ask questions and give guidance, but I avoid giving them the answers. They still need to solve this problem on their own.

Emma and I meet again in the temple, as we do every week, but she looks troubled.

"It is very concerning that they lost the wood M-TOG on your first trial run. Don't you think, Mr. Burke?" Her mouth is pressed into a thin line. "Do you think they will be successful this next time?"

"I don't know. But I can tell you that they are getting better. In time they will be successful."

She does not appreciate my answer. "We are running out of time. The city is losing faith that they can complete the move without you directly doing the work yourself. Will you reconsider and get personally involved in the project? It would guarantee success if you did. I am growing very concerned that your new stance of not helping is going to jeopardize our ability to move the M-TOG. Should the M-TOG be lost in the move, we will surely suffer. Are you willing to take that chance, Mr. Burke?"

"You are correct that I could help. But it would miss the point. This project needs to be completed by Remons. I am not a Remon. I am only a temporary stepping-stone. If they can complete this project on their own, they can complete anything. It is important that

I stay on the sideline. It is more important to have them try and fail, than to have me do it for them. If they fail, at least they have learned something. If they lose the M-TOG in the sea, then I suppose you are back where you were when you commanded your M-TOG to be burnt to the ground." Having made my point, I realize I might have pushed too far. "Trust me on this. We will get the M-TOG moved and your people will grow from it." I leave the temple reminded of the mural again. Of how I let down Remo before. I do hope that I am right about this.

Before I head back to the team rebuilding their equipment, I stop by the school to see Em. I put in a request to her to have her physics students make an important device. I give her a book for reference and have her figure out the rest on her own. Emma agrees and promises to have it completed in time.

The second generation of the raft, cart, and wood M-TOG takes less time to build than the first time, but it is still months to complete. Trent gives his cart four axles instead of two. He also works out a better design with Evelyn to load it onto the raft. Instead of strapping the raft in place with hemp cable, they build a small dock that the raft locks into with steel pins keeping it from moving in all directions. Evelyn's wider base raft also helps to keep it stabilized. She also installs outriggers on all sides of the raft to give it extra stability and safety factors. Evelyn isn't going to risk another crash. So, she practices going down the river with now eight bamboo stick operators and a team of twelve harnessed Water Foxes to keep the raft at a walking speed when traversing downriver and then tow the raft back upriver to repeat the practice run.

"Are we ready to take the wood M-TOG down the river again, son?" Aden asks Maynard.

"Almost there, Dad. I'm loading the ballast rock into the baffling compartments now. We should be ready in a few minutes."

The team looks more confident this time. Trent moves the skids into place and jacks up the wood M-TOG. Wearing his horned mask, he gives a sharp horn blast. His Water Foxes have the balanced wood M-TOG onto his four-axle cart with ease. The Water Foxes have an easy time moving the cart to the river on the crushed rock Trent had received from Alex's North Remo road project. With the widened raft locked into the dock, the cart rode onto the raft without a single soybean seed dropping in the new bottle I attached.

After an award of Orc tails and rest for the Water Foxes, Evelyn attaches her harnessed team of Water Foxes to act as the raft's brake. Two of Trent's men knock out the dock locking pins with sledgehammers to set the raft free. Eight Remons with bamboo sticks walk around the perimeter of the raft carefully steering it toward the center of the river to set up for the slow descent to the beach.

Evelyn rides the raft to direct the Water Foxes to swim upstream keeping the raft from going too fast. She wears a horned mask similar to Trent's to give the correct messages to the Water Foxes. Different commands for faster, slower, swim right, swim left. She has done an exceptional job training them. She cautiously eases the raft down the river. It never reaches a jogging speed. Instead, I leisurely walk along the river's edge all the way to the beach while keeping pace with the raft.

The raft easily passes through the delta after two large boulders were moved out of the way. Previously, Evelyn tied her harnessed Water Foxes to each boulder and pulled them out of the way. Once the raft is past the delta with the waves hitting it, the Water Foxes are redirected to pull the raft away from the delta to a landing spot on the beach. The raft hardly bobs sideways with its larger deck and stabilizing outriggers. Once the Water Foxes pull the raft onto the beach, I walk up to the M-TOG and inspect the soybean seed bottle.

I look back at the crowd and smile. "Zero seeds fell. Congratulations, everyone!" The students are ecstatic. Trent and Evelyn hug. Aden gives his son, Maynard, a congratulating pat on the back.

***

By the time we return to North Remo, Lemmy and Alex are anxious to show us their completed projects. Alex had cut a wide and gentle road through the North Remo forest. At no point is there a sharp turn or steep grade. He had paved the road with crushed rock after help from Peter and his men. Peter had built a waterwheel-powered rock crusher near the foundry.

Lemmy's freight ship is everything he had hoped for. The largest ship in his fleet by far. It has an enormous back gate that flips down and locks in place to allow the cart to roll on and off the ship. All the pieces are in place now to do the remainder of the move. The entire team is ready to depart the North Remo beach. We will take Lemmy's ship to South Remo to pick up the cart with the wood M-TOG.

"Mr. Burke!" I hear Em's voice as we are loading the ship. "My daughter, Joan, will be joining you on the trip." I give her a perplexed look. "You will need her to help operate the barometer you had asked us to make. I think it will be a fine idea to use a barometer to keep an eye on bad weather."

Joan quietly joins us on the ship bringing her water barometer with her. It is a simple device: a U-shaped glass tube with one end closed and the other end open to the air. It is attached to a wood board with graduation marks scribed along the tube. Joan finds a place to sit and opens her notebook to start taking notes. "She's a little shy, Mr. Burke. But she will do well. She's been reading all the books she could find in the library about meteorology. She's very excited. I think she'll be a big help."

I thank Em. She is an amazing person—becoming headmaster and raising the entire education state of the entire Remo city.

Lemmy's Water Foxes pull the great ship out to sea and we depart to South Remo.

After two days, we arrive at the South Remo beach where the M-TOG and raft are still secured. Lemmy maneuvers the ship to face away from the beach so that his Water Foxes can tow it to shore backward. Once the ship is grounded, Lemmy drops the back gate.

When it falls, it leaves a gap of a few meters between the raft and the end of the gate.

"How are we going to pull in the cart?" Evelyn asks Lemmy. "There is not enough room for the Water Foxes to pull within the ship."

"Aye, that is why we have these." Lemmy points to four pulleys at the front of the ship. Lemmy's men route hemp cable through the pulleys and attach them to the raft and the other ends to harnessed Water Foxes. "We will pull the whole raft to the gate. Then we can simply roll the cart from the raft to the boat." Lemmy puts on his horned mask and gives several blows to direct the Water Foxes to pull away from the boat in the opposite direction that the M-TOG needed to go.

The Water Foxes dig their paws deep into the beach sand but are unable to get the raft to move. The many weeks it had been on the beach must have caused it to sink into the sand from the occasional waves washing up, helping to settle it deeper.

"Aye, this is not good. We do not have any more Water Foxes to help pull. We are stuck," Lemmy says, taking off his horned mask.

Aden gets the team's attention. "Let's think of some ideas. How best can we safely move the M-TOG into the ship?"

Trent raises his hand. "Can't we just pull the cart off the raft, then back onto the gate?"

Maynard doesn't wait for anyone else to respond. "Do you see that?" he asks pointing to the soybean seed glass. "We can't afford to let the M-TOG drop off the ramp, then try to ramp it up the gate! We will certainly fail the glass bottle test! Besides if the Water Foxes can't pull the raft, they probably can't pull the cart up onto the gate's edge."

Evelyn offers the next suggestion. "We have four pulleys. Why don't we rearrange them to get more force generated? We can remove two of them and attach them to the raft. Then we can route one hemp cable through all of them back and forth. We'll attach one end of the rope to the front of the ship and the other end will be pulled by Water Foxes. We would be getting four times mechanical advantage!"

"That could work," Aden says. "There would be some things we would need to figure out, though." He gestures at the rope and pulleys. "That's a lot of force to put on one hemp cable. We've never stressed one cable that much—or the mounted pulleys. It's a really good idea, but we should do some tests before we go through with it." He leans back, looking at the rest of the assembled Remons. "Any other ideas?"

The group is silent. I keep my mouth shut. Finally, a small voice in the back of the group speaks up. "Why don't you fill in the gap between the raft and the gate with sand?" Everyone turns around and sees Em's daughter, Joan, speaking. "We can shovel sand into the gap. The four axles and wide wheels of the cart should be fine going over the sand. If we get going, we can have it done quicker than taking off the ship pulleys."

Everyone stares at Joan in surprise, as if forgetting the girl could talk. She'd silently kept her nose in her meteorology logbook the entire time.

Aden gives her a smile. "That sounds like a great idea. What does everyone else think?" Everyone nods in agreement. Lemmy has only two shovels on his ship. While he and Aden shovel, everyone else moves sand with their hands. I would be able to fill the gap in no time if I had Bearpaw with me. I sit on the side while the team quickly moves the sand into place. After a few minutes, Lemmy puts on his mask again. He instructs his men to cut the hemp cables holding the cart to the raft and move the pulling cables from the raft to the cart. With a few horn blasts, the Water Foxes easily pull the cart onto the deck of the ship. It rolls easily once on the deck and stops at the wheel bumper ahead of the center mast. Lemmy's men secure the cart with wheel chocks and hemp cable for the journey back home. Everyone thanks Joan for the simple solution that solved the issue so quickly.

Lemmy has his Water Foxes pull the freight ship back out to sea to make the journey back home. While the team is securing the deck for the journey back home, I have a funny thought and discussed it with Lemmy. "You know, Lemmy. You dragged me off the beach in a similar way. Now you are going to do it with the M-TOG. It seems you are an expert at this line of work."

"Aye, you're right. It turned out well that I dragged you across that beach. You can return me the favor by playing travel music from the Old Ones. It will bring us good favor for the sail home. So Sing the Old Ones."

***

I sit next to Joan during the ride home. She reminds me of Em when she was younger. Joan keeps meticulous notes during the journey.

"How is your mother doing?" I ask, trying to get a conversation going with her.

Joan looks up from her notebook. "She's fine. She's busy with her headmaster position so we don't talk much. She drives me really hard. Sometimes I wish she would give me a break." She pauses and looks up to me. "Do you know why I'm studying meteorology? It's so that when I am old enough I can leave Remo. I'm ready to explore. I've been studying celestial navigation on my own. I've found that the rings in the night sky help keep you oriented easily."

Joan stops herself to inspect her barometer again, then writes down the reading into her notebook. She looks west into the mountain range. "Mr. Burke, I think we have a problem."

I follow her gaze. Dark clouds are coming up over the mountains. "Don't tell me. Go tell Aden and Lemmy."

She jumps up to find them, pointing back toward the mountains. After a short deliberation, the team decides to go a bit farther to find sanctuary from the storm in a cove Lemmy is familiar with. Lemmy knows every meter of this shoreline. I don't even get up off my seat. I let them handle everything on their own. We set out again after the storm passes and the waves subside.

Alex meets us at the North Remo dock when we finally arrive a few days later. The ship's gate drops and locks in with the North Remo dock allowing a secure path for the cart to roll off. Trent's team harnesses the Water Foxes to start the pull up to North Remo on Alex's completed road.

Brumpff!! Brumpff!! Trent wails from his horned mask. The harness cables all tighten as the Water Foxes pull the cart out of the ship, onto the dock, and up onto the road. Alex leads the way back home. He estimates that the trip should take two hours. Alex has done a beautiful job with the road construction. The Earth Romans would certainly have been jealous.

After an hour of the Water Foxes pulling, they start to slow, then finally stop. They are whining and licking their paws. When the team looks closer, they find that the Water Foxes are leaving bloody paw prints on the crushed rock road. Trent's horned mask is ready to bellow steam from his anger at Alex.

Aden jumps in before anyone can say something they would regret. "Let's take a break. Trent, please set the cart's wheel chocks and let's sit down and discuss what to do. It is a good time to eat something anyways."

The team sits at the edge of the road eating and discussing. Trent does well to not blow up at Alex. Instead he holds his tongue while others talk. Aden brings the discussion into order. "We need to discuss how to fix this problem. What are your thoughts?"

Alex starts. "The crushed rock is too sharp. I should have realized that. I'm really sorry. We need to dull it somehow. Maybe we can have the foundry make something to roll along the road to flatten and crush the rocks more."

"That sounds like a great long-term idea. But we would still need to tow the roller using Water Foxes. We can't put their feet through the punishment. Do we have any other ideas?"

Trent finally breaks his silence. "I don't care what we do, but we need to take our Water Foxes home to heal. We can get fresh Water Foxes to finish the job, but this group is done. We need to take them to the infirmary and bind their paws with Bandage Leaves until they heal."

Evelyn brightens with an idea. "What about shoes for the Water Foxes? We can have the leather shop make them for us." The group nods in agreement.

After the students' break, they unhitch the Water Foxes and walk them back up the city. Since they are no longer pulling the cart, they appear to fare better walking on the stone path.

***

After a week of the leather shop working nonstop, a fresh group of Water Foxes are outfitted with shoes. They walk oddly initially. Trent got them to forget they were wearing them by having them shepherd Orcs in an open field. Once the team is satisfied, they return to the cart. Within an hour, they are at the city limits pulling the cart with fast-paced Water Foxes. They follow Alex's road around the perimeter of the city into the school's campus.

The final resting location for the M-TOG is an open area in the center of the school campus. Trent had dug a ramp just like in South Remo so that the cart deck would line up with the ground height. Trent directs the Water Foxes to gently park the cart in position, then move the pulling cable to pull on the skids. With a few more horn blows, the Water Foxes have the wood M-TOG into its final resting position. With eager excitement, Trent's men use their steel rod lever arm to remove the skids from under the wood M-TOG.

I hear panting and see smiles as the final hemp cables are pulled out of the way leaving the wood M-TOG standing on its own. The class of students look at me to go inspect the soybean seed bottle. I walk up and inspect it.

"Congratulations, everyone! Not a single seed has fallen!" The students cheer and start clapping. "But you need to do it all again. You need to move the wood M-TOG a second time." The clapping stops and the smiles disappear.

Aden walks up to me. "You said if we move the wood M-TOG without dropping any seeds, we can move the real M-TOG. What is the deal?"

"Did I say that? What I meant to say is if you move the wood M-TOG and *I don't accompany you*, then you can move the real M-TOG. We only have one M-TOG. The extra practice can't hurt."

Aden is not amused. He takes a moment to collect himself, then turns to address his team.

"We can do it, everyone. This next time will be even easier. We can even improve. What do we want to do differently next time?"

Shouts from the crowd come out. "More shovels for the South Remo beach!" and "Plenty of fresh Water Foxes with leather shoes!" and "Smooth the sharp rocks on the road!".

Aden looks relieved that his team is not throwing their tools to the ground in frustration, but instead are eager to go again.

"Wait!" Evelyn interrupts. "The raft is still at South Remo. We need it here if we are going to move the wood M-TOG back to South Remo."

Lemmy gives her a smile. "Aye, another trip on my ship to pick it up at South Remo. I can't think of a better way spending the next few days."

Chapter 25

When I tell Emma my plan during our weekly meeting in the temple, her entire face frowns, leaving wrinkles from age and displeasure. "You're not going with them? Is that not a grave mistake?"

"No. And I won't be going with them when they bring back the real M-TOG with the Oracle in it." Emma gives me the widest eyes I have ever seen. I point back to the motto still painted on the side of the temple wall. *Happy, Healthy, and Prosperous by Inquisitive Learning.* "Notice that it doesn't say *Happy, Healthy, and Prosperous by Mr. Burke.* It is important that they do this by themselves. If I am there, the city will think it was me that did it. We need to give all the credit to them."

"But what if they fail? What if they lose the Oracle? Bringing back the Oracle is the most important thing to the future of Remo. Is it not?"

"No. It is not the most important thing. The most important thing is having Remons solve this problem on their own. If they can do this, they can do anything. That is the most important thing for Remo. And if they fail? You can blame me. I will be the Oracle Fool in addition to the Night Thief."

"I hope you are not making a mistake, Mr. Burke. If you are wrong, we will never forgive you."

I leave the temple to spend the next several weeks working at the university with Em. It's good to take time off and let the students continue without me.

Em catches me in the university workshop. "The old Nick Burke would not be here," Em interrupts me while I'm tuning a drum. "The old Nick Burke would be the ship captain moving the Oracle right now. You've changed, Mr. Burke. Why are you here?"

I put down the drum and give Em a smile. "Do you remember when I returned from being captured? I had been away for weeks. When I was gone, I realized what I was doing wrong. I was treating you wrong. My behavior is what caused the North Remons to suffer so much. Me being here, tuning this drum is the right thing for me to do. When I am tuning this drum, that means someone else gets to move the Oracle. They will learn from it and will teach others to do even greater feats. It may not look like it, but I am building a civilization right now in this room."

Em gives me a comforting smile with her hand on my shoulder. "I'm glad you feel that way, Mr. Burke."

I stand up and give Em a hug.

Within a few days, the team retrieved the raft, moved the wood M-TOG back to South Remo, then moved it all the way back to North Remo. When they arrive, Joan is sent to retrieve me from the university.

I walk into the center area of the school campus to find the wood M-TOG returned to its place and a row of smiling Remons looking back at me. I casually walk up to the M-TOG and inspect the soybean seed bottle. "Good job, everyone! No dropped seeds!" Their cheers and hugs subside quickly waiting for me to tell them to do the practice run again. "Looks like you are ready to move the Oracle. You are free to do the move as soon as you are ready. But I must tell you, I will not be going with you. You must move the Oracle on your own."

"Mr. Burke, are you sure about this?" Aden asks. "We need your help. What if we run into problems? The real M-TOG is still inside the log building you made. The solar panels are on the roof. They need to be properly removed and secured. We have never done that before."

"You will figure it out," I say. "I trust you. Take all the time you need. Ask me any questions you want. But you will be the people that move the Oracle. Not me."

***

A week later, the team is rolling the Oracle into North Remo. Being the third time they had moved the M-TOG, it is routine at this point. Aden, Evelyn, Trent, Alex, and Maynard ride the cart like a parade float. All of Remo's eyes are on them. The heroes of Remo. I stay at the back of the crowd that follow them all the way to the school campus.

All told, it took the team about two years to get the Oracle here. I could have done the move myself. I could have done it much quicker. And at the end of it, I would have been the hero. No one is noticing me standing at the back of the crowd. And I could not be happier.

Trent expels the last blows from his horned mask to have the Water Foxes pull the M-TOG off the cart with its skids. The entire city is there to see the event. Trent's men cut the remaining hemp cables and remove the skids from under the M-TOG.

The team never turned off the Oracle. They were concerned that if they shut it off, they would not be able to turn it back on, so they had attached the solar panels to a simple structure they had built to the top of the M-TOG.

Aden addresses the immense Remo crowd, "Today is an important day. It is the day that the Oracle has returned to us! Her knowledge will serve us for a millennium!" Cheers erupt from the crowd. "Oracle, I would like to introduce you to the great Remo!"

"Very good, Aden. I am pleased to meet everyone. I am the Oracle. Please let me know what I can assist you with." A wave of cheers hits everyone's ears.

It is easy for me to see from the back of the crowd being Space Yeti height. Lemmy finds me easily. "Why aren't you up there with the rest of 'em, Mr. Burke? You were the brains behind the move. You deserve the recognition."

I look to Lemmy. "No, I only helped the team figure out how they can do it themselves. They did the real work. They deserve the credit."

"Aye, you have turned into a humble one, haven't you. When did you get so soft on me?"

I put my hand on Lemmy's shoulder. "Enjoy this Oracle, Lemmy. Try not to burn this one to the ground." Lemmy let out a hearty gut laugh.

***

Today is Em's fiftieth birthday. I've spent my last years standing in the background. Keeping an eye and giving guidance. I've since stopped teaching at the university and instead have been giving guidance to the professors themselves. Em treated me as her advisor in her headmaster role. She now has a fully-fledged education system, including graduate university courses. Over the years I've faded away. When the city figured out that the Oracle could play all the Old Ones music I could, the demand for me dwindled. They started music classes to learn the One Ones music from the Oracle so that they can play it anywhere. I could have been a god to these people. Now I am barely noticed. And I couldn't be happier. Because I know I've made it. The civilization I've always wanted is blooming.

I've had a simple life for the past several years. After the Oracle was moved, I've taken a pet. A pet goat. I named him John after my dad. I brought him home to my barn after he was weaned from his mother. He has a black coat with white-and-brown markings that remind me of Floats. For the past eight years, he has been by my side. I never used a pet rock with John. Instead I trained him to stay beside me and not wander away. When I am not summoned to give guidance, John and I take long walks into the area around Remo. It has been a satisfying end, but I now need to finish my plan.

I meet with Emma for one last time in her temple. The years are gaining on her. But she has more left in her.

"Are you sure, Mr. Burke?" Emma exclaims, "You are leaving us?! Remo is bigger than ever! Since the Oracle joined us we are now over five thousand citizens. The edge of the city has surpassed the Oracle road. We have new construction expanding our city! Are you going to leave now and not enjoy the success?"

"Yes. I am afraid that I must leave. I am at my half-life. I only have fifty years left before my HE-TEG finishes. I need to find the other Nick Burke. I need to make sure his body is properly disposed of. If he wasn't, he is a liability to your descendants. His HE-TEG is nuclear waste and it needs to be disposed of properly. He made this problem. I need to fix it. It is important for all your future descendants on Prasares." Emma nods her understanding and then looks at the mural behind her.

The Remons had painted over the third scene in the mural. What previously showed the Night Thief, now shows the M-TOG surrounded by the five Remons. Aden, Maynard, Evelyn, Alex, and Trent. Emanating from the M-TOG are the same wavy lines from the previous two scenes. I am not shown in the scene at all. I give Emma a smile to thank her.

Leaving the temple with my goat John, I walk to Em's house. When I arrive, I find all of the original South Remon citizens having a party. They don't know that I am leaving. They are having a birthday party for a group of grandchildren from the group.

"Em, I need to talk to you," I say, inviting her away from the party. I explain why I need to leave. She understands. "I need you to do a favor for me. Please take care of John. He has been a good goat and I'd like him to have a good life. I don't know how long it will take me to find the other Nick. I may be back in a year. Or I may never see you again. Either way I want to let you know that I am very proud of you and I love you." I see a tear drop from her face, then she gives me a hug. The same hug to my chest when she was born.

"Mr. Burke, please before you go, we have something to show you," Em says before I could leave. She leads me back to the party where kids and adults have their own acoustic instruments. Drums, horns, and even string instruments. "We want to play you a song. We wrote it ourselves." I take a seat with my goat and listen to the best original song I've heard since I was a little kid. Driving drums. Pumping horns. And soulful strings. Em's daughter, Joan, even sang. They made it on their own. I didn't even know about it.

I stand up clapping when they finish. "That was amazing! What is the name of your band?" I ask Em.

"We're called The Remon Redemption," she says, giving me a smile.

I say my tearful goodbyes to the rest of my people. Em's husband, Chase. Aden and Ava. Sophie and Luke. Their children and their children's children. I leave John with Em and give him one last scratch between the horns. I walk back to my barn to retrieve two friends.

I dust off Bearpaw and Sting and reattach their scabbards to myself. The white bands where I had previously taken them off have now disappeared into the darkened Space Yeti suit. I have not worn them in twenty years.

I walk down to the beach by myself. The sun is setting and the rings starting to appear in the sky. After an hour's walk I arrive at the beach to say goodbye to one last friend.

"Aye, I was able to make the boat you asked for. It should do well to sail the great sea. Please do bring it back in one piece, my friend." Lemmy smiles with a sniffle in his voice.

I thank him with a handshake and a hug, then push the boat off into the sea.

The rings in the sky look spectacular amongst the night sky. What now? Where do I go? I need to think like Nick. Where would he go? Where would I go in his situation? I head due east into the open sea. It is a calm night. I can only hear the light waves splashing up against my boat.

My dad would have never expected this to happen when he signed me up for the digital clone program. His son's D-Clo has set up the first interplanetary colony. Ever. In the history of mankind. If my old business partner, Jerry, had really sent out hundreds of me into the galaxy, I hope they are just as successful as I am. For the first time I feel like I've repaid my dad for the gift he gave me.

This is going to be a long trip. At least I have good music to listen to. COMMAND LOAD PLAY.

AFTERWARD

I really hope you enjoyed this book. It is the first book I've ever written. It started as a hobby to give myself a break from work and be creative. If you're considering writing, I highly recommend it.

Please leave a review on Amazon if you liked the book. Did you know that only 1 of 100 people leave book reviews? If you can spare a few moments, it would be a great help.

I also want to thank all the people that helped me throughout the process. You know who you are and I am very appreciative of your support!

If you find any typos feel free to send me an email at matthewgdick1@gmail.com. No one is perfect. Not even Nick Burke. Also feel free to drop me an email if you have questions or want to discuss any thoughts about the book.

As an extra treat to you, there is a readers-only blog you can find more discussion, insights, and blog posts about the book. You can access the readers-only blog at matthewgdick.com and use the Password:

PrasaresMTOG486

There are still many unanswered questions. Why are there no land animals in Prasares? Why does Aden look so familiar to Nick? And the biggest question of all: why did the North Remo Nick leave and where did he go? All these questions and more will be answered in the sequel book: SPROUT. Stay tuned!

Made in the USA
Monee, IL
26 July 2020

37050803R00135